The Enterprise

"Testimony"

ii

The Enterprise

"Testimony"

By Antonio Berry

Self-Published with help from
MIDNIGHT EXPRESS BOOKS

To get in touch with the author, you may write him at:
Antonio Berry
POBox 1393
Ocean Springs, MS   39566
Or by Email
Tonyberrysr64@gmail.com

Self-Published with help from
MIDNIGHT EXPRESS BOOKS
POBox 69
Berryville AR 72616
(870) 210-3772
MEBooks1@yahoo.com

The Enterprise

"Testimony"

By Antonio Berry

ACKNOWLEDGEMENTS

Special thanks for supporting me during my struggles of incarceration goes to the hero in my life...My mother Shirley, Aunt Vera, Uncle Billy and Sister Sharon...Each made this journey easier than it would have been otherwise... A big shot out to my Children and Grandchildren. The acknowledgment list of people that I wish to acknowledge is too long to remember or to list them all so forgive me if your name doesn't appear it has been a very long time.

Treyshawn Coleman
Christian Lewis
Jashaun Millender
Nylan Harper
Centrell Millender
Jordan Millender
Keelan Harper
Tony "Manie" Berry III
Andraya Lewis
Antonio Berry Jr.
Antrice Berry
Latara Berry
Veronica Thompson
Dorsey
Potrene Campbell
Linda Crandle
Juanita Moore
Lavern Williams
Paula Williams
Antonio Tampa
Johnson
Anthony Morrison
Ossie McCauley
Cameron Singleton
Wanda Williams

Gwen Lett
Hilda Faye
Thomas Holloway
Diane Costic
Chanda B Taylor
Grenita Dubose
Kirtisene Dubose
Evette Williams
Marion Dubose
Toscha Dubose
Robert Coats
Debbie Rouse
Charles Williams
Regina Barnet
Tonya Winston
Lolita Viverette
Kellie Rankins
Antonio Law
Kevin Davis
Benjamin Crandle
Lashundra Crandle
Michelle Boone
LeKendrick Johnson
Donna Jenkins
Kenneth Sparrow

Will Wade
Bobby Tate
Miguel McNair
Gerald Duffy
Darrell McDougal
Luis Pineiro
John Williams
Celidore Nelson
Gabriel Bolder
Archie Williams
Chuck Stennis
Donnelly Gulley
Leon Pickett
Micheal Hopkins
Tommie Gholar
Beatrice James
Darquist Williams
Terry Dennis
Irma Ramirez
Byron Williams
Willie Williams
Antonie Armour
Jeremy Fondren
William Howard
Duncan Waton

Andre Mays
Micheal Berry
Darryl Berry Jr.
Anthony Woodland
Allieson Preyear
Sonja Jackson
Kristen Lewis
Aaron Wells
Jason Armstead
Donald Jackson
David Callahan
Michael Page
Zelda Andrews
Betty Rankins
Jermecia Grear
Douglas Braithwaithe
Sonja Patton
Cozel Berry
Melvin Jones
Amond Harvey
Terrance Liddell
Willie Scott
Aaron Earl
Joe Dixon
Jerry Hampton Jr.
Patrick Armstrong

Shelby Bolden
Jessie Hall
Shirley Ann Wells
Eric Bozeman
John Lee
Jamichael Jenkins
Darrell McQuiddy
Horation Johnson
Jeremy Wade
Troy Marks
Katrina Stallworth
Curtils Wells
Mickey Torrey
Lenin Angoma
Clarimae Campbell
Forty Thompson
Donald Huckabee
Harold James
Buck Jordan
Delrick Pettway
Debra Burts
Pauline Rogers
Sharon Woodland
Desiree King
Calvin Quinn
Bettie Wells

Roderick Washington
Reginald Sweet
Thurmond Hayes
Ahmad Rashad
Hamad Ali
Edward Grimes
Steve Paul
Carlos Beaver
Nelson Williams
Corey Hobson
Peter Kenny
Jose Guero Garcia
Henry Butler
Herman Cline
John Kelly
Larry Johnson
Angelle Vonderpool
Ericka Littleton
Jerry Williams
Brent Lewis
Abimael Cruz
Williams Rivera
Michael Frazier
Desmond Johnson...

PREFACE

This book is the true testimony to the beginning of Tony Berry's demise and havoc created by his reckless behavior. The saddest thing about such a life style is, you are too trapped in the behavior and addiction of the game to whereas you have no vision or understanding about the chaos and destruction you have caused your community and many innocent lives. All for the sake of big money fast.

It's true we did not manufacture the guns or produce the alcohol and drugs. But, we indirectly pulled the trigger all the same, sat in the driver seat of a vehicle while alcohol impaired and distributed the drugs in the streets of our communities. Denial is deadly and it's only when you are taken out of the realm of what has become a normal way of life and your level of consciousness is elevated that you realize WOW!!!!!!! What was I thinking about???

The only way to rectify and make amends to the situation you help create if possible is, to attempt with a diligent sincere effort to give back to society, community and the lives you have negatively impacted and taken away from. We leave family, friends and others to suffer and struggle in an environment created by the selfish, inconsiderate behavior pattern that's not fit for the animals in the wild. I speak this while telling my story to acknowledge to the readers that in no way am I glorifying my past life style. Let's right this wrong and I long accepted responsibility for my actions.

Antonio Berry

2

CHAPTER 1

It's an early dewy morning on July 31, 1992 when I make it back to our recently purchased home in Jonesboro, Georgia Clayton County. Janice was reluctant to move from Mississippi, she was tired of moving from State to State. Our business the Number One Fan Shop was left in charged to be operated and managed by someone that Janice had personally trained for the task. This store consisted of NFL, NBA, MLB and all college teams' apparel. Jogging suits, jersey's, hats, caps, banners, sun glasses, shorts and other sport memorabilia such as, fan tags, buttons, bumper stickers, perma pennants, trash cans, wall posters, NFL helmets, NFL miniatures, NBA B'ball encyclopedia, fresa delindo spray, NFL and NBA clocks, duffle bags, jackets and helmet mail boxes.

The stores Footlocker, Footscene and Hibbits didn't have anything on the Number One Fan Shop when it came to sport apparel. The Fan Shop always incorporated fashion with product. The only exception was that these stores sold an assortment of shoes and the Fan Shop did not. All the other apparel that you could purchase in the other stores you could purchase the same at the Fan Shop at a fraction of the Price. It was the only store of its kind with in a fifty miles radius.

Also the Fan Shop was known for and sold the latest in the music hits, in stock was the latest CDs, cassette tapes, 45 and album record, video tapes and the Marvin Gaye Collection. If you wanted the Miami Sound such as, Jam Pony, Disco Dave, Uncle Al or my favorite J.T. Money the Fan Shop had it for you. Customers were always welcomed through the door with low playing soft melody music depending on the weather and season. In the summer it was Fresh Prince "Summer Time". The Fan Shop was advertised on a T.V. commercial and WBLX radio station. Janice, children, nieces and nephews participated in the 1991 Xmas T.V. Commercial thanking the customers for patronizing the Fan Shop and wishing them a Merry Xmas. The Fan Shop was on the map.

The plan had been for us to move to Georgia in an effort for me to break rank in this game that had a strong grip on me and will not let go no matter how hard I tried. The business idea I had was to open a You Buy/We Fry fresh sea food market. It would have a convenience store and a deli with cooks and store items in one area and fresh seafood in the other. Customers could purchased seafood and have it cooked to go with fries, potato salad, coleslaw, hamburgers, hot dogs, grits etc.

My step-father Richard was a Captain on a boat of the largest fishing industry in the world which was Omega. I had access to as much and different variety of seafood as could be hauled off the Coast. Private fishing boats were always available to purchased fish and shrimp. I had spoken with some of the workers on the different boats at the dock and they had assured me that once the boats docked and the company fish was separated from the fish that served no purpose to the company that they would call me to bring my delivery truck to the plant to pick up what they had gathered for me. I would be on a daily stand by awaiting their calls especially when I will only be paying pennies per pound.

It was only a five hour drive from Moss Point/Pascagoula Mississippi to Jonesboro, Georgia south of Atlanta. . I had a friend with a u-haul business and I intended to spray the U-Hauls with ice at the local ice house and use it for hauling the seafood each day. This would work for the five to six hours necessary to make it to Jonesboro with the seafood. The Fan Shop and other multi-real estate property I had acquired would be self-sufficient in taking care of themselves with common needed maintenance applied with extra while I concentrate on the developing of the seafood market.

Everything is wonderful and couldn't be better as the plan came together. I have created a legitimate income of $15,000 to $20,000 a month and still reaching. This had been my goal from the beginning. I'm now able to write checks for thousands of dollars from legally established bank accounts without any worries from the IRS. The dope game is gradually fading out of my life, is what I'm thinking. Although I'm dipping in and out of the game the motivation and thrust to mash the gas is no longer there. My most interest is in the change I'm so desperately trying to achieve. The most involvement for me is attempting to assure the guys who I thought was genuine and partners continue to make money and live the life style of a baller and what they had come accustomed. This would prove to be a fatal way of thinking.

Janice and I had married after living together for eight and a half years. I'm attending church regularly on Sundays with my family and trying very hard to completely walk away from the dope game. This dope game has gripped me and will not let go like that bad gorilla called a Jones; I have that Jones and it has me down bad. It's an everyday constant struggle for me that I'm losing with every passing hour and minute of the day. To have a habit for big and fast money is just as worst if not worst as having the habit of using drugs. They both can

Antonio Berry

lead to destruction.

CHAPTER 2

Janice had traveled to Mississippi while I headed to Texas.

I had been in Houston, Texas all week and we were expecting to meet back up in Georgia at the end of the week for the weekend. Sometimes I would take a female friend on the road for company and to spend time with. This particular time there was two reasons other than company for my female friend from New Orleans by the name of Angelle to be on the road with me in Texas. One, was for her to drive the stash car and two, for her to drive and bring back home with her the Cadillac in my yard at the house in Georgia. I purchased this automobile for Angelle as her personal vehicle.

On the way leaving Houston instead of taking the flaming route of interstate 10 East heading for the coast of Moss Point/ Pascagoula Mississippi, we routed from Houston by way of highway 59 North towards Lufkin and Nacogdoches with our target destination being that of Interstate 1-20 East. Jackson, Mississippi is our intended first stop where my partner Red- Charles is awaiting our arrival. This is a seven to eight hour drive and we took these drives as if they were around the block to a corner store.

On Angelle arrival in Jackson she checks into a hotel and immediately page me with her location and room number. I can now relax only temporary because the mission is only half completed.

Angelle had left an hour prior to us leaving Texas behind her heading in the same direction. This was for the purpose that if she had any automobile problems or law enforcement mishaps I would immediately be aware of it. I have two passengers riding with me for road company and we make it to Jackson with our first stop being at Red-Charles restaurant Big Johns. After spending may be an hour or two in Jackson chopping it up with Red and making sure he was satisfied we ride out again in the direction of Jonesboro, Georgia.

Angelle once again is on Interstate 20 east bound rolling and eating up miles better than any truck driver I've ever seen or known. She was made for this type of driving and didn't have a problem with it no matter when or what time I called she was ready. She would drive ten or eleven hours, rest two or three hours and be right back on the interstate. The only problem I had with Angelle was her obsession over me. When she loved she loved hard and was serious about it if she gave it to you. Other than that she was definitely a winner.

The house that Janice and I had moved into was located in a community in which there was only one way in and one way out. It was on Channel Road that consisted of a mixed race of people. There were blacks, whites, Spanish and Vietnamese citizens that made up this community. The yards were green, spacious and nicely manicured all with middle and upper class vehicles parked in the drive ways. We were very suitable for this community and actually a little too much with the candy Benz and truck. Nobody is familiar with us and we know nothing about anybody in this City.

I have no intentions of doing anything illegal in the State of Georgia. Hopefully they let me live a peaceful life here is what I' in wishing and praying for. My plan is to leave the dope game behind me in the past.

The Enterprise "Testimony"

As soon as I walk into the house after leaving Angelle at the hotel I attempted to call Janice in Mississippi to inform her that I have made it back to Georgia and that she and the children can return whenever she's completed the task she thought was necessary for her reason being there. Janice also wanted to bring back what remaining items we had left behind that would fit in the trunk of her candy blue AMG 190E Benz such as, remotes, lamps and pictures etc. Janice Benz was candy blue with gold mirrors, gold fender trims, and gold emblem package, Benz Lorenzo rims with the gold center piece, sec grill, low-profile Goodyear GT eagle tires, AMG kit with light tinted windows and a nice pioneer sound system. It was definitely a reflection of the status of my involvement in illegal activities. She drove and pushed it like a baller's woman.

Antonio Berry

CHAPTER 3

RING RING RING!!!!!!!!

I could tell it's a white man's voice that answers the house phone at our home in Mississippi with a simple hello. I quickly hang up thinking that I must have dialed the wrong number. I re-dialed and once again the same voice says hello. I hang up again and called my mom's house. My stomach is beginning to turn upside down with all sorts of thoughts going through my mind about what could be going on. I had no idea that the time had finally came.

On the second ring at my mom's house another white man's voice answered and he asked if I was my step-father Richard; I answered yes. Then he asked if I wanted to speak with Shirley and once again I stated yes.

I asked my mom what was going on and the first thing my mom said I'm ok, they're just taking my house apart.

I said ok and hung up and fled the house in Jonesboro heading for the border. I didn't know if the house was surrounded or not but I knew this was some serious shit going on and I had to make a run for it or be caged in like an animal. Clayton County at the time was known for racial profiling and its racism. I could be killed if not careful in this city and county by these red-necks.

I was constantly being asked by friends in Atlanta why did I move to

Clayton County? I would answer that I was only trying to get settled in up here and that it wouldn't be a problem moving later. Several other locations I had visited for one reason or another was not suitable. One home the rooms were too small for our furniture. Another one was in a bad location on the west side of Atlanta for my family to always be traveling in the direction of home or myself for that matter. The would-be robbers could recognize the vehicles and after frequently seeing them, begin to salivate. The third home was down south in Union City and that ghetto was out of the question. I had made my mind up to move two or three days after being in Jonesboro.

A couple of the guys that had helped me with the moving was leaving out of the community and drove into a road block. The person on the passenger side produced an ID that they later discovered had expired. Although he wasn't driving they circled the neighborhood until they notice the burgundy Cadillac in my yard that the guys had been driving. This was a pre-empt text to pay us a visit. I looked out the window and there were seven or eight police cruisers in the front of the house pointed in all direction and as to block in the parked vehicles in the driveway. I opened the door to the sound of a helicopter hovering above and I'm like what the hell is going on.

May I help you sir? I asked the policeman. Yes, the passenger in that burgundy vehicle had an expired drivers license and it's invalid to produced as an ID.

I stated he wasn't driving but this red-neck wasn't hearing any of what I was saying.

The next noise I hear is the crackling of the policeman radio from the helicopter informing them that there is a white vehicle in the back yard. This was the Cadillac I had purchased for Angelle. Now it's about five policemen at the front door when one asked what the foul odor was coming from inside the house. They then requested to come inside to search. I stated yes, I didn't have a problem with it because I knew there was nothing in the house to be worry about. Janice stated no, they can't search and became hostile towards the cops which cause me to wonder if she had something in the house I didn't know about. They grabbed Janice to turn her around to place cuffs on her when I stepped in and said let her go and told her to let them search it's not shit in here. The ghetto had come out of Janice and she was adamant about they didn't have a search warrant and we didn't have to let them search our home. I knew this also but I also knew that we had been smoking weed and the children were there and this could bring unnecessary attention and a potential problem.

One of the officers took the liberty to sit on the couch and I immediately asked him to get off my couch and do what he s going to do because I paid $30,000 for this living and dining room set and we don't sit on it. I was really just being arrogant and getting off on them in the only way I could without giving them a reason to arrest me. They searched and one of them found $5,000 I had in the bedroom and asked what was the money for and I explained to them that it was our petty cash to help us settle in our new home. They stated that if they came back and we was ever again smoking marijuana around the children that they would contact the children service department and seek to have them taken away from us. I responded that this was the reason for the children being outside when they pulled up because we don't smoke around them. I knew this was not just about some invalid driver's license when the occupant was a passenger in the vehicle.

At the end of the search they asked again for the driver's license and discovered that Little Larry (R.I.P) was using Kevin's driver's license and arrested and hauled Little Larry off to jail. On their way out my nephew Buck said that one of the cops asked him how could they afford them vehicles; another confirmation that this was not just about some invalid Identification. I looked out at them over the vehicles and said hey, about the vehicles, they're all paid for and closed my door. Larry's mom had to send school picture books and all sort of papers before they would even consider releasing Larry. It took about ten days to spring Larry out of jail and I contributed most of them days as a result of my arrogance. So because of this episode my mind had already been made up to move away from Clayton County the first chance and time I get to find another home.

After hearing the voices answer the phone at our home and my Mom's home in Mississippi, I fled the house and had the guys to drop me off at the Days Inn on Jonesboro Road and I-285 where Angelle was waiting.

Duffy had previously called home from the federal prison in Talladega, Alabama and informed us that our names was being mentioned by every law enforcement agency from Mississippi, Alabama, Florida, Louisiana and Texas. Inmates that was there in the prison with Duffy and had knowledge of the activity on the coast was letting Duffy know that the authorities was asking them about the flux of drugs in the Gulf Coast area and wanted to know who was the largest supplier of cocaine on the coast. They had an idea but couldn't put the puzzle together or figure out how this enterprise was operating without being the major subject of an investigation or net being under a close microscope to bring down.

The Enterprise "Testimony"

They're now thinking that this group of people is much more than just some average hustlers that have come up with a plan to distribute a small amount of cocaine for pocket change. To them it's unbelievable and impossible because nobody is being arrested or busted with drugs that alleged they're either working for or the drugs belong to this enterprise. No currency, drugs, charges, investigation, absolutely nothing is leading back to this enterprise except the fact that names are being mentioned to them by a few criminals that only thought they had an idea.

It was totally impossible for or to send anybody to one of us to purchase or talk about a drug deal. This was not happening even in that day and times. We would not discuss anything on the phone remotely close to drugs. If it was that important then we would travel ten or twelve hours to talk and in some cases Jeff would fly to California. The fix would definitely have to be in to bring down this enterprise. It has now settled on me as I reflect back on these calls from the federal prison by Duffy. Only one thing to do now and that is to begin the run for my life. They begin their chase with me as their prey.

Antonio Berry

CHAPTER 4

This is the start of the beginning of the end. The summer of 1987 is fast approaching and money is falling in my lap like a rain forest between Mobile, Alabama and Mississippi. I'm having more tax-free street money than any law is going to allow a twenty-two year old street hustler to have. The cities of Moss Point and Pascagoula Mississippi have never seen this degree and style of hustling in the dope game that the enterprise is leveling through the gulf coast. The dope game was being mixed with the artfulness of the slum game. The coast was being changed forever and would never be the same again.

Dope peddlers are coming from as far as Tallahassee, Florida east, Baton Rouge, Louisiana west and Jackson, Mississippi north to purchase cocaine from the hustlers in Moss Point/ Pascagoula Mississippi. Playa's from all four corners and the center of the United States of America was docked on this coastal area to distribute their product. To name a few there was the Panamanians Alex, Alvin and Keith from New York, Florida Tony from Tampa, Lucky, Duncan and Philly Dog from the west coast call crew just to name a few. The coast was full of out-of-towners and the money was plentiful. Some initial plan was to come and vacuum a bank roll and move on. Most never left the area until the Fed gave them a one way ticket to federal prison.

The coast was changing forever and the dope game was changing with it. Ounces of crack cocaine that once sold for $1,200 to $1,300 are now selling for $750.00 to $800.00. In the early 80's, ounces of powder cocaine sold for $2,500 to $3,000.

I had a get rich marketing strategy that I intended to apply to the dope game trade which was to sell cheap but sell plenty and make money in the volume that was sold. My connection had a never ending supply of the best butter cocaine in Miami and this coast of smokers has ever smoked. I was able to obtain cocaine as easily as a glass of water.

Everybody from hustlers to smokers was wondering and trying to figure out how this dope I was pushing could be so cheap and money still being made. They could not understand how a profit was being made. The area loved Tony Berry and his crew that's associated with the best and cheapest crack cocaine that's being distributed in the local area. The entire enterprise crew is making money like a printing machine, riding, partying and dressing like celebrities and the coldest playa's to ever set feet in this State. Jeff and I are riding most days back and forth to the surrounding Cities in his red low-rider blazer with the black rag top. The stereo would be blasting to the sounds of Eric B. and Rakim "Paid in Full" and "Dead Presidents We was on one and wasn't going to be stopped. The smokers are having a feast and can't sleep. After a pick up is would be Too $hort *"Ain't Trippin"* or *"Freaky Tales"*.

The old hustlers or the one's that was trying to muscle their way into the dope game had no idea of the plan I had in mind or what they was about to come up against, there was complaints that I was making it hard for them to sell their products and make any profit because I was giving dope away which couldn't be the furthest from the truth. Some actually thought I couldn't be making any money, was crazy and wouldn't last long in the game. I would tell them all the same things

18

which was I can get cocaine like water, I'm not trying to be greedy and I'll make my money in the volume that I'm going to sell. I believe what had to be the most arrogant and hurtful statement to them was when I would tell or force them to sell their products either when the enterprise was out of cocaine or out of town. . . I had no intentions of ever being out of product no time soon not yet anyway and intended to leave them not much of a choice.

I had begun the building of this empire with the direct selling of crack cocaine pieces out of my own hand. This would be the crack cocaine that Snap and I would bring home with us after weeks on the road slumming down in South Florida. I would hang out in the Carver Village all night occasionally falling asleep in my car while serving the night smokers and runners.

The smokers had more love for me than most hustlers. Some hustlers was out to cross or rob you, the smokers would watch while I slept and let me know when the police was rolling through the hood on Live Oak Avenue where Carver Village was located. The smokers wanted to protect the source of the best and cheapest crack cocaine they had ever had the opportunity to smoke until recently that was being put on the streets of the coast by Tony Berry.

The fiends wanted the Miami dope and if it wasn't butter and a product they knew was part of Tony Berry's enterprise they didn't want it unless it was the only crack cocaine around. Some hustlers would ride to find my crew so they could buy double up and some smokers with the same intent would do the same also. Everybody was shown love when it came to buying crack cocaine from the enterprise crew. They would ride the entire area until they found my brother

Darryl or his friend Roscoe. Darryl and Roscoe favorite hang out spot was the busy bee club off Machpelah Road in Moss Point. These were times of the beginning before things drastically changed.

This area of the State of Mississippi belonged to the 5'7", 140 pound little man of a giant. I had eased the area dope market from the grips of so many that thought that had played for locks. My plan was working and I wasn't going to stop until I had more money than I could count. There's an old saying, if you can count it then you don't have anything. When you reach a stage to where you need help to count your money or a money counting machine then you can claim to have money. The slum game is now totally over and I had no intentions, thoughts or need to sell any jewelry anytime soon. I just couldn't see how the two games were possible to co-exist to be played at the same time simultaneously.

CHAPTER 5

Roscoe had a banana, four-door Cadillac with trues and vogues, doo-doo brown rag top and guts. We would stuff ten kilos of cocaine in the bumper and ride with the cocaine from Miami ourselves in the beginning. The interstates were not as dangerous as they had become later and nobody ever knew the times or the moves we was making. The game was being put on locks by the enterprise. I was never in a hurry and it was always more important to make it there safe rather than when we made it there.

With these ten kilos, the twist and the cooking skills I was applying to the cocaine I couldn't lose. I had perfected the skill and ability to turn the ten kilos of cocaine into six hundred to six hundred and fifty ounces all on twenty four grams and the dope would remain good quality. These same ounces would then be fronted to different people on consignment to hustlers from Pensacola, Mobile, Mississippi, Louisiana and Kentucky for seven to eight hundred an ounce. The amount fronted on consignment to each individual would range from one hundred to two hundred ounces each depending and it could and would more often than not in two weeks all the dope would be sold and the money ready to be collected. The goal was to make the drops every two or three weeks. This is 1987-1988 and dope was still being sold on street corners.

If the truth be told and some will tell it because they told everything else. The first to bring the B-12 blow up dope game to the coast was the cali crew but the dope was garbage. Tony Berry was the first to bring the B-12 with nobody being the wiser because the dope was good. Only my immediate associates were aware of the twist I was putting in the game so I wonder if they would tell the truth to that fact the same as the rest of the story. The blow up I was using at the time was called incense; no smell and no taste that you could purchase from the flea market in Miami for $500.00 a kilo. There would sometimes be trips orchestrated just for the purchase of buying the blow up and allowing the driver to earn extra money. The blow up had the exact look of crack cocaine' and was the best cut you could put on cocaine. The Cubans had perfected the making of this product and was getting rich with it.

I would take 485 grams of powder cocaine, which is a half of kilo, and I know what some are saying, but if you ever had or broke a kilo of cocaine down, it was never exactly 1,000 grams. Take another 150 grams of baking soda with 100 grams of blowup with water and place it in the microwave with the 485 grams of powder and cook it until it jells together as one liquid. This technique would produce anywhere from thirty to thirty-three ounces of crack cocaine, all of them weighing on a triple beam scale at 24 to 25 grams each. It was the enterprise that brought this blow-up game to town and put it to its full potential us.

If it hadn't been for my partner Jeff who we called at the time Kango it probably would have been years later if ever before Meatball and others had a clue about the no smell and no taste blow-up. Jeff showed his hand and Meatball begin to sell blowup over the counter of his store by the ounces. The USP truck was allowed to deliver the product because it purpose had yet to be discover and it wasn't a drug. It was a good seller because it allowed the hustlers in the area to stretch their product purchased from the enterprise batch even further. This was during a time when the area was not even yet familiar with the candy airplane paint being used on automobiles or the rag tops.

Upholster shops along the coast was amazed when they would see one of our vehicles and would often stop us traveling the streets just to have a closer look. Some had actually thought they were convertible tops. Although the Mercedes I had earlier in my hustling days was an older model it was Turk first then Snap and myself that set the bar in that area which caused other hustlers to begin setting their sights on exotic foreign automobiles such as Benz's, Jaguar's and BMW's. Before that it was the same as most common places during this era. There were Cadillacs, Lincolns, Chevrolets and Ford's. There was nothing wrong with any of these vehicles because I owned a variety of them myself. It was one of the games that were constantly being introduced to the coast.

Antonio Berry

CHAPTER 6

The hustle had been good to me and I've acquired and massed more than I had actually anticipated in such a short period of time span. I was on a serious grind for eight-to-nine months and with the life style came numerous of women's. Although Janice and I were together and life was good with no reason for me to have any outside affairs in the streets with other women's, but I did. There was no problem in our house hold besides the basic disagreements from time to time that • could be common with any couple but it was never to the point where it was needed or contemplating a separation.

I would occasionally take different women's on either serious business trips or manufactured trips in order to get away and spend time with them, Janice didn't questioned me or interfered with my street life and I took advantage of that. Nobody wanted for anything and not only did my house hold not want for anything I also took.: great measure and pleasure to assure that her family and any close friends we had didn't want for anything important and that we could be counted on in time of need. It was common knowledge that Tony Berry would always do and never say no or refuse a sincere favor. The area loved Tony Berry all except for a few hidden jealous hearts that would prove later to be fatal. There were snakes all around me and I was not keeping my grass cut low enough to see them or hear them sizzling. It could have been that I was just not paying close enough attention to the obvious. Jealousy is as cruel as the grave. Psalm 8:6.

Janice is operating the L&L Grocery store that we had opened in hope of earning a legitimate income. This business is not panning out with the profit I had anticipated and I'm seeking a way to abandon the idea. It's become very frustrating and I'm about to say "F-it" with the closing it down and swallowing the lost. I only allowed it to stay open longer because of the passion that Janice had for it and the sense of purpose it gave her day in and day out. The other reason was it kept her occupied while I did my devil work in the street. This way I didn't have to worry about her riding up on me while I was doing something or at a place I had no business. She didn't even have time to wonder about what I was doing.

A major concern for me at this time besides the protection of my family was doing all I can to protect Darryl and Roscoe and keep them out of the direct line of fire and heat from the authorities. Darryl is my brother and Roscoe is someone I took under my wings to try and give him the game and show him how to have something and hustle up on a bank roll. That will also prove to be fatal. They were the closest to me and target for the would-be robbers or authorities. Either could lead a direct path to me. I had to avoid the police and the suckers which is sometimes an almost impossible task.

I was hiding money from the burying it in my back yard, under the dog house, inside the walls and other places I had safes, I couldn't stop and knew I had to leave this area because I was becoming paranoid and had the feeling of being watched at every turn I made. I really wasn't being watched; it was only my mind playing tricks on me. There was never one person at this time that had been arrested with drugs who mentioned my name which I learned later. I had never been approached by a CI Undercover agent nor had I been the subject of any drug investigation during this time. I was not even on the authority's radar as a major playa. Hustlers was constantly being arrested in the area on secret indictments that would be served at midnight or early morning hour raids while everybody was asleep and the Cities was quiet.

I was never indicted or charged with a drug crime and I knew why and it was because I was very particular when it came to who I would deal with concerning the cocaine game. I consider myself to be playing the dope game same as I had played the slum game with finesse, constantly on the move, throwing curve balls and leaving most to wonder how is he making his money, some curves thrown can be like a boomerang if it doesn't cut the head of a snake. It will come back to hit you and cut your head.

In the attempt to try and prevent the brain of the enterprise from having a serious harmful problem I devised what I thought was a scheme to proposition a local mechanic to become my driver. This will also later prove to be fatal. His job would be the trafficking of the money to Miami for the purpose of bringing back the purchase cocaine to Mississippi. The same method of placing the money and cocaine in the bumper would be utilized. Jenkins was a local shade tree grease monkey mechanic that could barely read or write and was a high school dropout. How he made it to high school alone is yet to be understood and continue to be the subject of a major corruption investigation. You could only take your work car or what we considered a bucket of a car to Jenkins for simple repairs such as, brake pads, oil change or universal joints repair. You definitely couldn't take your automobile to him for major repairs.

I know I ask myself the same question. It calls into question how smart was I to have recruited him for such a potential detrimental mission. I have had a lot of time to wonder and think about the exact same thanks to Jenkins and the others.

CHAPTER 7

The Jenkin's family lived in a dilapidated three bed room home on blocks with more than five children and that's not including the parents. The house was located behind a business facing the highway that handmade tools. To get to the Jenkin's house you could travel down the side of the business or come from the back street of West Bayou. As I pulled up I noticed Jenkins and another occupant sitting in his raggedy looking burgundy Cadillac four-door sedan parked on the side of his parents' house.

The amazing look in Jenkins eyes when I pulled up said that he thought he had a potential automobile repair customer. It's hard for me to imagine how he could think this because it's written across his forehead but not only him—I would also have to be out of my mind to even consider allowing him to put a rag on this candy-blue gem. He may never be allowed to sit in it nevertheless touch it, the way he's dressed. I pulled up in one of my toys that was the 87 candy blue maxima with the Kaminari kit, five star Fittipaldi rims sitting on low-profile Fugi tires, gold fender trims with a black rag top and gold buttons. The stereo is blasting *Don't Stop The Love* by Keith Sweat. I had a theme song for every mood and vehicle and just the sight of the gem made love to some.

Jerkins' is in suspense as he steps out of his burgundy Cadillac with his trade mark twisted grin as if he's had a stroke that left him this way. He was one funny deformed looking dude but the purpose I needed him for didn't require beauty or to be handsome. His needed purpose only required a valid driver's license, ability and willingness to drive for hours at a time with the understanding that you had to be careful and mindful of what you were hauling. He can't seem to take his eyes off the Maxima as he runs his hand across the top and tells me how clean it is as if I haven't heard this no less than a thousand times. To him, he was telling me something new and I just responded yeah, yeah, yeah ready to move on to the real purpose and reason for me being at his house.

I have accumulated and stacked enough money to where I can now afford to send Jenkin's or anybody that's willing to travel to Miami to bring back cocaine with $150,000.00 to $200,000.00 and sleep knowing I can chance that amount and still be ok if things didn't work out as planned. The thinking was for me not to put all my eggs in one basket and have the resource to continue if things went astray. You don't want anything to happen or for you to lose your money but you always want to secure yourself just in case. I turned 24 a month ago in December and was definitely about my business for a young man and it reflected in the moves I was making. It also reflected in the image of my associates and the way in which I was making it possible for them to eat. They was having money and living the life style of a celebrity. I made sure they was able to make money in the same manner as I was, all the time going -against one of the major carnal rules of the game. This proved to be a fatal decision on my behalf. The more you do for suckers and unappreciative people the more jealousy you can cause. If you over-look and not notice this jealousy it could prove detrimental and fatal at a later time and date as I lived to learn. Therefore, you do you and keep the press on and suckers away because they will be your down fall and cause you too many regrets at a too late of time. Keep your feet on their necks because they will turn on you every time as I hope you never have to come to learn as I have.

What's up Jenkins? I have something I want to discuss with you that could be financially beneficial to the both of us. With this ugly grin that I should have seen was nothing but an upside down frown he tells me to talk to him trying to sound hip. I'm searching for a long distance driver with a dependable automobile, before I can continue to tell him what would be required of this driver he responded he can do it. Now I'm thinking this fool hasn't even heard me out yet, a sign I didn't take notice of. I continue to explain to him that the job will consist of taking money to Miami for the purpose of bringing back cocaine. The pay is good and it's simple and pretty safe with the idea of the stash spot on the car. The first intelligent thing he said to give the slightest belief he has bird sense is when he asked how will it work.

I'm listening to his every response and paying attention to his attentive behavior to determine whether I can detect if I can really trust him to reveal my business nevertheless about me and my hustle. He like the rest and most may have an Idea and opinion but don't know with certainty. I hope he can tell by my image that my involvement in this dope game is very serious, he may not know my business yet but I'm more than sure he has heard the word on the streets about who runs this city and most of the coast when it came to the dope game. I first asked him about the condition of his Cadillac and did he think it could make it back and forth to Miami with no problems? Jenkins gave me the ugly grin one more time and said yes with enthusiasm as if I had insulted him by asking a mechanic of his status concerning the condition and ability of his automobile. He still has no clue as to why his Cadillac and condition is, so important to the mission.

31

I continue to explain to Jenkins the reason the Cadillac is my preferred vehicle for this task. Some mechanic he was because he never knew about the space that existed between the bumper and the inside plate that created a hollow space. This space in the back bumper was wide and long enough to stuff and place multi-kilos of cocaine easily depending on the packing and wrapping of the cocaine. This was a stashed spot I had already been using for maybe two years prior and considered it safe enough and so safe that I had even traveled with the cocaine with Janice and the children. The only reason it's not safe for me any longer or anyone close to me is because of the fact that I could be a target of an investigation is what I'm thinking.

The reason for this belief is due to the unbelievable amount of money that I'm making and the life style I'm living with no problems or interference by the authorities not even a stop and search of the vehicles. If I was a target then I had to make sure that every attempt was a wasted effort, and blank mission for whoever showed their heads.

CHAPTER 8

A week has passed and day after day I've been spending time with Jenkins in an effort to prep him and making sure he understood the ends and outs of this mission he's about to take on. He has to know this is very serious and nothing about it should be taken for granted. You must not speed, look suspicious, smoke weed, drink alcohol and always pay your fines to assure your driver's license remained valid if checked. These trips must be kept a secret and the only people in the need to know every detail was me and my connection on the other end. I believe Jenkin's is now ready for his first road trip in the game.

I begin to prepare for the trip with the taping of $150,000.00 in separate bundles in brown paper bags with the use of duct tape as wrapping. The money was taped in a way that made it easy to slide inside the back bumper of the Cadillac. This model Cadillac had a plastic piece that set flat under the tag where you would pull the tag back to place gasoline in the tank. Once the screws was removed from the plate that connected to the bumper the lifting of this plastic piece allowed you to place a heavy object whether it was the lug wrench or the jack leg between the plate and the bumper, with this done you could pull back and separate the plate from the bumper leaving room for whoever is helping you to place either the money or the cocaine. There was plenty of room in this hollow space.

On this first trip I decided to convoy with him similar to an on the job training exercise. We packed up for a couple of days being gone and headed out for this eleven to twelve hours trip in the direction of Miami, Florida. We always exit in North Miami at the Calder Race Track where there was a Holiday Inn Hotel. Most of the time I would not stop until I reached my female Rhondetta house who lived off 191st street in Carol City. Rhondetta was my girl from Miami at the time who's brother Corey was best friends with the connection Cuban Shorty. Rhondetta was good people and with a Miami Beach figure. The entire family loved me and we were really tight once and had some good memorable times together. I use to even fly her to Mississippi when she had days off and wanted a short get away vacation. Cuban Shorty's father was the President of the port of Miami. This is one of the major reasons I was never short in supply of cocaine.

Rhondetta was a working young lady and had been working at this bank for a couple of years. She never knew when I was coming and I would sometimes be there when she arrived home from work. The only way the secret that I was in town would be revealed was if her sister, Tisha, knew I was there. Tisha was, and still is today, my buddy but she wouldn't hold it from her sister.

Rhondetta kept a boa snake in the house that was left to her care by an ex-boy friend. The snake had gotten out of the aquarium a few times and I wouldn't stay there either. I would take the entire crew there with me sometimes to her house. Mostly it was me, Darryl and Roscoe in a separate vehicle from Jenkin's and his girl-friend Felecia who he would often take with him for companion and try to keep her from behaving promiscuous in his absent.

While in Miami we would shop for clothes, shoes, hats, stereo equipment because Jenkin's also thought himself to be a DJ and any other items that would give the appearance that we had been on a shopping spree vacation in Miami. I introduced Jenkins to everybody and took him slow one step at a time through this procedure to teach him what I expected. I'm paying him $1,000 a kilo which will earn him $10,000 to $15,000 a trip sometimes $20,000 twice a month. He would sometimes make runs for the blowup a less dangerous mission and could still earn $3,000 to $5,000. He has never seen this much money in his life and probably will never again. This always made it that much easier to recruit and convince a person to agree with the trips. I have always believe in treating people fair with the belief that if you do then you have nothing to worry about when it came to their sincerity and loyalty. This turned out to be a fatal error and mistake to believe. Not with just Jenkins but the other most trusted friends and confidants as well. The one's you're good to and treat with genuine respect and love will sometimes deliver you to death. Matthew 10:21.

I was very close with Rhondetta entire family. Her mother Ms. Eloise treated me like a son and not only did she treat me like a son she always made me and whoever I would bring there with me feel like family. Tisha, Sue, Glenn, Corey, Zsazsa, Saycee, Shymeka, Tyesha, Quiteka, Shaquoria, the twins Zedrick and Kedrick. Even their father Ricky always treated me with great respect and love. This was a great family one that I would forever be grateful. The way I met Rhondetta was by chance because I had been going by her mother house with Glenn and Corey for years and had yet to see her due to she didn't live there and was always at work. She rode to my house in Orlando one time with Glenn to see me and on their way out the door I asked Glenn who she was and he stated his sister. I told her I would be down there to see her and within the next two weeks she was in my arm!

35

Cuban Shorty and Corey had been classmates and remained friends over the years. When Cuban Shorty got his first break in the dope game his best man Corey was right there by his side. In the beginning I use to go through Glenn or another friend I had in Miami named Yogi. Glenn Family asked me one day to talk to Corey because Glenn was sick with kidney failure and shouldn't be running around the way he does. That's when the relationship between Corey and I was formed that lead to my introduction to Cuban Shorty. We had a unique understanding and bond. He was very much trustworthy, responsible for his age and didn't play any games.

The Gang knew Tisha as our "G-Queen" that was always lying in the cut analyzing everything and everybody that came into her present. Her keen sense and sharp eye had long revealed the snake in Jenkins. If only I had listen and set my emotions aside. Tisha was also trustworthy and loyal. On a weekly basis she was burden with the task of counting $350,000 to $500,000. She had perfected the Enterprise Trademark of wrapping and packaging the kilos of cocaine that's to be transported by the Enterprise. When Tisha did her gift wrapping technique using the bounce fabric softener and duck tape old dog Lassie couldn't smell it. The chick had more heart in the end than most of the other busters in the Enterprise. It took heart and nerves for her on many occasions to deliver kilos of cocaine to buyers in exchange for duffle bags of cash... Tisha was an intricate part of the wheels in which the Enterprise road. It could have been the "G-Queen" and I against the world and the odds of survival would have risen to a much higher level.

CHAPTER 9

Cuban Shorty and Corey were in their early 20's and beyond their time. They was handling just as much cocaine in the City of Miami as other hustlers who names was ringing like a bell through-out the City and Dade County. The reason for this was due to Cuban Shorty association with the port of Miami. He walked the port as if he was the President instead of his father. Corey and I created a working relationship to whereas I would send the car with my money and he would pack and send the cocaine back up by Jenkins. For this and his loyalty besides him making thousands from me I would sometimes work this end for him. If he wanted to send a few extra kilos to be distributed by my guys who I was fronting on consignment or if he wanted it to be continued in route to relatives of his that resided in Mississippi I would make sure it was done.

I never had to worry about being robbed or dope that wasn't good or a top grade, every kilo I ever purchased from Cuban Shorty was good and a money maker. The business was great and everybody was happy and making plenty of money. From Yachts to Ferrari's was being purchased by this organization. You couldn't find one smoker in Jackson County, Mississippi that didn't believe or knew without a doubt they was smoking the best crack cocaine in the United States of America and on the planet. The cocaine that I'm bringing to Mississippi is being distributed through-cut the Gulf-Coast from Tallahassee east to Baton Rouge west. Nobody is the wiser that it's Tony Berry who has the type of grip on this dope game that has only manifested by the flux and quality that's being distributed and smoked by fiends.

There were other drivers I recruited beside, Jenkins that would sometimes drive on these missions. There was my friend girl in Orlando name Marla that would do anything I asked of her. There was Bobby who stayed loyal and true to the end. He would have been the only one I needed looking back but hind-sight is 20/20. He was dependable, well liked and didn't have a jealous bone or piece of envy in his body. I began purchasing 77-to-79 model Cadillacs whenever I came across one that I thought was a deal and would often placed them in Bobby's name. I also had other high-end vehicles in Bobby's name.

It was Bobby, his mother and older brother but Bobby was the man of the house and took care of his mother like an honorable son/man. Usually around the holidays I'll take a break and more so Xmas. I'll have the word spread to other hustlers to slow down in order for the children to have a nice holiday. If not their parents will spend any and all the money they could put their hands on smoking crack cocaine. Reflecting back I never considered it through-out the years but I guess it was trying to have a sense of balancing what I was doing with a inkling of morals but that's impossible. It's only two ways in life and that's the right or wrong way there's no in-between. Although society has a way and can dictate decisions that your spirit tells you is wrong but they becomes sociable accepted and advocated by the same individuals that passes and enforces the laws and Constitution upon us. They would call this political correctness.

My friend Yogi had been stopped and arrested in Pompano Beach, Florida while traveling to Orlando for us to proceed on to Mississippi destination being Carver Village. Yogi and another friend that was riding in the car with him were taken into custody after the authorities found cocaine stashed in the rental vehicle. He had thought it was a good idea to pull out on a Friday evening and blend in with the traffic on the turnpike. It would have been if he hadn't been in such a hurry and impatience. This was prior to the use of the Cadillac's. Yogi is another partner from Miami that I can say was good and loyal to me. I never had to worry about any games being played by him. He was always straight and trust worthy.

Antonio Berry

CHAPTER 10

Ring, Ring, Ring!!!!!

"Hello."

"You have a collect call from Broward County jail from inmate Yogi; would you accept the call?"

"Yes!!!!"

"What's up Yogi?" I asked.

"We was stopped and busted and I need you to call Nat," said Yogi.

Natalie was Yogi's girl-friend and the mother of his daughter. Nat explained to me that because Yogi was on probation for a previous charge that we needed to get him out of jail before Monday, it's Friday. Yogi had a bond of $150,000.00 and we have to move fast and spring him.

Yogi called me again in a state of panic and I assured him that we're going to make sure he's out before business hours Monday morning prior to his probation officer learning of his arrest. If the probation officer found out before he made bond, there would be a hold placed on Yogi.

Yogi had a couple of kilos he had left behind at his house. We devised a plan for Nat to deliver the cocaine to me, Darryl and Roscoe in

Orlando. Our objective is to take the cocaine up the road to Alabama and Mississippi to sell it and be back in Miami before sun rise Monday morning to spring Yogi from Broward County jail. This episode had happened in the beginning before serious business had started with Cuban Shorty and Corey.

Nat loaded the cocaine up in Yogi's black blazer sitting on chrome rims with large Mickey Thompson tires, lights across the top and a chrome bar across the front bumper. This was a big boy truck and when you seen one rolling through Dade County in these times you knew more often than not that the owner was pushing weight. With the cocaine loaded in the blazer Nat set her sights on the four hours ride it would take her to reach Orlando. I could make the ride in less time riding clean but it wasn't safe riding dirty to be speeding. In four hours Nat was pulling up in front of Dunwoody Apartment Complex in Orlando where Janice, the children and I are living at this time.

Darryl, Roscoe and I unloaded the cocaine from the Blazer and placed it under the hood of a GMC Blazer I owned and didn't waste another minute to hit the highway going to take care of the necessary business. Nat went south on the turnpike towards Miami and we went north towards Wildwood on our way to Mississippi. This was the first time that Yogi and my friendship had been put through a true loyalty test during a crisis. From that moment on Yogi and I have been very good friends. The cocaine was 100% pure and like always, there wasn't any problem selling it and the fiends loved the butter cocaine, we sold the cocaine and was back in Miami before sun up Monday morning. Yogi was out of jail before the Probation Officer made it to work and is now a free man and can deal with the lawyers and other business associated when these situations arises.

The Enterprise "Testimony"

Yogi eventually received a State sentence for the arrest in Pompano. He served most of his sentence at the Florida State Correctional facility located in Punta Gorda on Oil Well Road in Charlotte County. While there he would send me different inmate's names to mail packages (boxes) in with his requested items that were allowed to be sent to inmates from their family as a privilege. The main reason he wanted the packages and sent the names was because this was a method we used to send in weed for him to smoke. The way this would be done is, once I had the send in name, I would take a bottle of Sauvé shampoo that came in the black plastic bottle and pour the shampoo out and make sure the bottle is rinsed and dried.

I would then take the weed and secure it in several balloons squeezed very tight. It would sometimes be almost an ounce that I would drop in the bottom of the bottle. Before dropping the balloons in the bottom of the bottle I would drop a few specks of super glue in first and then drop the balloons. After the balloon has dried in the glue at the bottom of the bottle I would pour the shampoo back inside its rightful place from which it came. I then prepared the remaining items he requested with the shampoo to be mailed to the prison in the given name he provided. I'll find a female from around the way and pay her to send it from the post office coming from a fake name and bogus address.

Mission accomplished.

I always made sure that Yogi's commissary account was full and he didn't want for anything as long as I was on the streets.

Sometimes while visiting in Miami I would check in on his mother and sister and drop them money also for whatever was needed, he called once telling me how he had asked his cousins about some money and in exchange for the money they wanted him to sell them his automobiles for the favor.

When he told me this I was mad as hell at him for this. My response to him was to never ask them for shit because I got you and anything and more than you could need.

I made sure that all my places of businesses, homes and girlfriends knew to accept all collect calls from Yogi with urgent. It has been times I was traveling out of State and he would call and everybody was directed to tell him to call back in thirty minutes while I was being paged and located. I would be paged and call back with a number to give to Yogi to call while charging it to wherever he had called for them to let the operator know it was ok to put him through to me. His Mom, Ms. Lossie, once told him I was the only real brother and friend he had although he did have a biological brother. I was showing him so much love until his mom would let him know how blessed and lucky he was to have a real friend as such.

CHAPTER 11

On an early morning around 8:00am Mississippi Time 9:00am Florida time Yogi called. I had slept in late this day while Janice had already left to open up the store. For some reason the needed rest and sleep had caught up with me and I decided to just lie there in bed this particular morning thinking this could be an all day event. Yogi explained to me that Nat was trying to buy a car and needed some help with a down payment. I'm like serious and asked him how much was the car total. He began to tell me that I didn't have to do this or that or buy the car. I responded with listen, if you tell me one more time what I don't have to do I will hang up. At this moment in my life which is the late 80's early 90's I'm spending $40,000 to $60,000 cash, on and in, automobiles so I know whatever type of vehicle it is she's trying to buy can't be that much. I'm contemplating buying a Rolls Royce but know I will have to do some additional construction work to our garage in order for the Rolls to fit. So we called Nat on three-way.

Ring, Ring, Ring!!!

Nat answered on the third ring. "Hello."

"Nat, this is me and Yogi on a three-way. He said you're trying to buy a car."

"Yes, I am," said Nat.

"How much is the car, Nat?" I asked.

"No Tony, you don't have to do that I was just short of the down payment," responded Nat.

"Listen, Nat. I'm going to tell you the same thing I told Yogi. If you don't stop trying to tell me what I *don't* have to do, then I'm going to hang this phone up on the both of you and go buy you a car myself. Now tell me the price of the car."

"The car is $6,500.00," quoted Nat.

"Ok, stay by the phone and we're going to call you back in 10 minutes," I explained to her.

There's one person I know without a doubt in Miami that money is no limit when it came to him and me. It used to amaze friends sometimes how I would have them in the car with me riding around town and before you know it we would head out of state on an unplanned trip with no money or clothes. Whether it was Georgia, Florida, Texas, Alabama, Louisiana or Northern Mississippi that set above us, I knew wherever I ended up there was always somebody I could borrow a couple of thousands of dollars from until later. My word was platinum.

Ring, Ring, Ring!!!!

"Yeah," answered Corey.

This was Corey's trademark way of answering a phone. I never understood and didn't try to change it but I would always call him country when he tried to say I was country. I proceeded to tell him I needed a favor. There's somebody down there that I need you to give them $6,500 for me and I'll bring it or send it to you when the car comes down that way. I'm going to have them call you and you tell them where to meet you. It was just that simple and done without a question while both Yogi and I were on the phone.

Yogi and I hung up with Corey and called Nat. This was all done within ten minutes. I gave Nat Corey's phone number and explained to her that he's going to tell her where to come or meet him to pick up the money and Yogi and I will call her back in an hour to make sure she's good.

After an hour passed, Yogi and I once again were on the phone with Nat. She told us she got the money and you can hear in her voice the joy and appreciation and I knew Nat was genuine. This was not necessary because I considered her my sister-n-law and she was damn good people. I told her to never hesitate to call me about anything. She and Yogi thanked me again and Nat was on her way to buy her car.

I always made sure I sent Nat money for her and the children. She gave birth to a baby girl a few months before Yogi had to leave for prison. Kenyatta and Ne-Ne.

Antonio Berry

CHAPTER 12

The hustle continued with Cuban-Shorty never being out of a supply of cocaine and the best cocaine on this side of the Country at that. This was necessary and the key to building the drug empire in which I was seeking to build. I had plans and ideas to become a major figure in the underworld. The secret in the dope game is having a direct connection and a never ending supply of whatever type of good dope you're distributing. I had what every hustler dream of—a direct connection.

I finally worked up and found the nerves to try and convince Janice to close this guzzle of a business called L&L Grocery. L&L stood for Lameeka and Latara. It made me feel bad doing so because she never spoke of anything I did for myself, except maybe sometimes the mentioning of why I bought a specific automobile while having so many others. We continued to live in Orlando and I'm constantly in and out of Mississippi and Alabama with Jenkins as my main driver of the cocaine that's being shipped to these States. A majority of the time I would cook and turn all the cocaine into crack there in Orlando before it would reach its destinations. I did not know the difference in the penalties associated with crack cocaine as opposed to powder cocaine. Jenkins would have ten-to-fifteen kilos of crack cocaine turned into sixty ounces per kilo in his possession driving on the highway taking it to Mississippi.

Jeff and Chicken had recently been sentenced; Jeff first to nine months in a special R.I.D. program for first time nonviolent offenders. Kenny

D. was part of the Enterprise and is in Parchment State Penitentiary awaiting his release on parole.

I have paid to assure his release by sending $10,000 to be placed in the appropriated hands of the people that have the ability to guarantee his release when that time comes. I made sure nobody wanted for anything even while they were doing their time in State prison. This is not always the same when the shoe was on the other foot. Kenny would call sometimes stating he wanted to bet another inmate that's locked up with him on a Monday night football game. I responded with put him on the phone.

I could hear Kenny laughing in the back ground when I tell the guy there's no limit on whatever amount Kenny wanted to bet because it was covered. This would produce a chuckle from the both of them. The guys usually knew Kenny was serious by the pictures, money and packages he was receiving through the mail. Mississippi State Penitentiary had conjugal visits if you were married. If you weren't married all you need was about $50.00 to grease the officers hand for an on the spot marriage certificate. I have allowed many women's to use one of my vehicles to visit their man at the prison. There was numerous of children conceived as the result of these visits.

Kenny had been on the run from the authorities for a couple of years because of a previous charge in which he had been paroled. He was going back and forth to Florida with Darryl, Roscoe and myself. We protected him and done things in a manner that kept him out of harm's way. I thought we had a loyal crew at the time and the feelings were mutual. This turned out to be a fatal assumption on my part. The reason it was so easily to believe these feelings for one another was mutual was due to the many opportunities that presented itself for the cross to come into play and didn't. These three guys I thought would forever have my back and I could depend on them if nobody else. The thought process also proved to be wrong and a fatal disappointing way of thinking. As the saying goes, there's way too much monetary gains to be had for them to think any other way. Take away that element and the benefit factor then you can get to the raw soul and character of any man. This was another one of those times where I didn't keep my grass cut low enough to see the snakes or hear them sizzling but they were there in the flesh the entire time waiting to strike. I trusted in the people I considered my brothers. Jeremiah 9:4.

Kenny was not re-arrested and sentenced for the violation of parole until he decided he was going to do things in a manner differently than what they had been done for almost two years, in hind-sight it could be best that you resolve these types of matters so you can move on with your life and not have to always be looking over your shoulder or worrying if a simple traffic stop is going to result in your arrest a thousand miles from home.

He's on his way home now from the State Penitentiary and I informed him to get off the Greyhound Bus at Gautier Singing River Mall and call me because I will already be in that area. This is where I picked Kenny up and the look on his face gives the impression that he think he's dreaming and his first words was got dam man. I arrived on the scene in my candy green AMG 300E Benz with the sec grill blasting DJ Quik *"Tonight"* appearing as if the kit is going to drag the pavement.

The very next day he was given $30,000, an automobile, a shopping spree of almost $10,000 by Darryl and Roscoe and back in society as if he hadn't been gone for the past two and a half years. Not saying this is how it is most of the times for people returning from prison but this is how it suppose be if there's true playas on the other end of the field. There was a donation to Kenny by the other fellows that produced a half of kilo of the best cocaine on the coast. It was the bottom butter that they loved so much. Kenny D. was back and the city welcomed him with open arms. These types of playas, that gave this type of welcoming, no longer exists.

CHAPTER 13

The car load of cocaine that I would send to either Mississippi or Alabama Darryl and Roscoe would make sure everybody received what was meant for them as their package from me. The people who received the cocaine would contact me on the prices. If they called and say they needed to see me before I came to town and was finish I would give them the ok to give what they had to Darryl or Roscoe. I was taking care of the business in Florida as far as the buying, cooking, and packaging it for Jenkins to transport and whatever else was necessary to make it happen. Even with doing all of this I would still most of the times come to town and take care of most of the business myself.

What is more unbelievable is the steps I took to protect and keep them out of the line of fire whether it was the robbers or the authorities. It wasn't even necessary for them to sale or distribute their own cocaine, being I had trusted people that I'm already giving cocaine to on consignment I allowed and had no problem with them including a kilo or two of theirs in with mines to be distribute by the same people I'm giving cocaine. If I was giving one person three kilos I would allow Darryl and Roscoe to add another one or two with it. The people receiving the cocaine never knew the difference and assumed all the cocaine belonged to me. I didn't consider this to be anything major mostly being unselfish. In the end do you think it mattered? What do you think??

Prior to Jeff State sentence and incarceration, he, Tina bit, Janice, Meeka, Tara and I had gone on a cruise to Freeport Bahamas for a week. Jeff and Tina-Bit had yet to have any children and was enjoying and loving Meeka and Tara as if they were theirs. Once Jeff was released from the State Prison he falls right back into the groove of the enterprise as if he has never left. Jeff was buying and trafficking cocaine from California and would sometimes fly there just to party and shop. The cocaine was much cheaper but not as potent. Jeff loved to dress and stayed fresh and fly. Jeff had a system that he was using at the airport to increase his chances for his cocaine making it back and through airport security safely. When I compared the risk, quality and distance my money and cocaine would have to travel, I was never interested or convinced in obtaining cocaine from California. Turk introduced us to the Cali crew of Duncan and Lucky and invited them to town. They were some very good and trust worthy playa's. Turk did not stay in the cocaine game any length of time. He had a goal and plan and once it was accomplished he laid the game down. As a result of Turk laying the game down and leaving his people with Jeff, Jeff now has the best of both worlds. Jeff had me on this side of the globe and good people in California.

The first day I picked Jeff up after his release from State Prison we ride and turn a few corners with me catching him up on all the latest events and what has transpired since his absent away. Jeff could be considered a top dog in the enterprise and I felt obligated to him. We're smoking a joint of the best weed around while sipping on some Hennessey. The stereo is blasting to the sound of Too $hort "*Life Is Too Short*". We always gravitated towards the pimp, playa type music. I never charged or taxed any of my partner's more than what I was paying for the kilos of cocaine; another fatal mistake that most of them didn't deserve. Jeff is one of the few that did deserve it because he was real and stayed real throughout it. I was getting my money from the streets so it wasn't necessary for me to tax and get it from the pockets of my thought to be real partners. If you're going to be in the dope game you have to be fair, firm but rule with an iron fist is what use to be the rules of the game. At the writing of this book the game has drastically changed. Constantly test the character content of the human individuals that's your close associates and the one's that can do the most harm. It will pay large dividends to do so, believe me because I'm a living testimony to the truthfulness in that statement.

Jeff recognized by the structure of the enterprise that I've held it down and not let up off the gas with pushing this cocaine game. I still have good prices that I'm paying in Miami but a plus has been added to the business. This Columbia named Julio that I was introduced to through a mutual friend want allow me to spend my money with him for the cocaine and just rather leave ten to fifteen kilos with me at a time and would not come back sometimes for his money for more than a month. The price he was charging was only a couple of hundred more than I was paying in Miami with cash up front. The quality of the dope was the same. To be on the safe side when I was out-of-town when he came I would always have his money place somewhere that Janice could put her hands on it. It was a strict understanding between Julio and me for him to never leave any dope with Janice. He was to only take his money and see me when he sees me. I still had the business I created to run and was not depending solely on Julio for dope. Having him was something extra to do that I could handle with no problem and I admit it was profitable. This was the only time and only person I've ever had dope that I considered being fronted to me on consignment and it wasn't because I couldn't afford to buy it. I didn't believe in that and preferred to buy all my cocaine with straight out cash. I had too much of my own business to worry about and take care of to be burden with someone else's.

The conversation that Jeff and I were having lead to me agreeing with Jeff that I would allow him to have one or two of the kilos coming from Julio for the same price I'm paying for them. I was already allowing Darryl and Roscoe to have a couple of them with the same understanding. Out of the entire crew looking back with hind-sight Jeff had always been the most trusted one from the beginning and it was naturally I should have been able to trust my blood brother Darryl. Jeff did one thing during those days that I couldn't appreciate and disapproved.

I was totally adamant against it and I made that clear to him. Jeff and Chicken had never been what you would consider friends or cared much for one another and only tolerated each other for the sake of the enterprise. I was the mediator and glue that kept them together and constantly in each other's presence. Without me they probably wouldn't even speak. Jeff use to wonder and couldn't figure out why I befriended Chicken. Jeff had seen the evil crudeness in Chicken long before it was going to happen.

For one Jeff thought that Chicken wasn't good people or could be trusted to have him around and knowing too much. Two, Chicken was smoking crack on the pipe on the low off and on. It turned out Jeff was correct and Chicken was a bad choice of friendship I made. I wouldn't find out until years later based a situation and the discovery of the evidence.

CHAPTER 14

Sharon was Chicken long time off and on girl-friend and it wasn't anything he wouldn't do for her. He would even kill and face a death penalty for this woman. She would be with other men's or could have another man and Chicken at the same time and he always accepted it and took her back. I have to give it to Sharon she was and has always been a playa since I've know her in School. I knew Sharon before Chicken and she stayed involved with weak dudes and Chicken was the weakest. She had even had a baby for another man and the fool accepted this. What I will say is he loved and did for the little girl as if she was his own. He was good to them both the mother and daughter.

On a Saturday night Sharon and one of her friends name Mary was in the club partying and shaking their asses on the dance floor. Chicken was still in prison waiting to be release from the R.I.D. program with only a few months remaining. Jeff happened to be in the club this night and bumped into Sharon and Mary on the dance floor. He had already heard that Panamanian Keith had had Sharon and Mary both in the bed at the same time and this had Jeff curious. His story and understanding I received from him was while they was on the dance floor he begin to dance from one to the other. Their eyes were glistering and telepathy communication was made and one thing led to another and before the night was over he had them both in the bed together. He had said that he was definitely going to tell Chicken as soon as he made it home from the State Prison. I dreaded that day and wanted no part of it. I didn't like it and now I'm in the middle because if ask, I have knowledge of what happened. This is how much resentment there was between these two people, Jeff and Chicken.

We decided to take a trip to Miami and do some shopping at the two flea markets that we regular frequent. The one on 183rd street and the corner of 27th Avenue and the U.S.A. flea market further south on 27th Avenue. Jeff is fresh out of prison and although he was only incarcerated for nine months he insisted on buying a new wardrobe. The last thing Jeff needed was more clothes because he had shoes and out-fits he hadn't wore and enough close to open up a clothing store. We're ballin' out of control so it's no big deal to spend it like we're getting it. It's more dope thanks to us on this coast than can be imagine. Turk was always asking and saying to Jeff and me, Bro-n-Law you and Jeff have to stop and let it go because this is not a good look. Turk gave us the slum game and felt it was not good thinking for us to continue selling and putting cocaine on the streets as if it wasn't obvious what we're doing.

Turk was in the game for only a short period of time but entered with a plan that he was discipline enough to maintain and exit out with. He was and has always been very savvy when it came to taking care of his business. Turk opened a clothing store in Pensacola called T.G.I.F. (Thanks God It's Friday), moved his mother from Atticks Court where him, Jeff and his other siblings had grown up. He bought his mom a home out west and laid the game down and walked away and changed his entire life and style. He made it seem easy and simple but it wasn't that simple for Jeff and I as Turk had preached so many times to us. The ball was rolling and we couldn't see it no other way except the way things was going and to us it was the way we wanted it to roll and bounce.

There was another real close friend of ours that lived in Atlanta name Howard that we called GA. Whenever Howard would come down to visit us he would always say he felt uncomfortable based on our life style and the way we're living as if we was untouchable. It seems fictional to him. Howard was from Atlanta and had already experienced and been exposed to the sight of seeing how the FEDS operated and arrested hustlers in the dope game. They hadn't gotten that bad on the coast yet except in the Mobile area and our understanding of them were very limited to nothing at all. He would tell us how such and such was arrested and seizures that were taking place. The news would broadcast the seizing of millions of dollars in currency, automobiles and other property of drug dealers. He knew first hand that if Jeff and I slipped and became the subject of a federal investigation that we was done, cooked like a thanksgiving turkey and the snakes would show their heads. We couldn't chop them off because they weren't evident to us at the time.

It was almost never any violence associated with our crew except for maybe on one or two occasions when it was necessary to remind an individual to not get it twisted that we was still street and because we have changed the game and doing our thing on the low and quiet, they shouldn't forget we grew up in this area. We all at one point in our lives had been hell raiser but was now on some playa type time trying to have money with the use of more finesse than brute, more thinking than just action. On one occasion, Roscoe's brother Tracy couldn't hold his evil, mischievous and jealous characteristic inside his soul any longer. I should have taken his behavior as a Club Nouveau Jealousy warning for things to come. I didn't and that was another fatal error on my part., he laid and waited until Darryl and Roscoe retrieved some cocaine from their hiding place.

I didn't find out until later by his own admission that he went behind them and stole the remainder of what they had buried in where they thought was a secret spot only known to them. They accused the wrong person based on an assumption of something that had transpired earlier that same day. They beat the wrong man dam near to death about their missing dope. Neal was a good guy and when he told me he hadn't stole their dope I knew he was telling the truth. I sent Darryl and Roscoe to Orlando and told them to lay low until I can resolve this matter. Tracy was and is as slimy as they come. There's an old saying that goes back since Biblical times. The man in your house is your biggest enemy. Micah 7:7.

Learning this the hard way could sometimes be too high of a price to pay.

CHAPTER 15

The cocaine we're putting on the streets is good so it's selling itself for the people we're giving it to with no problem. Everybody is making money and buying whatever comes to their minds to purchase. There's $100,000's generated weekly by our crew. Benz, Jaguars, BWMs, Cadillacs, Jet Skis and four wheelers that's popping up from everywhere, the local business owners are loving and benefitting from the economy that's being created by the enterprise. It's like an epidemic that this area of the coast has never seen before. You couldn't tell us Mississippi was poor nor did we worry about the price of gas or anything else for that matter.

If one of us had a mystery and was having an affair on our main woman her appearance would be the reflection of the one she's in the bed with. We was definitely having it like Burger King our way and was seriously caught up into our activities until a person on the outside looking in would have reason to think and believe we must have thought and considered ourselves to be invisible. That's exactly what I said and mean invisible and not invincible. How we thought what we was doing was not obvious to the naked eye is beyond me...Stevie Wonders and Ray Charles could clearly see it. Why couldn't we. I guess for the same reasons I couldn't see the snakes in the grass but they were there waiting to strike.

After spending the weekend shopping and squandering a large sum of currency at the Flea Market in Miami it's time for us to prepare to leave the City Sunday Morning. We're going to make one last stop at the USA Flea Market and then be on our way toward the Turnpike in the north bound direction. I kiss Rhondetta on the cheek leaving her in bed with a nipple peaking at me from under the sheet. I tell her I'll call as soon as we make it home to let her know we made it safe. What I really wanted to do was crawl back into bed with her and have another taste of last night. I know this will only further delay our departure and it's time for us to be riding out. Besides it had already been an all night, off-and-on rodeo for the both of us.

Rhondetta and I use to enjoy one another's company and spending time together and were always able to laugh and joke around as if we had been best friends our entire lives.

Rhondetta and I never argued or talked aggressive towards each other. I had my own set of keys to her place once and came and went as I pleased. This was accepted by not only her but the other women's that I was having an affair who had knowledge that I had a main woman at home whom I was living with and raising a family. I admit I was very promiscuous during these times when it wasn't as dangerous of being a death sentence to be from one woman bed to the next one. This was the influence that the life style I was living had on a woman and she would more likely than not be satisfied with just being a part of it and accepting whatever situation that came her way. I know it was insane but that's what it was.

The reason we did not leave Miami that Saturday night is because a couple of us had time to think about a certain outfit or other items we had seen but didn't decide to purchase them until later. We're going to stop back by a few of the Flea Market stores and purchase the items we had passed up. Leaving USA Flea Market we traveled in the direction of 22nd Avenue and made a left turn heading north toward Opa Locka. Our intentions were to stop at this Amoco Service Station that sits directly across from Bunch Park, gas up and hit the turnpike making our way out of this City.

I'm driving Jeff's short burgundy square Cadillac sedan with the Cadillac rims, burgundy rag top, gold emblems and package. The Cadillac is fresh and in the game hard for real. We're cruising down 22nd Avenue blasting NWA *"Gangsta Gangsta"* and Special Ed *"I Got It Made"* smoking some grade "A" weed. We very seldom wear our jewelry in the City of Miami and rarely drive one of our vehicles with the out-of-state license plates while visiting unless I was living there and had made the place my home. I would always switch vehicles while visiting Miami. Rhondetta would often drive my car and I'll keep hers while she's at work or drop her off and leave mine parked. You had to be on your toes in this City and remember to never stop completely at a red light or stop sign. The newest form of carjacking was for the perpetrators to bump your vehicle from the back and wait for you to exit your car to assess the damage. You would then be confronted with a Glock pointing in your direction screaming for you to give it up and even if you give it up, you could still be shot. We have been at a drive-thru window ordering something to eat and noticed, on the inside, they're being robbed right there before our eyes while we're sitting in the car waiting at the window. These were some crazy unforgettable times but we couldn't see it for believing we had the world in our hands.

Antonio Berry

CHAPTER 16

We're cruising down 22nd Avenue towards the Amoco to gas up without a care in the world. We have now placed on our jewelry because there are no other intentions or reason for us to stop after this one stop. After gassing up we're going to point this Cadillac front end in the direction of the turnpike and leave the city of Miami in the review mirror. A peach color Cadillac Coupe Deville with two or three occupants pulled up beside us while we're cruising thinking about the fun weekend we've just had in Miami and getting back home to business. The guys begin to bob their heads in a gesture that I took it to mean they was listening to something on the stereo or meaning they was jocking Jeff's Cadillac. I didn't know nor did it cross my mind that they had another agenda waiting to play out. They saw us as marks.

There's a major mistake that's made by most people while visiting Miami whether it's to party, shop or tourist. People from other States have a tendency to naturally assume that because guys in Miami are riding in nice expensive automobiles that they could be boss playa's in the drug game and had whatever you wanted in the form of drugs. The automobiles could be stolen or high-ass payment is being made on it each month. Out-of-towners automatically assumed that these are some good guys to deal with because of the way they're rolling in the City. This has never been the complete absolute truth and many people has not only lost their money as a result of this belief but have lost their lives. Most Boss playas in Miami you will never know the extent of their collection unless you come to know them personally.

I'm draped with a large rope chain with a Mercedes emblem around my neck, a Rolex watch and a few rings. Jeff has on a fat link chain and several cluster diamond rings. Roscoe and I enter the Amoco to pay for the gas while leaving Jeff, Darryl and Snap on the outside by the car to pump the gas because there's nothing else we could care for besides a soda and chips. We have some weed and wrapping papers and fire.

While Roscoe and I was standing at the customer counter paying for the gas and talking shit to the clerk behind the bullet-proof glass partition, Roscoe looked to his left pointing to the clerk in the direction of the vehicle that he's paying for the gas. What he turned to see is the same guys from the peach Cadillac is outside robbing Jeff, Darryl and Snap in broad day light at the pump right here in the public eyes. They're waving pistols while screaming Nigga, give it up. The store manager sees it on his store cameras and comes from the back just as Roscoe and I are pointing to the outside and telling the clerk what's going on. The manager immediately tells Roscoe and me to come this way towards the back to his office.

The manager locks the door with us in his office; there are several monitors that show the activities in the store and around the outside of the premises. These cameras suppose to alleviate and discourage theft. One of the guys with what looks like a 45 caliber is running up and down the aisles screaming where's that nigga with the big rope chain as if I was behind an isle I would be foolish enough to stick my head out. He would have to be one of the world's dumbest criminals if he thought I was coming out. It was over in a matter of seconds but the manager is telling me and Roscoe to stay put until the police arrives. He had already pushed the alarm button and metro was on their way but seem like it was taking forever.

I'm insisting to the manager that I must be let from this back room because I need to check on my baby brother Darryl. If something happens to him while he's with or following me my Mom would have a heart attack. Nobody was harm but Jeff had been stripped of his jewelry and Darryl had run a few yards down the street and was out of harm's way. Snap just set there pretending he wasn't with us and was ignored by the robbers. This left Jeff in a daze state of mind and he remained that way the entire trip home. He couldn't believe he had been caught slipping and was jacked. Jeff is originally from Florida and has traveled all over the Country and back and never had this to happen to him. The clerk could have locked the door with the jack boys trapped inside but probably feared for her life also and didn't want to be the test dummy for the bullet-proof partition. There were little children across the street in the park that witness the entire scene as it happened. The children begin laughing and screaming to the top of their tiny lungs that MC Hammer got robbed. People have always said that Jeff resembled Hammer with his Gazelle shades on his face and Kango that was tipped to the side.

I did not call Rhondetta and tell her what had happened until we made it home. As far as Jeff, he was scarred from that incident. Months later Jeff was still talking about that day in Miami at the Amoco.

Antonio Berry

CHAPTER 17

Things could not be better for the Enterprise, we had a solid loyal crew is what I believed at the time and couldn't be told anything differently. The money circulating in this area of the Coast was so plentiful that it caused hustlers from all over to flock there becoming rich. They found it unbelievable and not to be the image they had formulated of Mississippi. A couple of them that came with the foolishness thinking that hustlers and the street playa's was soft and was some push over country bumpkins found something different. If you came to the area with the bull-shit you had a high percentage chance of being body bagged and shipped back to your family for a sad service.

There're two sides to every coin and some of the out-of-towners came to the area with the mind-set that it didn't matter and was willing to bring whatever heat necessary to do what they had and wanted to do. You had to be willing to kill some of them because they were willing to die before leaving this honey hole of an area. No outsiders has ever been able to completely take over because this home-grown enterprise had a real serious grip on the area and that left the rest to get in where they fit in. I have always tried to keep the peace and the heat to a minimum. Everybody knew that I had the ability and power to shut and slow the town down to a snail pace and put a cap on anything that had the potential of getting out of hand. With the pistol play and murders in any game you're playing it want be long before the law will be to see you. I was trying to have money and a large bank roll not funerals. Looking back some funerals should have happened and are necessary as a mean to justify the end. Keep your grass cut so you can see them. One fatal error and the Enterprise will come tumbling down to dust and nobody can or will try to save you. A house divided against itself will not stand. Matthew 12:25.

There was too much money to be made to allow the type of heat that shooting and killing will cause. It was some youngsters that didn't mind pulling the trigger and letting loose an entire fifty round clip if you looked at them side-ways. There was the village, the front on Machpelah Road, Tony Tip Top, Frederick and Second Street, Kreole Park and the Nikki Brown Crew, West Side, Krebs Avenue, Dupont, College Park, 504 Club, South forty, Blue Moon and too many project homes to name them all. All of these areas were a potential battle ground on any given day for a mass killing. When this much money and territory is involved you just never know what's going to happen.

You had to be on point, your best behavior and stay ready for the possibility of drama. Most of the people and hustlers in this area knew that my crew wasn't to be taken lightly or soft unless you were willing to go all out and bar none. For some this was too high of a price tag to chance it. There were some good people associated with my crew that lost their lives to some cowards. I called them cowards because that's what they were to have killed two of the best and kind hearted individuals you could meet. Chicken was fronting Mama Rose and Brock dope and their murders have never been solved in over twenty years. These two people would have literally given it up to the robbers without a fight. To kill them was unnecessary unless one thought about the possible consequences that could come behind a face seen during the robbery. There were rumors flying everywhere even one that Chicken had given them some bad dope.

Mama Rose and Brock was in the cocaine game. Brock was a real good dude that I had known all my life and was a good hustler that everybody loved except some coward. He was left to die behind a dumpster at an Eden Street Apartment Complex in Pascagoula. Mama Rose was stabbed multiple times in her home on Jackson Avenue in Pascagoula. Mama Rose would give anybody the shirt off her back and was as sweet as they come. Both had to know and trusted their assailants. Things were heating up behind the murders. I have hoped, wished and prayed that these perpetrators be apprehended and the full weight of justice be tossed in their laps.

The day has come and we're waiting on Chicken to arrive from State Prison within the next week. I have pleaded with Jeff to leave that issue concerning him, Sharon and Mary alone and let bygones be bygones. He insisted that he's going to tell Chicken what has happened with the justification being Sharon was no good. I believe it's more to hurt and crush Chicken which he knows it will. He knows how weak and blinded Chicken is when it comes to Sharon. I'm thinking, who is Jeff to figure that anybody else is no good after the stunt he's pulling. I know this drama could have the potential to cause animosity and the possible break down and destruction of the enterprise. This is my main reason for trying to keep a lid on it and Jeff mouth closed.

To only say that Chicken was in love with Sharon would be a huge understatement. He was the definition of blinded with deception and there was too much at stake not to be able to see the forest for the trees. Eve caused Adams to eat the fruit from the forbidden tree. Chicken had already eaten too many pieces of fruit from Sharon's tree and there was no turning back because he was full of fruit. This changed the course of history forever. Genesis 3:1-5.

71

Antonio Berry

CHAPTER 18

I continued to do a great deal of traveling to and from Georgia, Texas, Florida, Mississippi, and Alabama two or three times a month at the least. If it wasn't me and one or two of the members of the Enterprise it would be me and my lady friend Theresa. She was very pretty, classic and sexy but more important she was intelligent. I'm at the car wash having the vehicle which I'm driving down to Miami cleaned. I decided this time it would be the maxima. I received just as much jocking in the Maxima as I did in the Benz or Jag. Jenkins has already pulled out heading to Miami with the money to pick up and bring back the cocaine.

I received a page from Chicken family house phone number and returned the call. It could have been anything because the entire time he was incarcerated in the State I made myself available if they needed anything. His little sister Kim answered the phone on the first ring.

"Hello?" she said.

I responded, "Somebody paged me?"

"Tony, Todd said come down to the County jail in Pascagoula and pick him up he just arrived by van from the State Prison. If he calls back tell him I'm on my way as we speak."

The van had delivered several guys home from the State Prison who had either finished a short served sentence or it could have been decades. We hadn't expected Chicken home for another week so this was a surprise and it could have been that he was trying to sneak up on Sharon. I borrowed another vehicle and pulled out to pick him up. When I arrived at the County Jail there were inmates up on the 4th or 5th floor that knew me by sight and was screaming out the window that Chicken left instructions for them to tell me that he had caught a ride to his Mom's house and for me to meet him there. I guess the ten minutes it took me to make it from Moss Point to Pascagoula was taking too long for a person leaving prison. Chicken had only been gone nine months which probably seemed like nine years while worrying about Sharon. He wanted to be quickly removed from the vicinity of any penal institution and probably would have begun to walk if necessary.

I tell the inmates in the window thanks and headed in the direction of Chicken Mom's house. I was always receiving messages or request from home-boys in our State Prison or County jails to send them something or could I do this or that. These were small tasks that I never had a problem with. Some would call for me to help them make bond that wasn't a part of my crew or enterprise. I would often have to tell them to call their family and tell them to contact me. Calling me from the jail regularly wasn't cool and could give the impression that they worked for me. This was not true but most knew I would help them if I could.

I had been helping Chicken and his family the entire time he was absent from the scene. Everybody was in the yard when I pulled up welcoming him home. We hugged and pounded for a minute before I explained to him what I had going on and that I hadn't expected him home for another week or two. I was in the middle of handling some

74

business and time was of the essence. I had just sent Jenkins to Miami with $300,000 about five hours previously to him calling with the intentions that I would be trailing behind him. Chicken response was that he needed to see Sharon.

The first thing that comes to my mind is that I best get him away as soon as possible or he want be leaving. I know this is eating him up on the inside because he really wanted to surprise her. You can believe one thing and that was by now Sharon was aware of the fact that Chicken was home. Word spread around here like the flu. The only person who received news faster than the people in Jackson County, Mississippi was GOD.

"Pack one outfit and let's go; we'll buy you something down the road," I say to Chicken.

"I have to see my probation officer within 72 hours of arriving home," stated Chicken.

"It's Friday and I'll have you back by Monday morning man, in time to see your probation officer. So stop tripping," I say to him.

We talked for twenty more minutes with Chicken family and were on interstate 10 east bound on our way to the city of Miami.

We arrived in Miami in time to catch a couple of hours of sleep before waking up going to the Flea Market. I had to get Chicken fresh and told him there was no limit; something he already was aware of. He picked eight or nine out-fits, two to three pair of shoes, several Kango hats and a few pieces of jewelry to welcome him home. Chicken was not situated same as Jeff before going to prison. Jeff had clothes he hadn't worn and money he left behind and was ready when he walked out the prison gates to his freedom.

Chicken was broke but I had considered him my friend partner contrary to everyone' s believe that he was a bad choice of friendship. My plan was to help him become financially stable this time and make it a focus of my attention as a project. Hopefully he would not continue to smoke crack on the low thinking I had no knowledge of his behavior. I had always stressed the fact to any partner and friend that if I had it they also had it. I never was selfish and never charged my partners one dime more than what it cost me. Again I was collecting my money from my business associates in the streets and not my partners thought to be friends riding next to me. Not knowing one day it would be revealed that the feelings were not mutual. If you're sitting in prison as the result of a bad choice in choosing Chicken as a friend I regret you was not able to read this story in time to avoid the pain and hardship that contributed to mines and so many other's demised. A bought lesson is sometimes the best learned lesson but sometimes the price can be too high for the class. They were in sheep clothing. Matthew 7:15.

CHAPTER 19

The business is taken care of with the packing of the cocaine and giving Jenkins instructions to stop in Orlando before going any further. This is where I'm living with Janice and the Children. The Townhouse Complex was now Ashley Pointe and it was a very quiet setting with a large populated County police officer residing. It was one of those complexes that had free security besides the front guard stations you had to enter before coming on the grounds of complex. It seemed as if the entire Orange County Sheriff Department lived there. This was evident based on the patrol vehicles that was scattered about in the parking lot mixed among the plan vehicles of the tenants. It wasn't a concern for me because I wasn't carrying on any drug dealing in Orlando so it didn't bother me except on one occasion when we pulled in off the road and several of the patrol vehicles had their lights on and flashing. Somebody had attempted to steal a vehicle from the parking lot and was apprehended. They had to be the dumbest criminal and a desperate one to think that they could get away from all these green and whites in this parking lot. Nevertheless I would still have ten to twenty kilos of cocaine in the town house waiting to turn them into 1,200 ounces of crack cocaine. The only people that can ever hurt you are the ones that know your business and are close to you.

It was like a dope factor with the cooking in the townhouse with the wrapping and packaging of the cocaine to be shipped up the highway. The cocaine would always be unpacked out of the Cadillac on Oak Ridge Street in the last stall at a self service carwash. All the dope is cooked into crack and divided into 50 ounces bundles to be placed once again into the Cadillac bumper.

Duck tape and bounce fabric softener would be used to minimize any smell that could be detected by law enforcement and drug sniffing dogs. With the dope packed, stuffed in the bumper and bolted down tight, the car would then be washed for any finger prints, residue with dishing washing detergent taking extra notice and effort to clean superb in the area of the back bumper. At $800.00 an ounce the Enterprise will circulate $960,000.00 dollars from the cocaine that's in the bumper, within three weeks all the cocaine will be sold and all the money will have been collected. These are the years of 1989 and 1990 when hustlers was able to stand in one spot on the block seven days a week 24 hours a day and not worry about the jump out boys on a regular basis.

Jenkin's has left once again five to six hours prior to Chicken and I leaving behind him on his way to Mississippi with the cocaine. Some of the cocaine will be distributed and eventually find its way to Pensacola, Louisiana, and Alabama. I've always preferred him to leave no later than 6:00am during the weekdays. This enabled him to take his time and flow with the traffic while blending in through the toll plaza in the City of Wildwood, Florida and arrive in Mississippi during the time when there would be a flux of work traffic with people on their way home from their daily jobs, Jenkins would take and park the stash car in a secluded designated area that had been picked or a house garage of someone that's expecting his arrival. I would call him, Darryl or Roscoe to determine if he's made it there safe and that everything is secured.

The Enterprise "Testimony"

Since I'm on my way there on this particular trip, the distribution will not be done until I arrive for no other reason except I'll be there to help with it. Sometimes the business would be taken care of prior to my arrival. Jenkins was earning $1,000 per kilo, expense money which was always more than needed because I always wanted him to be comfortable, satisfied and able to shop if he desired. He had moved in with his grandmother who was very elderly and needed assistance around the house. This was only after he had made several trips and needed no more to perform mechanic work to survive. His grandmother shortly afterward passed away. I bought Jenkins a truck and Grand-prix and this is not to include the special Cadillacs I owned for these trips to transport the cocaine. He would keep them as his own vehicles on many occasions. This fool was in a win/win situation and probably talking about it and regretting today how he fucked a good thing up by sending me to the grave yard. There were always three or four of these Cadillac's around waiting to be utilized.

Jenkins grand-mother has passed and the family was undecided as to what they were going to do with her home. The side of the family that lived in California really wasn't interested and had no intentions of maintaining such an old house is what Jenkins was saying. Since Jenkins had been living there and taking care of her I suggested to him that he inquire with his mom and other family members concerning selling it to him and let me know their response. A week or two later he said that they gave him a figure of $28,000. An hour later I was counting $28,000 out to him for the purchase of this home. Some months when I took a break I would still give Jenkins $4,000 or $5,000 on general principle to put in his pocket. To say I was good to him would be an understatement. Did he appreciate and honor the love and friendship? Answer to be revealed.

Antonio Berry

CHAPTER 20

We have made it back to Mississippi in time for Chicken to see his Probation Officer without him being in violation of his court order. I gave Chicken 6 ounces to give to someone else to sell for him and told him to put that money in his pocket, he gave the six ounces to a guy name Paul P. The next time the car leaves to go down south to Miami for cocaine I'm going to place enough money in the bumper to buy him a package of cocaine that would set him financially in good shape. I've done the same for all my partners that came home from doing either State or County time in prison or jail. Would these same individuals give me the same treatment if the shoe was on the other foot? I doubt it very seriously. Within a week enough money has been made and collected to prepare for another trip to buy more cocaine with cocaine belonging to the Enterprise still being circulated on the Streets.

I'm preparing to leave for this trip when this Guy name Dave approached me with the request to purchase a kilo of cocaine. I told him come on Dave you know better and know I don't get down like that. I knew him and his large family of brothers and sisters well and if it had been anybody else approaching me with this conversation I would have immediately thought it was a set up. I've known Dave for many years and he was cool but he knew he wasn't going to be able to purchase a kilo of cocaine from me. I responded further by stating that the prices of cocaine has went up so high and were dam near too high for me to make any money. This was so because the prices had risen after the arrest of General Manuel Noriega.

"My cousin Said he can get them in Orlando for $17,000.00," stated Dave.

"That's where I'm living and about to head for in about an hour or two. If they have them in Orlando for that price, then you need to follow me down there so I can buy 10 or 15," I told Dave.

He hesitated and I explained to Dave that another fact was I don't want to be responsible for anybody else's money. This is due to the fact that if something was to happen I may be able to take the lost and continue on with my business. This may not be the case for the next man. I've seen this cause a major problem because one person is now broke and the other one is still hustling and having money as if nothing has happened. The man that's broke is thinking that the one with the money and still able to hustle owe him or having second thoughts whether or not the money was really taken, lost or robbed for. I didn't want to be involved in something of that nature simply because it started out with me trying to do a favor. I didn't need anybody else's money. I had more than enough of my own.

"I trust you Tony. I know you're not petty and know you're a long ways from being broke," said Dave.

"That's just something I don't feel comfortable doing," I responded.

I had an idea that suddenly hit me like a ton of Bricks with Chicken in mind. He knew Dave just as well as I did and Dave knew Chicken was deep in the mist of this Enterprise. I tell Chicken about the idea I have. I explained to him that Dave wants to spend $17,000 but I told him that I don't believe in taking other people money and mixing it with mines and that he couldn't buy a kilo for the $17,000 he was trying to spend. I tell Chicken if he come ride with me to Miami and then Orlando and help me cook up all the dope that I'll put $5,000 with Dave money and buy and extra kilo and turn it into 65 ounces. He can give Dave 30 ounces for his $17,000 and he kept the other 35 ounces for the $5,000 and the dope will still be good. Chicken response to this was.

"Are you serious man", asked Chicken.

"I'm dead serious," I told him!

This was the beginning of Chicken first time having a substantial amount of money and change of demeanor. Everyone saw it coming but me. I seen it but was not paying close enough attention to what was obvious and labeled it as something other.

We as humans have a tendency to not want to believe and always giving people the benefit of the doubt. This is not always good to do and can be very fatal. Take heed and act on it accordingly. The grass was too high and I was too blinded to see, understand and recognize that I was soon going to be betrayed. Matthew 17:14.

Antonio Berry

CHAPTER 21

Red Charles was from Jackson, Mississippi and had plenty of money. I had always heard about him but we had yet to have the opportunity to be introduced. Red served prison time in the same program as Jeff and Chicken for receiving stolen property. While there Red and Chicken developed a friendship that flourished and one that they would take to the street from prison. They would often talk and reminisce about the day when it would come time for them to be released. In their minds was a hatched plan to come together and see what they could make happen in the streets. Chicken had told Red about me and our friendship. Red had also heard my name ringing in the circle of street hustlers and knew I was causing waves and had the coast on locks.

Almost a month after their release Red decided to visit the Coast. By this time Chicken had stacked him a fat bank roll. I was in town and hadn't yet left to head home to Orlando and had the opportunity to formally meet Red for the first time- Red had been making money since he was in his teens and was well known in the Jackson and the down town area. He had long been a millionaire before I was half-way there. Him and his wife Arleen was and still is some of the best people I have ever met and always treated me like family from day one. They owned and operated Bonnie Liquor store, Big Johns Restaurant on Medger Evers and a game room down town. They also owned several pieces of properties. Red was also known for his professional gambling skills whether it was cards, dice or noting/dragging across the Country Red knew the hustle and how to execute.

Red and I developed a relationship like no other; he was very trustworthy and dependable. Whoever gave Red the game also gave him a set of morals and principles to go along with the game. He knew how to be a friend, loyal and cherished the bond, he seen the same in me and that I had a connection of a never ending supply of cocaine. He had also knew that Chicken came home broke, was somewhat a smoker and in a matter of a month you couldn't tell he wasn't able to buy a pair of payless shoes the previous month. The Relationship that Red and I built was one that had no limits when it came to doing favors for each other. Red had his own money and was deserving of paying the same price as I was paying and that's what happened. When we both got the game from the older playa's that's how it was given to us and we was to give it to only the one's that deserved it... That would soon change and a black eye put in the game. Everybody that met Red loved and respected him. He's a legend in Jackson, Mississippi underworld and many other places across the United States of America. Keep pumping Red.

There was times Red and I have traveled to different places, besides taking him to meet all my people in other States we would go on shopping sprees, Daytona, Florida to spring breaks or just follow the car that Jenkins was driving down and back from Miami. We had money to burn and often threw some in the fire. We would double date to a movie with our wives and some NFL games in the New Orleans Superdome. Our most pleasant and memorable time was when we took a vacation cruise through the Caribbean. It was the Bahamas, Grand Cayman, Jamaica and Cancun. It's a memory I will never forget. This is the life style we were living and the next planned trip we had anticipated on was to travel to London and Paris.

The Enterprise "Testimony"

To give a small example of the type of weight that's being handled and moved around by the Enterprise I misplaced a kilo of cocaine one day. This was very dangerous to do and let me tell you briefly why and what happened as it relates to a close call and scare. I'm preparing to send Jenkins off to Miami on another cf many trips.

"What's up, Freddy?" asked Red.

"Nothing much Red. Just lying here taking it easy and talking to Janice about to fall asleep."

"What's shaking?" asked Red.

"Let me call you back."

"What's up Red? I wanted to call you back on the chip phone."

"Do you have anything lying around I can get until I score something?" asked Red.

"I may have one left," was my response to Red's question.

"Let me get it for some people of mines and I'll give it back to you and soon as I score."

"You got that," was my only response.

We had chip phones that cost $3,500 and you were stealing air time for free. You couldn't receive incoming calls but they couldn't be traced, bugged and there was no phone bill that came with it. Chicken, Roscoe and I, and eventually Bob, had all bought us a phone from this white guy friend that was selling them in Pascagoula, he was a good guy and wasn't going to just sell them to any and everybody but we had been around for a while and he trusted us. Red and I talked back and forth for several minutes and he agreed to pay a driver to deliver the kilo of cocaine to him. These phones was very safe to talk on and we had tested them on several occasions and knew without a doubt that nobody was on the other end listening. If that hadn't been true the Enterprise would have long been dismantled and crumbled. Technology hadn't advanced to that stage at this time.

I called Darryl and asked him to contact one of our child hood friends name Bryant who we called Lil' Dick Vitale and check to see if he wanted some extra money. The only thing he would have to do is drive the Cadillac with the kilo of cocaine in the bumper about 35 miles south of Jackson to Red. Red had built a 5,000 square feet home on 18 acres of land with a pond. Darryl is told to tell Bryant that Red is going to pay him $1,500 to bring it. Red was going to return the kilo once he purchased his own supply. These were small favors done between us regularly. If either wanted to borrow $200,000 or more all needed was to ask.

The Cadillac which Jenkins is going to drive to Miami is loaded with more than $400,000. It's me, Roscoe, Darryl and Snap that's at the service station in two separate automobiles gassing the Cadillac up to be dropped off to Jenkins. Roscoe has a 45 caliber pistol playing with Snap while talking shit. We're relaxed because the money is hidden in the same place as always which is the same place where the cocaine will eventually be hidden. I feel more comfortable with money than cocaine and had begun a bad habit of taking $400,000 as no more than $400.00. We take and dropped the gassed up Cadillac with the money off to Jenkins at his House on Jackson Streets. I gave him his traveling expense money and told him as always to be careful and don't leave at a bad time to where he want be able to place some miles behind him before having to stop and pull over to rest if necessary. I prefer for him to drive most of the night trying to make it as far as he can and most of the trips he has been able to drive all the way without stopping and only resting when he arrives in Miami. I had no plans to travel behind him on this particular trip. The next time I see Jenkin's he will have the cocaine in the bumper. This is what I had been thinking and hoping would be the case.

Bryant is sent in one direction on his way to meet Red outside of Jackson at Red's newly built home, Jenkin's is on his way in a total different direction to Miami to meet Corey and Cuban Shorty for another purpose. I'm home in bed trying to fall asleep after a busy day orchestrating these two trips. I never fully rest or relax until any trip is complete.

Just when I begin to doze off to sleep around 11:30pm the house phone rang.

Ring, Ring, Ring!!

"Hello?" I answered.

"What's up, Freddy?" asked Red.

"Bryant should be there by now," I said.

"He's here, but nothing is there," said Red.

"Say What?" I responded thinking 'Am I hearing right?'

"Yeah, he's here but there's nothing in the spot," said Red.

"Hold up," I said, "Let me call you back."

I get up out of the bed and go to the garage and call Red back on my chip phone that's in the car. I need to make sure this conversation can take place with as much understanding as possible. How can nothing be there?

"Now what did you say?" I asked Red again.

"Bryant, aka Lil' Dick, is here and we took the bumper apart, but there's no package inside."

"Let me call Darryl and I'll call you back in a minute," I told Red.

"Darryl, Red said that Lil' Dick is there but there's nothing in the bumper," I said.

"There wasn't anything in the washing machine where you told me to look so it wasn't anything for me to put in the bumper," said Darryl.

I snapped and blew a stack, "Are you stupid or what? Why didn't you call me and let me know you didn't see anything where I had told you to look? Then in that case, why did you still send Lil' Dick to Jackson knowing he didn't have shit in the car?"

Then it hit me. I had been so busy and thought about moving the last kilo I had but never took it from under the seat of the Cadillac that was in the garage. This is the same Cadillac that was packed with $400,000 for Jenkin's trips to Miami. I intended to bolt the bumper back in place, remove the kilo of cocaine and it completely slipped my mind. I made a terrible, what could be costly, mistake. But if Darryl had only said there was nothing in the washing machine where I told him to look, it would have reminded me of where the kilo was. There was so much cocaine being moved around until I had forgotten about this one block of dope. These kinds of mistakes were not good for a business; this was serious.

Jenkins is now on Interstate 10 on his way to Miami, he has no idea that a kilo of cocaine is underneath his front seat sitting right below his ass. The $400,000 is secured in the bumper. To think earlier I was driving this same vehicle with a kilo under the front seat while thinking I'm safe. The fellows were bull shittin' around at the service station not knowing how close the Enterprise was to tumbling down on a fluke. It would have honestly been all my fault. I called Red and explained to him what has happened and that I have to drive the interstate trying to sandwich Jenkins in before he make it to Wildwood and the Turnpike. It's Jenkins and his girl-friend that s in the Cadillac but I have to try and save him. I reached Corey by phone and explained the situation to him and that I needed him to come up the turnpike and help me to sandwich Jenkins in before he make it to Wildwood. Sumter County was one of the hottest Counties in the State of Florida and dope traffickers were constantly being arrested in this area. I watched it on the news every other day while living in Orlando. This is how we worked together as a team and it was necessary and too much involved to allow this to be a fatal mistake without trying to prevent it.

Antonio Berry

CHAPTER 22

Earlier that day I had traveled to New Orleans in Angie's maxima that I had bought her for her birthday. I considered Angie closer to me than any of the other women in which I had an affair. The game she has today came from the teacher she had in the past. The taste she has acquired in automobile, homes, clothes, traveling and restaurants all came from what she had come accustomed to by getting a taste of the life style of the Enterprise. I had left my radar detector in her car and she lived ten miles in the opposite direction from the direction I needed to travel in order to try and catch Jenkins - I decided to buy another one at the truck stop in Escatawpa and exit onto interstate 10. I have to save Jenkins. Take heed that, no one deceives you. Matthew 24:4.

It's me, Darryl and Roscoe that's riding 100mph in Janice Benz 190E and I'm pushing it while roasting Darryl for not thinking also. I instructed Roscoe that if we're stop let them take me to jail and keep going and catch Jenkins. He could bail me out on his way back but we have to stop that Cadillac. I haven't turned on the stereo because I'm busy with the cursing of Darryl for not having enough sense to do some type of thinking with the telling me there wasn't anything where I had told him to look for the kilo. He had recently spent $36,000 cash on a brand new showroom GMC wide cab truck, wood grain, side boards and blaze rims. I'm letting him know that it's more to this than just Spending money. Here I am about to lose $400,000 one kilo of cocaine and two people's lives about to go down the drain. You're about to cost me a million dollars because all you focus on is spending money and having fun. I was pissed the fuck off to where I hit the steering wheel a couple of times emphasizing my point.

When we do finally catch up with Jenkins it was only because he had did something that I was totally against and had told him many of times not to do. He left the house at a bad time of night when he couldn't make it too far without becoming sleepy. He was only able to drive a couple miles east of Pensacola before pulling in a rest area. We had almost passed him when I glanced to the right and spotted him parked between two 18-wheelers asleep. I'm the first one out of the Benz and tapping on the driver side of Jenkins window. This episode has caused me to become so upset until I had diarrhea. I took this business serious because it had become a way of life for me. Jenkin's looked up in a state of shock as if what the hell is going on.

He had to be wondering if he had really left his drive way or had he fallen asleep in his yard before pulling out. He opened his door and I reached in under his seat and grabbed the kilo of cocaine and he hugged me dam near falling to his knees at the sight of the block. His legs had buckled at the sight of the kilo. I should have seen the fright and weakness in him at this time but made a fatal mistake of not recognizing the signs. Roscoe had already called Corey to inform him that we had Jenkins. I assured Jenkins that I will always come to save him and he never had to worry where I stood. I would later find that the feelings weren't mutual. We opened the hood of the Cadillac and stashed the kilo and had Jenkins to follow us back as far as Mobile to drop the kilo off to this fellow named Zeth. My fatal error as such was what contributed also to my demised.

There were very few incidents that I can remember which could have been a catastrophe for the Enterprise. It was always a major concern of mines to protect this organization and everybody associated. If not we wouldn't have lasted or made the type of money we did for the period of time we was having it our way. It was like Burger King is what I use to think while all the time deceiving myself. Jeremiah 37:9. Money is still being made by some of the former members of the Enterprise but it's not being done for the period of time they've been doing it without working for the devils.

Antonio Berry

CHAPTER 23

While living in Orlando for three years I would often wait for the call that everybody was out of dope and the money had at least been made if not yet collected. I was never in a rush to do anything and two of my main themes to the fellows were. If you're always known to have dope and predictable then it will be that much easier to be caught with it. This is the reason that no member of the Enterprise had ever been caught with dope in their possession. The money is going to always be there whenever the dope is available. The other theme was. Hard work dedication and staying true to game and the game will be true to you. This is what I thought would produce longevity and success in the dope game. Nobody was hurting or in the need of anything. This method of thinking would have to be practice by each and every individual that's a member of the Enterprise.

Strictly from boredom I would still on some occasions ride and try to sell a few pieces of slum jewelry in the Cities of Daytona, Winter Garden, Winter Park and other local areas while living in Orlando, Turk would visit and stay for weeks at a time and we would ride together. Turk has long quit the game. I'm riding but this is not my main source of income and method of getting paid and my heart isn't in it anymore. It's more for fun and to keep Turk company. I had been discouraged by the slum game turning its back on me. This is what I want to believe as justification for what I really want to do when all the time it was me that turned my back on the slum game after it had been good to me. The slum game made me the hustler that I became and allowed me to travel across the Country and live off the land. The only other activity I had going on in Orlando was the creeping with other women and shopping. Nobody in this City knew me so it was fairly easy to get away with it without my business making its way back to Janice. Meeka and Tara had visited Disney World so regularly until they begged not to be taken there anymore. I had a habit of pushing Janice and the children off on anybody that we knew who came down on vacation. Most people from around our way would be told to make sure they called us when they arrived because we were home town people that knew the area and was established there. We really wasn't what I would called established and it was more that we had wealth and was able to do as we please and lived a good life. Tara blurted out one day and said, Daddy we don't want to go to Disney World again. I laugh because it seemed that my baby knew and realized my only reason for always sending them to Disney World was so I could run the streets. At times I would have all my children there in Orlando together. Meeka and Tara were Janice's daughters so they were there with us at all times. Janice would make sure the children had a summer vacation.

I had even met a couple o£ women's there who I was spending time with while still occasionally going to Miami visiting Rhondetta. The one's in the Orlando area was Marka in Orlando and Tonya in Sanford. Both of them were cool and very good people but with opposite personalities that I had to make adjustments when dealing with each. It wasn't a problem because they were easy to get alone with and just wanted some time spent with them. They knew I had a woman at home and never tripped with me or did things to bring attention to our relationship. These are the only type of relationships I would be a part of because I definitely wasn't going to leave Janice or break my family up for the streets. I was tricking but not going to be tricked. If this worked for them then they could enjoy and live the life style that the enterprise was living.

Marka and I met one evening after she and some of her friends and cousins had noticed Darryl, Roscoe and Nunie riding around Orlando in my maxima. She said later that she had been seeing that car and wondered who it belonged to. I told her I got that response all the time. Even on the interstate while traveling people would dam near break their necks trying to look and was always complimenting me on how clean it was. The fellows were out this particular evening turning some corners while visiting. That was something they did regular when there and Janice would constantly be saying I needed to keep them out of my cars because people would later think it was me. One day Janice and the children were coming from down town and spotted one of my vehicles at a store. There was a woman in the passenger seat but the driver was missing. She took the next exit and came back that's when she seen Turk come out the door of the store. When she and the children arrived home there I am on the couch watching television. She said it again then that I need to keep them out of my cars because just like that somebody else may mistake it for me with another woman or somebody else's woman in the car.

I said to myself if only she knew that I wasn't a saint. I always thought she had to know I was a hot commodity and the type of money and life style I was living it should be obvious that women was going to be chasing and jocking.

Turk had been visiting Orlando when Marka came into the picture of my life. After Darryl and the others made it back to the hotel room at the Days Inn on 33rd Street they was talking about these broads that was jocking the maxima and screaming and pointing as if to say there goes that car I've been telling you'll about. I asked them what neighborhood it was in and they said it was the Richmond Heights area. I was familiar with this area and it wasn't too far away from here. We jumped back inside the maxima and I put in Too $hort "I Ain't Tripping" and set out on a mission to capture our latest prey. I was hoping they hadn't left and would still be in the neighborhood. We turned the corner and there they were, hanging out in the front yard on a warm summer evening in their sunshine state attire. Some had on Daisy Dukes, others with halter tops and slides. Their hairdo was fresh and looking like some young tender Roni's.

They were told what hotel that Turk and the fellows was staying and to follow us. I'm living in Orlando so Janice and I have a Townhouse we're leasing, The Roni's trailed behind to the room where we was all introduced and had a few laughs, I have to say this because it was true,, We was some pro's when it came to catching broads. We had conned and tricked females across the Country so this wasn't something new to us the prey just didn't know how seasoned these dudes was they're about to get involved with. I asked them did they want to have dinner with us and if so follow us to Bennigan's on the trail which is what the locals called Orange Blossom trail. By this time unbeknownst to us they had already chose which one of us they each wanted and Marka and I had the same taste and thoughts in mind. She was choosing me at the same time while I was locking eyes on her. Marka was almost twenty and two years out of Jones High School and I was twenty four. She was 5'7, 140, fine as hell, tender and fresh. She was yet to be tainted and drove for miles when I came into her life. This mean I was getting a warrant on my investment.

Everybody was eating, drinking, laughing and having a blast of a good time. I leaned over and whispered in Marka ear to let's make it for the door and we eased our way to the car. One by one we all performed the same James Bond act of leaving Turk sitting at the table with a $300.00 tab. He paid it but walked out the door to the car screaming that he wanted his money. This was the first real laughter that Marka and I shared together. She experienced the relationship that all the fellows had. Somebody was always being humorous but we did give Turk his money back and paid our half on the bill. I guess you could have called us a bunch of pranksters.

Marka would later accompany me on trips and wouldn't allow me to leave town without her. She had recently escaped and went through a break-up with her very abusive boy-friend and was now living with her mother Ms. Jenny in Lake Mann Garden. He had bought her a white Toyota and taken it back not knowing about me. A car was the furthest from Marka's mind at this time especially when she knew I had so many and was pushing some hell-u-va rides. I had been shot in the arm trying to flee the scene of an attempted carjacking in the project on Ivy Lane. Turk and I had came the back way on Colonial coming from Daytona Beach working and stopped in the project on Ivy Lane to buy a couple bags of weed. On the way out there were two guys that called out something in our direction that neither Turk nor I understood.

Turk originally didn't even see them and the only reason I notice them was, because I'm the driver and had to look in both direction before pulling out in potential traffic.

I shifted the Jaguar in reverse to back up to try and get a better understanding of what they were saying, the first guy to the car was fast approaching Turk side while speaking at the same time which sounded as if he was asking if we was from Pensacola. While asking this question he was sticking a pistol in the window on Turk side. Turk grabbed the pistol and scream hit it bro-n-law but at this same moment I was already mashing the gas. I was able to see the second guy in my side mirror coming around from the back side of the car and he was pulling what looked to be a chrome 9mm from his waist band, I mashed the accelerator giving the Jaguar all it could take. Jaguars has a very slow acceleration and I was shot in the arm by one of the 10 or 15 shots fired by the perpetrators before running the stop sign and crashing nose first in a ditch, I was unable to make the turn at the corner stop. The ambulance arrived on the scene and although it was only a arm wound I was hauled off to the hospital to be examined. When Turk initially called Janice and told her I had been shot she thought he was joking and said for him to stop playing. That was one call she always dreaded would come one day. Janice knew I was a potential target by the would-be robbers and law enforcements.

The hospital staff allowed Janice, Meeka and Tara to come in the room where I was being examined. The bullet had gone straight through my upper left arm by passing any main arteries and leaving only bullet fragments in the wound. Some of the fragments were able to be removed and the rest would have to remain unless I wanted major surgery performed on my arm leaving that arm numb, sensitive and aching whenever there was bad weather. It would remain this way for years to come. This shooting episode has caused me to never again leave the house without my automatic Bersa 380 unless I'm going slumming and back home. I would cruise with it in my lap when riding the City and especially during the night.

CHAPTER 24

Although the shooting had taken place in the brightest of the day I still wasn't taking any chance or trying to get caught slipping without my 380 Bersa. Marka ex boy-friend has now heard about this new playa in town and he's pushing weight and has taken one of the local boy's girl. She didn't have her mind on him and became involved with this out-of-town baller. The town is screaming and he's embarrassed by what has happened. I wasn't putting any dope on the streets of Orlando and the only illegal activity I had going on there was cooking dope and traveling the interstate/turnpike. The sight of me made it obvious that I had it going on somewhere and wherever it was I was clocking money hand over fist.

After a late night of Marka and I hanging out, I pulled into Lake Mann Garden to drop her off at her Mothers. We said our goodbyes and that we'll see each other tomorrow and she exited the car. As soon as she closed the car door she broke out in a sprint run towards her Mother's apartment door. At the same time I looked in my review mirror and spot this old school square Lincoln pulling up behind me bouncing on its shocks. I was blocked in with one bullet in the chamber ready to let loose if necessary. I was paranoid and willing to go out in a blaze. This 6'6" monster of a guy exited the Lincoln and walked to my driver side window and asked me if I was Marka's man. I told him there she is; ask her questions not me. He looked back and pointed to the driver of the Lincoln to let me out. If he only knew what I had on my mind and how he so made the right decision. He didn't have anything in his hand

and mine was on the trigger. The only thing I'm thinking about was the fact that I had recently been shot and wasn't taking any chances. He didn't have to tell the driver to let me out because I had already formulated a plan in my mind to shoot everything that stood in my way.

This man was so in love with Marka that once he discovered where I lived he came by the Townhouse and asked Janice to ask me give him his woman back. This was some of the weakest shit I had ever seen and couldn't believe it. I pretended as if it must have been Turk or one of the fellows this guy seen in one of my vehicles. I believe it was more of her being with me and not doing bad and depending on him like he had hope she would come back running to him. If she had became involved with a scrub and someone unable to do for her and wasn't having the type of money that he guess I was having then he probably would have been able to accept it differently. I'm somebody new in this City and have trapped a local street thug woman. When in reality I didn't steal her as much so as he ran her off and into my arms. On top of it all his behavior wasn't helping his cause in the slightest bit. He was very embarrassed and humiliated by this turn of event.

It was me, Marka, Qwanda (R.I.P.), and Kim one night that was riding around playing the lottery scratch off when the guy brother pulled up beside us at a red light. We were in Janice's Benz and he was in his two-door Coupe Deville Cadillac. I knew then that I had to drop the girls off at home because it wouldn't be long before the guy received a phone call. I was 100% correct because less than ten minutes after making it home I looked out the window in the face of this 6'6" dark-skinned monster at my door. I opened it with my 380 in my hand and asked him what he wanted coming by my house. He stated that his brother had called and said that Marka was with me. I said man I'm home with my wife and children and you have awakened my partners and other people in my house that's looking out at this crazy shit. There was nobody in the house but me, Janice and the children but I had to bluff this monster, he said I see man and turned around in defeat. If he had half a brain he could have easily touched the hood of the car and blistered his hand because it was still hot and the engine hadn't been shut off for a good 15 minutes. He would continue with the foolish behavior in an attempt to cause her to stop or scare her into stop being with me. He even asked me to call him when I had her at the hotel.... I asked him was he retarded crazy because I wasn't that type of playa. None of the above tactic by him would prevail because I was a real coast playa.

Marka continued to travel the highway with me when it wasn't a trip that Janice and the children would be taking. I had to take them sometimes and especially on holidays. Marka would actually cry and be seriously sad if I left her in Orlando. Once she asked me why didn't I take her because she had seen Janice and knew I didn't take them. That woman loved going to Mississippi and had became knowledgeable of the area and the people there. She would frequent the area as if she had lived there her entire life. I would tell her most of the time before leaving Orlando that I was going to be busy taking care of my business and wouldn't have time for her like that. She would still insist on coming and say she'll stay in the hotel. I had eventually bought her a small car to ride in when she wasn't driving one of mines. This was cool because Janice was not living or in town. Everybody came to know Marka and she begin to feel like a local.

Antonio Berry

CHAPTER 25

I met Tonya while confirming money that had been sent via Western Union to me in Orlando. She was employed at the downtown office on Orange Avenue. She had a home in Apopka, a small city north of Orlando. Although most of the time she lived with her mother in Sanford as opposed to Apopka. Tonya had recently been in an automobile accident and was going through therapy. Prior to her accident, her long time, off-and-on boyfriend of two years had been accidentally killed while trying to calm an argument between two friends. She had one son and hadn't dated since his death.

Tonya was a gorgeous woman, 5'5", 120 pounds with the skin color of brown sugar. She was as sweet as any woman could be with a soprano voice and puppy eyes that won me over. Tonya was definitely house wife material and I probably would have taken her to be just that if not for Janice currently holding down that position. I met several of her family members who was all down to earth and made me feel at home. I would sometimes visit her mother while Tonya was at work. When Tonya would make it home and discovered that I had visited her Mom she would, become angry when I say to her that I'm not coming back to Sanford today. I was bored and took me a ride to see her Mom. I tell her I had nothing to do earlier and would see her tomorrow. This was really winning her mother over and I have always enjoyed making my women friends parents feel special. Tonya and her mom had a wonderful relationship and communicated as if they were sister with great respect for one another.

This was a very decent family in which Tonya came from. I only remember one of her sisters Shelia that was in the military and stationed in Texas around this time. There were days when Tonya would remain in a hotel in Orlando and leave from there for work the next morning. We would lie around together until may be 11:00pm to 11:30pm watching television after cuddling for a couple of hours. One night while leaving from her home in Apopka traveling south on Orange Blossom Trail I noticed on the right hand side there was a field which seemed to be a group of people and what appeared to be a barn fire.. Once I made it home I turned on the television to watch a few minutes of the news and smoke a joint of weed before going to bed. The news was broadcasting that the barn fire I witness was a KKK meeting. I use to mess with Tonya about I wasn't trying to get caught coming from her house in the middle of the night. I could come up missing.

I was always taking lunch to Tonya and her co-workers at the Western Union. They loved to eat from the Olive Garden on Colonial. They use to fall head over heels thinking me and assuring Tonya that she had a sweet man. Tonya could be very feisty and hard to deal with at times. Here we are traveling down Orange Blossom Trail (OBT) on our way to the Florida Mall. From out of nowhere we was pulled over by this State Trooper that I had not noticed coming up behind us. OBT is the main throughway in the City of Orlando so there, was always a large number of Highway Troopers cruising up and down the trail. For no other reason except having an out-of-town tag which is normal in Orlando but also being black in a expensive candy green AMG kitted out Mercedes Benz we was pulled over by this trooper. He questioned the ownership of the vehicle and asked was there anything illegal inside or in the trunk. Most of my vehicles was custom and gave the appearance to be newer than they were. I stated no sir and it wasn't anything illegal nowhere in the car because being stopped for no apparent reason has happened to me on several occasions.

The trooper asked Tonya if he could search her purse, she begin ranting and raving saying no and telling him he did not have any right or cause to search her purse. This behavior by Tonya caused the Trooper to become alarmed and he called for backup. Now he's thinking we have something to hide. This shit is about to get crazy right here in the middle of the trail. I know for sure there's nothing in her purse because prior to leaving the hotel five minutes ago I was rambling through her purse looking for my keys. Tonya was only being rebellious the way she could be sometimes when she feel aggravated and this was one of those moments for her. I know for sure it's not that time of the month it's just Tonya being Tonya.

The true reason the trooper is suspicious is because of the foul odor of the marijuana he smells coming from the vehicle.

I knew from the beginning that this was his reason for asking if there was anything illegal inside the vehicle. We had left the hotel smoking a joint but I was not about to ride with any substantial of anything illegal in this vehicles. When he walked to the car he could smell it. This Benz turned too many heads and attracted too much attention from on lookers as well as law enforcement. Two other yellow and black State Trooper ford Mustangs (Bumble Bees) pulled up with more troopers, I stepped in and calm her down and told her to let them search her purse. Tonya gave me a look as if she wanted to take my head off for going against her wishes and argument with them. I can see a much bigger picture becoming of this scene and it want be pretty for us. This could become blown out of proportion all because of Tonya mean streak.

The search was done and we were allowed to proceed on to the mall with only a warning about the odor. As soon as we were rolling and out of sight of the troopers I gave Tonya the tongue lashing of her life damn near went postal on her. I asked her if she was stupid or just plain retarded for what she pulled back there with the troopers. I attempted to get my point across to her that she was about to cause them to tow my car and that having it drug on the back of a truck could destroy my AMG kit.

The car is not in my name and it's possible the owner will have to be the one to get it out of impound if they decide to retaliate and all for what? You being stubborn knowing that you didn't have shit to hide. I'm trying to avoid all trouble. I really was concerned about the fact that I could be with Janice, or her in this vehicle one day and the same officer notice the car and pull it over with Janice driving. Besides this one incident, all the other times that I spent with Tonya was some pleasant moments.

I actually had two women's by the name of Tonya. The other one was Tonya who was my young, slim red bone that stood about 5'8. She was a tender Roni that I enjoyed spending time with when I wanted some feisty moments and also some good laughs. She was from Moss Point and I have taken her places with me on several occasions. She was good people that wasn't any different than the others when it came to being impressed by the life style I was living and the environment that was being created as a result of my behavior and activities. On one particular trip to Orlando t she claimed to be pregnant from me. I believed her, and to this day, she still has love for me and I never mistreat her. She's one of my babies' Mother.

Antonio Berry

CHAPTER 26

Janice and I decided that after Meeka's school year ended we're moving back to Mississippi. First we must have additional work did to our home on Charles St. in Moss Point to accommodate the furniture we have accumulated. The girls should each have their individual bed rooms. There's also Tody, Lil' Tony and Antrice alone with their cousin that will be spending time with us.

I seek out my father's cousin Roy for a construction estimate. I had thought the hiring of him would be a good idea. The home was originally 1,400 sq ft and valued at a little more than $50,000. My intentions are to increase it to 4,800 sq ft with a fire place and raising the value to five times that amount. I never reported any of the addition to the tax assessor office knowing this would have increased my yearly State and County taxes. At the time of my arrest and seizure the home at 4,800 sq ft was still listed at the same original value.

Roy gives his estimate and agrees to a suitable time frame. I explained to him the urgency of completion. The new school year begin for Meeka in August and we're trying to be in no later than the end of June. Tara's transition will not be as complicated as Meeka's. I could have chosen a more morally carpenter than Roy. I made a fatal error at attempting to have the money and job remain in the family. Another decision based on my emotions and self-righteousness will prove to be fatal. Roy was deacon so surely he was going to do right by his first cousin son. The snake will bite you every time. The end was much worse than the beginning and not worth the price I must now pay for a few pieces of lumber and nails. 2 Peter 2:20.

Bob, Tracy, Kellie, Doug and the one guy from Mobile name Punkin were pushing some of the cocaine weight that I'm sending to Mississippi to be distributed by the enterprise. The female Kellie and Doug who was Kenny D. brother was the best people hand down and proven later not to have any snake venom. Kellie would even call some times and let me know when she would be visiting her husband in the State prison just in case I came to town and she wasn't around. I always assured her that if she had anything she wanted to give me that she could give it to Darryl, Roscoe or anybody she knew that was associated with me. That was something I never worried about was whether my money would reach my hands.

Kellie and I had a short flame and then decided we were too close of friends to destroy it. Kellie was a very good and decent woman and I made it clear to her that anything she wanted all she had to do was ask and she wouldn't have to ask twice. Once her husband Cat was released from State prison he wanted me to begin giving him the package of cocaine that I had been giving Kellie while he's been in prison.

I explained to him that she had been straight with me and I didn't think it would be right or fair for me to do that to her. The smart and wise thing for me to do was to back up before a problem arose and let her know I was, and will always be, in her corner and she was very understanding of this decision.

The way I came about dealing with Tracy was through his brother Roscoe as a favor. This would be one favor I did for Roscoe in which I should have refused because it had an everlasting detrimental poisonous effect. It's a true saying about hind-sight that it is 20/20. Although you can't believe nothing you hear, and half of what you see, at face value—still make that extra effort to pay close attention. The most deadly snake is the one right before you that has the upside down frown taken to be a smile. And desired favor against him, that he would send for him to Jerusalem, lay waiting in the way to kill him. Act 25:2.

I received a phone call from Roscoe saying he needed to speak with me about a matter. The first thing came to mind is, something has happened that we have to look into. It wasn't as serious as I had thought r he only wanted to explain to me that he and Darryl had been selling Tracy a few ounces of cocaine real cheap and in a way that they really couldn't afford and still make money. Their only reason for doing this was because Tracy was Roscoe's brother. At this time Darryl and Roscoe was breaking and cutting their dope into smaller pieces and making more money and as much as possible off each package they purchased. Roscoe asked me was it possible or would I start Tracy off by fronting him some dope. Based on Roscoe recommendation I told him to have Tracy come talk to me in person. My GOD was this conversation ever a fatal mistake. How was I to know that Tracy was a desert rattle snake and his bite would be fatal?

Tracy informed me that he only has enough money to purchase two or three ounces of cocaine. I explained and gave Tracy the method in which the enterprise operated. You didn't need any money if we took you in and that all you needed was your trust, loyalty and to be straightforward. Second, how much can you handle because I know this is about to be something he has never imagined, he had been

115

paying $900.00 to $1,000 an ounce for the couple of ounces he had been buy around town. I'm about to introduce him to the first large sum of real money he has ever had in his possession. The first package of dope I gave Tracy consisted of ten ounces of the best crack cocaine on the coast. This was the Miami butter dope and it would make him a instant celebrity dope dealer in the streets. The price I quoted him was for $800.00 a piece. He did the same as everyone usually did when I gave them the quota when they were lucky enough to deal with me. He didn't believe or think he had heard me correctly and asked me was I sure. I only smile and said yes, you heard me correct because there's enough money for everybody.

CHAPTER 27

Tracy would come to not only want his share of the money but death and total destruction to many others and the enterprise. Never share all your pearls before applying the ultimate test of loyalty or sincerity. You have to create a real life scenario to determine where a person is at mentally and with their loyalty to you. This is very important when dealing with others in the capacity that could cause great harm. If not it could be too late by the time you learn you've been dealing with a snake and a worthless worm.

As my business relationship with Tracy progressed I begin to supply him with as many as 200 to 300 ounces at a time for $750.00 an ounce. He was always straight and never short with my money count. My win came with me cooking the dope and I wouldn't change that for years to come. I would also allow Tracy, on occasions, as I would do with the others to purchase a kilo or half a kilo whichever he wanted for the same price as I was paying. You couldn't lose when dealing with me and every one of them knew this too well. This was to assure that everybody had more than enough more and was beyond satisfied. You would think so anyway. It was no different with him as with the others when it came to giving my love and loyalty. I put forth extra effort to make sure he understood that if I had it so did he.

Somebody had decided that Tracy shouldn't have the corvette he- was riding in and set it on fire and he hadn't yet became financially stable before this incident. He called me with the news and the first thing I tell him is to go to my Mother's house and pick out one of the cars inside the fence. Roscoe and he had told me one day that they wanted to move their mother from this area in which she was living. My first response was to tell her to find one. She found one and my second response was to tell her to do the paper work. Tracy wanted another corvette to replace the one that had been set on fire. I had sold one of my vehicles to Corey in Miami for 30 ounces and had recently purchased Janice a Benz. To help Tracy with the buying of another corvette I gave him a deal on the 30 ounces. The car was going to be bought regardless I was just doing it from a win/win point of view applying good economic. I told Tracy to give me $15,000 for 15 of the ounces and keep the other 15 ounces to put towards him another corvette. Then once he had sold the dope I took him to Orlando where there's this famous corvette car dealership in Winter Park. Was I sweet or what? I know it now.

This is the years, between 1989 and 1990, when $100,000.00s were being shuffled around as if one dollar bills. While this is happening I failed to read the first sign of a potential harmful problem. This was after Tracy had stolen cocaine that was buried by Darryl and Roscoe. They had arrested General Noriega and the dope prices had increased tremendously to almost doubling in the price. The price of cocaine became sky high and scarce in supply. If you was able to obtain any you were blessed and paid a high price for it regardless of the number or amount of kilos you were purchasing. The car was loaded with money and sent to me in Florida to take care of the business on that end. I purchased what I could and sent the car back with the instructions not to bother or touch anything until I arrived in town. This was one of the times I let some people that I was fronting buy dope for my price. I needed to explain to them what has happened and what needed to be done before distributing it out.

I arrived in town late that night and I let Jeff know that I couldn't obtain all the cocaine we had initially sent for. The next morning Jeff relayed this information to the crew. Everybody took it in stride except Tracy. The problem was something small to the point that everybody had to accept half of what they sent for meaning Tracy would only be able to receive a quarter of kilo of cocaine. Even with this being the case Tracy knew he could still depend on receiving the cocaine I would front to him so, there should be no problem. I believe it was more about the person delivering the message than the message itself. Jeff assured Tracy that these were my instructions due to what was happening down south in Miami with the dope trade. This was one of the times that I even accepted to shorten myself and really didn't have to in all actuality. I did this in order to be able to accommodate the crew with a portion of their request and for a show of loyalty on my behalf. I could have easily claimed what I had intended to purchase and divided the remainder between them. I had no obligation to do what I was doing except I preached loyalty, sincerity and was standing on it and leading by example. It was my connection, thinking and effort that kept the business operating. Opening your hands to the poor and needy isn't always good and Tracy, Chicken, Bob and a few of the rest came from a poor family. Dt. 15:11.

Tracy did not accept these instructions too well coming from Jeff. An argument had ensued between the two when I finally arrived on the scene the next day on Jackson Street in Moss Point. Tracy was screaming that he wanted his money back or he was going to call the police. The boy was a real Ho. I'm tripping like what the hell is going on and then the amount of money he had sent to Miami was pocket change and not even a third of the amount of dope I was fronting to him. I should have taken heed then but made a fatal error of not doing so. I didn't take him serious about calling the police concerning a couple of thousand dollars. I say give me ten minutes and I'll be back with your money. I gave him his money and didn't deal with him for more than a year and it should have been forever. Tracy began to deal with a connection from California and the dope was not as potent as the Enterprise dope. He was not having the same type of money in the amount he was having with the Enterprise and couldn't compete. He had also managed to bring heat to himself from law enforcement. His mother's house was raided as well as the apartment in which he lived in Mobile. The DEA found and seized $69,000 in his mother's freezer and a couple of thousands in Mobile. He had never suffered a lost or attracted any heat while involved with the Enterprise.

I was aware that Tracy had resentment towards Jeff and was jealous of him same as I knew and understood the tension between Jeff and Chicken based on similar reasons. This resentment was Tracy fault and own doing because of his weakness. Tracy didn't like the fact that Jeff had an affair with a woman that he was attracted to. Jeff had told Tracy about the episode with the woman and I think it was more of Tracy's perverted thoughts in his mind that captivated him while listening to Jeff describe the times he spent with the woman. I have many days and nights of regrets for not taking notice and acting on the weakness that was displayed so many times by Tracy's action and behavior. The boy is a born weakling and when these white folks is done using him as a register informant and toss him to the wolves that is if the Mexicans don't discover his secret life first, he will be cooked. Stick a fork him, he deserve it. This was another instance where eve was about to destroy the Enterprise. If you see a snake on the side of the road, kill it or pass on by but never pick it up. The snake will do what's in its nature to do and that's to bite and poison you.

The year has passed smoothly and things had been quite. Everybody was avoiding and ostracizing Tracy because of his behavior with Jeff and his lack of understanding. Even his bother Roscoe was feeding and playing him with a long handle spoon. I saw him one day appearing as if he had cancer or some other related disease that was eating at him from inside outward. We spoke and I told him that I had heard about his misfortune and the seizure. The connection from California was pressing him about their money and was adamant about they didn't give dam about what the DEA/police found or seized in his Mother's house. To take a lost was not that easily done by some organizations and he's now grasping what he had with the enterprise. This is what separated and exposed the one's that was faking and perpetrating in the dope game. Looks can be deceiving but the truth has a way of revealing itself. Tracy realizes now and knows he had the best thing he could have ever had in the palm of his hands. He had a connection with a enterprise who never was in short supply of cocaine or money. It's often you don't miss your water until your well runs dry.

It was Xmas time and the holiday spirits are obvious and I always slowed things down around this time of the year. In my mind I tried to create a sense of balance and decency in the dope game but that's impossible. I would ask other hustlers to slow it down in an attempt to allow the children to have a better Xmas and holiday. Some cared and some could care less but who was I to dictate a set of morals and principles one time a year. I had been pumping dope throughout the communities of States and Cities all year and now I was asking those that probably couldn't afford to stop and take a vacation. I gave Tracy

$3,500 to shop for his children with the understanding that it's going to be alright after the holidays and that I will be calling him. Another fatal error on my behalf because jealousy is the rage of a man. Proverb 6:32.

I would buy and give the children gifts. My nieces Chasity, Keshia, Lisa, Ce-Ce, Nephews Mike, Bussie, Buck, Fat-Albert, Jermaine, Terrell along with my children Meeka, Andraya aka Tody, Lil' Tony a/k/a -Man, Antrice and Tara would all have some of the most wonderful Xmas imaginable because I was going to make it happen for everybody.

CHAPTER 28

Bob who most called by the name of BC was a local nobody.

I was always questioned as to why I allowed him into my circle because of the tree and roots in which he sprouted. The saying that a limb doesn't fall far from the tree is such a true statement that's confirmed in the reflection of BC. Bob was having a teenage love affair with one of Janice's nieces. I had noticed him in different hood areas of the County and assumed he was hustling crack cocaine unguided. To me he was the same but had a slight edge and different from some of the other youngsta that was wild and having fun. He had gotten lucky and discovered the economical dynamics of the cocaine game and was trying to come through the door but with no real guidance on what was necessary and required to elevate to the next level beyond street corner hustling. I had no business trying to be his teacher and it would later prove fatal for me to do so.

When I encountered Bob for the first time face to face we were both visiting Chicken mother's house. I took a liking to him and thought he could be cultivated into a loyal friend and hustler never a foe. He was already a family friend of Chicken's which should have spoken volume to me but I missed it. Chicken invited him on a trip to Florida which I said was ok. This had to be in the top ten of the worst mistakes I'd made in my life beginning with allowing him to participate traveling to Florida and trying to broaden his mind and thinking in the cocaine hustling game. Bob would later testify for the Government to his beginning which constituted this first trip he made with me. You have to let the dead stay sleep and never awaken them to the truth. He learned how the enterprise operated and it was deadly for him to have such knowledge.

The second mistake that I made after agreeing to allow him the opportunity to travel down to South Miami would put the nails in my coffin. The second fatal mistake was to let Bob earn money by dealing and associating with the enterprise. It has been said since the beginning of time that men will be unthankful. 2 Timothy 3:2.

I took Bob under my wings and tried to teach and groom him on how to spread his wings and fly same as I did Darryl and Roscoe. I was attempting to give him the game as it was given to me. This was with some morals and principles incorporated with loyalty. It's impossible to change the stripes on a tiger. You can and should sometimes only seek to make them extinct and in the case of Bob extinct would have been a better choice for mankind. In the past some Countries and leaders sought to destroy an entire blood line which one came from. Whether it was being a thief, traitor, adulterous or plain untrustworthy you and your entire blood line would be destroyed. Life experiences had led me to trust and agree that there's nothing wrong with this belief. How could I believe otherwise when it's dam what a person say and more of what you know to be a fact and this is something I know to be a testimonial fact.

The first thing I did as a gesture of initiation into the enterprise was to make sure Bob could purchase cocaine at a special price regardless of the small quantity he was buying from local dealers around the area. His hustling increased and he was beginning to make a name for himself. It didn't hurt or take away from the cause that he was now having the best grade of dope and people would see him associating with the enterprise. The Enterprise had that type of effect and it was desired by everybody who considered themselves a part of this hustling world. Bob friends would envy him and seek to position themselves in the same like as he had become. This is not how the game goes; you don't recruit just to increase your numbers. You have to be chosen and sometimes the people who are doing the choosing make bad decisions and choices as so I did.

The hustlers that were close to Bob's age envy him because they knew Bob had become connected. They knew he could now obtain cocaine from a direct source and that was rare. It wouldn't be long before Bob was swimming and surfing in large sums of money and all the other finer things that came with this game and the way the Enterprise was executing it. The predictors was 100% correct and on the mark. Bob would live and sleep in the Village all night selling crack cocaine and not only couldn't stop didn't want to stop. The transformation was unbelievable to him and he was experiencing a phase of the game he did not know existed. Overnight he had accumulated a sum of money that would consider him hood rich, he now wanted to purchase a vehicle that best reflect his status and ride flossing in the town. His status had elevated and he had tasted the comfort of riding in Mercedes, Jaguars and BMW's. Besides riding in some of the members of the Enterprise vehicles his then girl-friend Tammy family had always seen to it that she pushed a nice girlish BMW for her own personal vehicle.

Bob asked me would I take him to Florida and help him find a Mercedes Benz he could afford. This made me smile because I seen his growth and maturity in the game. I have always enjoyed seeing my associate's progress and he was stepping his game up. I told him I would be leaving in two days and that he was welcome to ride with me. He doesn't know I'm not going to let him come back without a Mercedes even if I have to purchase it for him. He had another two days to hustle and I would help him with the finding the type of vehicle he wanted for the statement he wanted to convey to his peers. This was another attribute that the Enterprise was known to create; a life style that most could only dream about but never have the opportunity to live. The life style could be too costly and most of the time it is. It's great while you're living it. It's all good until the wicked is revealed. 2 Thessalonians 2:8.

It was me, Bob and Germaine traveling east on I-10 blasting the car stereo to the sounds of Rob Base and D.J. E-Z Rock "*Joy and Pain*" and Slick Rick "*Teenage Love*". We're smoking some of the best skunk weed in the Country at the time while thinking the world is ours and nobody has it better not even scarf ace. I would ride through the Village often and pick up Germaine and we would turn a few corners. Bob and Germaine were best friends and partners in the streets. Germaine was good with me and respected the game. He was cool as I detailed in the book "*Coast Playa's*" He had hustling skills and came from a tree of hustlers. His father Jimmy P. is one of the coldest pimps to ever walk the planet. Jimmy was born and raised between McComb and Pascagoula Mississippi. Germaine had his father's blood and it showed in many ways when it came to his survival skills in the game and streets. The ride from Mississippi to Orlando took only about seven hours and appeared shorter when you're enjoying the ride without a care in the world and paid in full as Eric B. would say.

The Enterprise "Testimony"

The next morning after waking up in Orlando and eating the breakfast Janice had prepared we set out for the day to find Bob a Benz. We rode I-4 west spying each exit in search of Bob his dream automobile. Plant City is where we exit and pulled into a used car dealership and finally found a vehicle that Bob would be satisfied with flossing the town in. It was an immaculate older model one owner 280 Mercedes for the price of $8,800. It was clean as a whistle and had been well maintenance. This would serve him good for the purpose and moment as he continued to elevate in the game. Things were sure to become better as long as the Enterprise existed and loyalty persisted. By the time we arrived back in Orlando after being gone most of the day and the purchasing of the vehicle Bob had decided he wanted to have a imitation convertible top which we called a rag top placed on the Benz before going back to Mississippi. The next morning we dropped the Benz off at this shop that does most people vehicles in the Orlando area. It was two days later and the appearance of Bob's Benz was totally enhanced. I suggested to him that he should also buy a set of rims that would high light the new look while he was at it. He was hesitant and stated that he wanted to save enough money to purchase some more cocaine to hustle and recoup the money he had spent. I encourage him to buy the rims with no worries and that I was going to make sure he was ok. He had no idea what I had in mind.

Antonio Berry

CHAPTER 29

I had assured Bob that he could spend every dime in his pocket because I had his back and that he would be just fine. This was also to test the trust and faith he had in me and my word. I stated to him that when I send a car up with a package of cocaine it will include instructions with his name on them. My word was known to be platinum with anybody I had ever given it to. I'm about to elevate Bob life to a notch above hood rich status and he has no idea of the change about to take place. Will he appreciate it and show the same loyalty?? Who knows at this moment and stage of the game?

Roscoe had previously been informed concerning what to do when the car arrives to Mississippi with the cocaine and as it relates to Bob. Bob was to receive a package of 30 ounces with the instructions to call me. Nobody was able to quote him a price but me. This was my special favor I was doing for one who I chose and thought was worthy and I wanted to see him having some real money. Not always the best way to think but I had the ability to make such decision.

Ring, Ring, Ring!!!!!

"Hello?" I answered.

"Freddy, this is me, BC," said Bob.

"Did you receive that from Roscoe?" I asked Bob.

"Yeah, I got it," responded Bob.

"What's the ticket on it?" asked Bob.

"Give me $700.00 a piece," I responded.

"You serious?" asked Bob.

Bob couldn't believe his good fortune and was ready to get busy with his hustling. He knew the cocaine he had just been given without spending one dime was cheaper than he had ever been able to obtain it for and that it was the best cocaine on the coast with the likely hood of a never ending supply. It was going to be hard for other hustlers in the street that wasn't a part of the enterprise to compete with him. He's now calculating with nothing but dollar signs glistening eyes. This was better cocaine and cheaper than most of the cocaine he had been paying for with his cash money. It was definitely a larger supply. Bob would eventually begin to earn the type of money that allowed him to live the life style of a baller. He was purchasing any and everything he ever dreamed of or went to bed at night and desired the next morning. The early model Benz had been put out to pasture for a newer model 300E. He had taken an S-10 truck and had it customed with a top on the back and equipped with $30, 000 worth of stereo equipment with gold wire and the works. He purchased motorcycles and Jet Skies was only another few of the items that the youngsta was buying.

CHAPTER 30

The urge to relocate has once again set in my bones and blood and the plan was to move back to Mississippi. I'm so caught up in my own little world until I have not rationalized this decision as I should. The ability to see the potential harm this move could cause has been removed from my better senses. I've became content and in a dangerous comfort zone as if I'm living an honorable legit livelihood. On the outside looking in the life style to others is only one that you see in the movies. Trouble sometimes is never far and could be lurking around the corner or for that matter sitting beside or under you with an upside down frown. When the grass is too high you can't always see the snakes which are why it's important to keep it cut. At the same time I didn't know they could be so cold blooded and treacherous. Isaiah 24:16.

Roscoe and his woman on the side Tonya whom he was having an affair had introduced me to her cousin Angie during one of the short weeks I was in town. I've completed the task of purpose for me being in Mississippi and now I'm ready to leave back out; heading to Orlando. Meeka will be out of school for the summer in a couple of weeks and we're going to move back to Mississippi before the start of the new school year. I gave Tonya a $100.00 bill and asked her to tell Angie to have dinner on me and I'll see her upon my return.

Angie was 5'3", 120 pounds, brown eyes with a brown sugar complexion. She was fresh one or two years out of college and employed at Singing River Hospital working as nurse interim. I guess my first impression on her was a pretty good one and the $100.00 bill given to her as if it was a $1.00 bill didn't hurt the cause at the time. To me I only thought of it as an apology for not being able to keep the dinner date. I wasn't in Orlando 24 hours before Roscoe was calling asking me to call him back on my car phone because someone wanted to speak with me. This means he either wanted to talk to me about the business or he needed me out of ear shot from Janice.

Ring, Ring, Ring! ! ! !

"Hello," answered Roscoe.

"What's up, man?" I asked.

"Somebody wants to speak with you," said Roscoe.

He passed the phone and it took only one word for me to realize it was Angie. She wanted to know when I would be coming back to Mississippi and thanked me for the dinner. I explained to her that it would be a week or two before I returned but she will be the first person I'm expecting to see. She had a long time off and on boyfriend that she basically took care of to say she had one although he had a job. Angie was feeling that her and her then boy-friend relationship wasn't progressing and that made it much easier for me to wrap my fingers around her heart.

Angie was living at home with her parents and driving the same Toyota Celica she had driven for the four years she attended college at the University of Southern Mississippi.lt was a vehicle passed down to her from another one of her family members. Angie was a pretty woman and looked the part to ride in the Benz and other similar prestige automobiles of the life style that I'm accustomed. She was a head turner when riding or driving one of my vehicles. I introduced her to the finer things in life with the appreciation same as Janice had come to adopt.

I would rise up sometimes from reclining in the passenger seat to see males in other vehicles jocking Angie while we're traveling the interstates. I would look over and smile at them and tell her to mash it. She once told me not so long ago that the only place and thing that I never did or taught her was to ski. Think about it, Angie. I set the tone for you to even have those desires for such.

She and I would rent hotels at least five days a week in order to spend some time together. After about three or four months and $5,000 to $6,000 at $75.00 a night for a hotel I suggested she begin looking for an apartment. It was beginning to appear that Angie was going to be around for a while. It was nothing I wanted she wouldn't do and it was only one thing I didn't try with her and that was having a ménages à trois. In my heart I know she wouldn't have refused me that but I didn't take her there and wanted her all for myself. She was a lady in the streets and a cold blooded freak in the sheets and wasn't anything wrong with that. When you're a king, that's how it suppose to be.

The first place of living that Angie had of her own to live was the Lodge Apartments on Eden Street in Pascagoula. The tenants were mostly middle class working families and they were very quiet living people. Around Xmas I usually made it a point to try and spend quality time with Janice and the family. We'd ride from one relative to another dropping off gifts and to Daddy and Mudear house to exchange gifts with my Mom's side of the family. This particular Xmas I bought Janice and Angie a fur coat from Persian in Mobile Mall. Janice coat was long and cost $6,500 and Angie coat was short and cost $4,000. I gave Angie her coat the night before with the understanding that we would not be spending Xmas day together but I would come by for a minute and check on her. We had been together Xmas eve day well up into the night sexing and lying watching television.

It's Roscoe, Bridgett and their son Lil' Roscoe that were at Janice and my house on Xmas day. We were drinking eggnog and talking while the children were playing and having fun with Lil' Roscoe, who was a toddler. As Roscoe and his clan was preparing to leaving him and I had been able to sneak a conversation in discussing us riding to Pascagoula to see Angie and Tonya for no more than a ten minute stay. I picked Roscoe up at his house within the next fifteen minutes and we headed in the direction of the Lodge Apartments with the intentions of being there ten minutes at the most. We walked in the Apartment hugged them and talked for a minute or two and was back out. I mean I probably didn't even feel on Angie's breast before turning around. It was a good thing we didn't stay any longer.

Roscoe and I walked out of the apartment into the fresh air and around the corner where then I heard a voice calling my name, Tony, Tony, Tony! I knew immediately it was Janice although it would be another second or two before I seen her. When we made it to the car there she was standing there blocking us in with her Benz. She asked where was I coming from and I responded buying a bag of weed. Bridgett had called and told her that we were going to see Angie and Tonya. Bridgett was nosey, messy and always stayed in other people business.

The worst part was her man couldn't keep her straight and not keeping shit going all the time. Now that Janice know the whereabouts of Angie's resident and my home away from home it's time to relocate Angie. Janice didn't know the exact apartment number but she was too close for comfort. If she had known you can believe Janice would knock. I should have seen this weakness in these dudes with their inability to keep their women in line. Each one of them has always traveled with different women when visiting us in Florida and not one time did Janice get out of line with them or their guest. It wasn't going to happen on my watch.

Antonio Berry

CHAPTER 31

Angie relocated and moved to the Carriage House in Gautier.

I was more relaxed with this move and my vehicles being parked and seen in this area because it was out of the way and a more upscale living. I had been driving her Toyota back and forth to Mobile, Atlanta, Louisiana, Miami and Houston. The engine began to give her problems alone with other small maintenance needed after a recent trip which I had driven it to Miami. I replaced the engine with a practically new one. Angie had never mentioned about wanting a new car and was in love with her Toyota. I changed the color of it from blue to white and she was just as satisfied. The last straw was when I had her to bring me a package of cocaine that I'm suppose to meet her at her parents' house to pick up. I pulled up in the drive-way and she came to the door. I was already confused and wondering why her car is not in the drive-way when pulling up. The cocaine is stashed in a spot inside the Toyota. She said that the drive shaft came out and her dad and brother were gone to tow it back from the I-10 bridge.

This incident prompted me the coming weekend to take her car shopping and it would be a birthday gift as well as a needed necessity. I insisted because she had no business having these kinds of problems when I'm riding in several different Mercedes, jaguars, Cadillac's and other vehicles. She represented me when seen by most people because it was common knowledge that Angie V and I was having an affair. We went to Mobile that coming Saturday and found her a Maxima on

Airport Blvd at the Toyota Dealership. It was serviced and she picked it up the next day. Angie was my number two and did things deserving of me spending money on her occasionally.

Angie was a doll and could be convincing, feisty and rebellious sometimes also. She almost made one serious mistake with me that had me thinking about leaving her alone and calling off the affair. She blurted out one day that I don't have Janice doing all the things she's doing for me. I talked to her with as much venom in my voice as a poisonous snake without biting her. I screamed that Janice had paid her dues to me and she's not Janice and if she ever say that again or I believed the thought crossed her mind I was going to stop seeing her. Janice wakes up every morning and make sure the stores are open, the children don t want for anything and if I had any construction work going on anywhere she would make sure it's attended to while I was lying up out-of-town probably in a hotel with another woman. The things Janice do is what allows me the time you and I have to spend together I explained this to Angie. If not I would have to be doing them because they had to be done. Whoever Angie is with now I'm sure they can't do anything with her because she was broke in by the best and another man will never be able to lead her by the nose ever again.

For the next two years Angie would do more traveling with me than Janice. Unbeknown to Angie I had to straighten another woman name Shelia that didn't believe she had to respect Angie in her position. Shelia said one day that she would respect Janice but not Angie and I was left to tell her the same thing. She was going to respect who I told her to respect or leave me the hell alone. She knew Angie was my number two and plus Angie was deep in my business, knew too much and had seen it all. Whenever I would pull up to the chevron station at the corner of Second and Frederick Street Shelia son would run across the street from his grandparent's house up to the car not knowing whether it was me or Janice in the car. He was a good boy that had no idea so, I asked Shelia one day to slow him down with it just in case it was Janice in the car and she had possible heard something about the affair we was having. I didn't want to give Janice any indication that it may be possibly true concerning Shelia and I. As time went on I gradually slowed the pace of visiting her at Compass Pointe on Chico Street in Pascagoula. Shelia had called and called but I made it clear that she had one time to cause me to believe she was trying to be messy and start a problem and it will be over. Everybody had their position and I always believed in them knowing where they stood. Janice was number one hands down and Angie was number two and the others just were in a long line. The fact remained at the time that I wasn't and never gave it one thought about leaving Janice for any of them. Some was worthy but a bird in the hand most of the time is better than the two in the bush.

Angie purchased a personalized tag for her Maxima that read "2Angie". I went ballistic and didn't call her for several weeks. She had Roscoe, Tonya and anybody she could think of and had come to know calling me. I had to back up because she was hitting to close to home base. I've even had to ask Chicken and Roscoe to talk to their women's about being in other people business. On one occasion I had Marka in town and we stopped by Chicken and Sharon house and can you believe this weak ass dude had the nerves to tell me that Sharon didn't like me bringing my other women's there with me. I'm like what does my women friends have to do with her? I'm there to see him and for him to even mentioned it lets you know how Sharon "Eve" had done him with her panties/apple. Roscoe woman Bridgett was constantly telling Janice about Roscoe and Tonya and me and Angie. It was insane.

CHAPTER 32

There are several other dealers that's scattered about on the Coast that's obtaining cocaine coming from the Enterprise. If it wasn't broke it didn't make sense to attempt trying to fix something already in proper working order. I had a grip on this dope game like no other has ever had in this area. Many would imitate but it would never in the history of the Coast and the dope game be duplicated again. The bar has been set and it's high. Some has tried to cross it and came close but the era and times are not the same. I've always enjoyed being self-employed and the distribution of cocaine and running this Enterprise seems very easy. Usually when something sounds too good to be true 99% of the times it's not true. My surrounding was many evil men and imposters. 2 Timothy 3:13.

The first thing I did before becoming settled in good after moving back to Mississippi was do something I had promised my Grand-Ma Big Momma I would if I ever became able. This was my Father's Mother. She had been living in the same trailer since moving from Miami in the late 60's early 70's. I was willing to buy her a home somewhere else but she insisted she didn't want to move from the property she was already living. I asked about remodeling the house in the back that Uncle Collie her brother had built for their mother Grand-ma.. She said no because that was the only place their brother Uncle John had to live. I had another idea that I was sure would work and I'm going to do it in the morning. She really was in for a surprise and I just hope it wasn't too big of a surprise for her to handle.

I called Big Momma the next morning and told her and my father's sister Cozet to be ready I'm coming to take them somewhere. Big Momma had no idea and couldn't imagine where I was about to take her. I took her to the mobile home sales lot off Hwy 90 and 613. We exited the Benz and a salesman was there to greet us being certain he had some sure buyers and he was correct. I told Big Momma to look around and pick which one she wanted and she looked at me as to say what did you say? I said pick any one of them. She had never had central air or a dish washer and I'm about to make sure my grand-ma taste some of my accumulated wealth. She was always more than good to me, Eric, Darryl and Sharon. She became my legal guardian in order for me to attend school in Pascagoula after I was expelled from the entire Moss Point School system. I was in the 9th grade and had cut another student with a broken bottle and puncture his kidney. It had already been established that I wasn't to be taken lightly and would stand my ground.

Big Momma is looking around like a kid in wonderland at the prices on each mobile home. I chimed in and said don't worry about the prices Big Momma just pick the one you like and would love to have. In her mind she can't phantom the one's to our left and continue to look at the ones on the right that's in a lower price range. I take over and asked her what about this one? It had a price tag of $18,000 and it caused her facial expression to change as to say are you serious. The salesman walked us in the direction of the $18,000 price tag and gave us a tour of the inside. From the glisten in my grand-ma eyes she was about to be the happiest woman on the planet. I asked her if she liked this one. She said yes. It was a three bedroom, den, living room, two baths, large kitchen and central air and heat compared to the two bedrooms, small kitchen, small living room, one bath and more than twenty year old trailer she has been living in.

I had a scheduled trip to leave the same night of the day we went to the mobile home lot. I counted $23,000 and placed it in a brown paper bag. Before going in for that night I carried it to Big Momma and told her not to tell anybody she had it. The only thing she is to do is call Cozet and ask her to come take her back to the mobile home lot so she can talk to the man again. The next morning when I awaken in Orlando, Florida at the holidays Inn on Orange Blossom Trail I walked to my Jaguar and picked up my chip phone and called Big Momma. She stated that she had been to the mobile home lot and paid for the trailer. They were going to give her a couple of days to organize and removed her property from the old trailer. I then called a guy to build her a utility house and told him I'll pay him when I make it back to town. My grand-ma was the happiest woman in the world.

Antonio Berry

CHAPTER 33

The Enterprise was up and moving like no other organization this coast has ever seen. From Pascagoula/Moss Point, Mississippi, Miami, Florida, Mobile, Alabama. Houston, Texas the Enterprise was known and on the map. I have moved back to Mississippi and spending most of my days and nights with Angie. There were other females on occasions that I would share moments with but the main two was Janice and Angie. It's time now for me to figure out a plan to legitimize my persona after the selling of the grocery store L&L. This wasn't going to be hard because of the education and knowledge I had acquired from my family. My grandfather Lawrence use to take me to his shops with him regularly and I dreamed of the days when I could own my own businesses and become successful.

Daddy as we used to call him was one of the first black men in the State of Mississippi to own a liquor store back when the County provided the license for such business. Daddy businesses consisted of a liquor store, convenience package store, laundromat, and a barber shop. He was employed at Ingalls and a retired veteran from World War II and him and Mudear was a heaven-made team and head of the family. Throughout my hustling days I have always had thoughts in my mind to one day own several business same as my grandfather. It was never a established thought of mines to have these streets as a career and I didn't plan on doing this until I die. No way was my thinking that shadow.

I always tried to encourage the main players in the Enterprise to legally invest their earnings and make it work for them in a manner that would avoid any problems with the IRS. We weren't going to be able to continue with the spending of U.S. currency the way we was doing and never have any serious problems.

Most members wanted to buy automobiles, clothes, jewelry and have fun. I have to admit I was guilty of this behavior also with the buying of a talking parrot name freeman for $3,800, adding an addition of a 30/30 room to the house for a squirrel monkey to be kept in, three Rottweiler trained canines by the names of Mercedes, Porsche and Jag. A 50-gallon fish aquarium with two Jack Dempsey and one Oscar that people said wouldn't be able to survive in the same tank. The pets even understood the high quality of life style they were living and settled for the cohabitation agreement, when I started this mission I had a plan and although it's hard for me to stop I still intend on fulfilling that plan. I've owned a grocery store and will now attempt other business ventures. Chicken was the only member of the Enterprise that I had success with convincing to invest his earnings. He was a good street hustler but uneducated when it came to paper work. Considering he was a high school dropout he did fairly well but was only going to be able to excel so far. We brained-stormed and decided to open a legitimate jewelry store. After traveling selling jewelry for years we had a full text book of knowledge when it came to gold and jewelry and its value. The plan had been for us to open and begin operating it ourselves until people learn and begin to patronize the business. Then; Janice and Sharon could work out a schedule between them and operate it while we moved forward with other ventures and our street hustling. This was going to cost us at least $90,000 each but who's counting?

CHAPTER 34

Coast Jewelry is open for business with its grand-opening. Customers are skeptical at first because of our slum jewelry reputation. The doubt quickly subsided once the word spread that everything we had in the store could and would withstand any gold test. The most popular seller was the l0kt although we had 14kt, 18kt and 24kt. The store was set up basically the same as the flea markets in Miami but with a real store front quality. The keys are ready to be turned over to Janice and Sharon for them to take charge. They have agreed on days and times to be equally shared among them with operating the jewelry store.

In less than a month I had begin to ride some mornings by the store at 10:00am on Sharon's days to open. People had been saying on particular days that they were coming to the store in the morning and it wasn't being open sometimes until past 11:00am and sometimes 12:00pm. I was usually up and out riding early hours because I was in the process of opening a sport apparel wear store.

I had called Chicken after 10:30 on several occasions only to discover that Sharon had yet to get out of the bed. All he would say is she's just waking up. I'm like to myself 'is he serious' after we have spent almost $200,000 opening this place and he can be this casual about it not being open for customers. This went on for several months until I decided to let him buy me out and move on. The business of selling jewelry was slow and picked up only during the holidays and valentines. Other than that we had a lot of lay-a-way plans and jewelry in the safe waiting to be completely paid. He would have to deal with Sharon laziness on his own because I didn't want the headache. Chicken and I came up in different teachings whereas I came from a business and political family and he was allowed to be a 10th grade drop out.

I was a born go getter and so was Janice. Owning and operating our own business wasn't new because we had owned and operated the grocery store L&L with a deli. I heard word that Benny was trying to sell his sports apparel shop named The Number One Fan Shop on Main Street. The store was not fully stocked with a lot of empty space. It was noticeable that either he was trying to sell it or wasn't interested in operating it any longer. I discussed the ends and out of this type of business with Benny and was able to see the potential the business had with the investing in stocking it with the right sport items. All it took was what I already had and that was money. I gave Benny $35,000 cash for The Number One Fan Shop and immediately spent another $50, 000 in stocking it.

The Fan Shop was busy daily year round from opening to closing. I would even open sometimes on Sundays for a couple of hours after coming from church. I would leave church heading to the store. The only other retail business I had ever witness as busy was a liquor store and the selling of crack cocaine. I believed Janice and I had found our calling and my way out of the street and game while maintaining the same life style. I even tried a towing truck business and to be honest this was a joke because I was more enjoying the tow truck that was a fully loaded hydraulic row-back. It had the capability to tow one on top while dragging one behind. It was cleaner than most of the well known established tow services in town trucks.

CHAPTER 35

The money is not just raining in from the streets but the legitimate business is doing its part. It has been nothing but work on top of work for the last several months and a vacation is in order. Red and Arleen, Chicken and Sharon, Claude and Loraine, And Janice and I are planning to take a carnival cruise vacation to the Caribbean. The cruise ship will be pulling into port at the Grand Bahamas, Ocho Rios, Grand Cayman and Cancun. Claude is a native Jamaica and we're going to visit his family while there. We leave one week early to enjoy the festival of spring break that's happening in Daytona Beach before going down to Miami to depart.

The cruise was a great experience and one that would be impossible to forget. It's time to return to the business of the streets and store. While on the ship I called and arraigned for Jenkins to make a trip to Miami to pick up a load of cocaine to be waiting for my return. Nobody except Jenkins had knowledge of the cocaine that's in the bumper of the Cadillac that is now parked in Janice Sister's garage. I had also two automobiles in the paint shop expecting to have them painted when I return from the vacation. Janice, Claude, Loraine and I drove my candy green AMG Mercedes to Miami while Red, Arleen, Chicken and Sharon drove Red's 380SEL. Red found the power of my Mercedes unbelievable to be a six cylinder. We had never had the opportunity to have them both on the highway at the same time. There was always bullshit talking from each other about once that day come when we had both Mercedes on the highway at the same time what the other one was going to do. It was no longer any doubt after this trip.

Before we departed the cruise ship Claude and Red wanted to keep the good Jamaican weed we had gotten in the mountains of Ocho Rios. I was of the mind to flush it down the toilet. It was grade "A" weed true but we could get more in Miami. Claude had to check in with immigration at each port of entrance because of his dual citizenship of being a United States of American citizen and a Jamaica native. While Claude was checking in we all had to gather in the lobby of our individual deck floor outside the cabins. The White 18 wheeler truck driver the Snowman on Smokey and the bandit was on our floor. He would not answer to his stage name and to tell you the truth the bastard responded snobbery.

I was not convinced by Red or Claude to keep the weed and flushed it before closing the cabin door to stand in the lobby with the rest of the vacationers. They called floors one at a time for departure of the ship in Miami port. I was lucky to have flushed the half ounce of weed or I would have went to jail for attempting to smuggle drugs back into the U.S. regardless of the amount. As we were departing the ship the port authorities ran the dogs through Janice and my legs and I'm like what the hell. We had on a few pieces of nice jewelry but Arleen had on some real chunks that were some noticeable, outstanding pieces. Maybe this was one of those times where I could have not had on anything and would have stood out among the crowd. I had saved $2,000 to pay Corey for the stereo system I had asked him to have hooked up in my Benz to add to what I already had in it hoping it would sound like his Jaguar.

As we're coming through the gates at the port into the parking lot I can hear music in the distant of the lot and it's clear as a concert but I'm yet to detect the direction in which it's coming from. I see Corey afar waving us in the direction of the car and it's the same direction as the music. This causes me to smile because I know he has hooked my stereo up to sound same as his jaguar the way I asked and wanted. He opens the trunk and I'm flabbergasted at the sight of what I see. There are two 150 watts precision amps and two 300 watts precisions amps across the floor deck with a Plexiglas box holding four 15 inch speakers inside facing each other. Across the back window deck on the inside was four 10 inch quarts speakers. There are 8 inch quarts speakers in each door with tweeters at the top corners of the windshield. Inside the glove compartment is a pre-amp to balance the electronic cross-over on the trunk deck floor sitting beside the precision amps. I have never had a sound system of this magnitude. I'm thinking like dam my Benz is competition ready and I'm all smiles. Corey then handed me a receipt for what it had cost and what I owed him and when I seen it I almost vomit. I screamed what the hell and all he said was I told him I wanted it to sound like his jaguar. It sounded better than his Jaguar but for $7,000 I would have placed music in seven vehicles. I decided to spend the $2,000 I had saved for him at the flea market and would send the $7,000 back down by Jenkins in the Cadillac. Party Down stereo had done their thing on my Benz.

I hadn't made it off 1-75 onto I-10 west towards Mississippi before blowing one of the amps. I wasn't used to this type of stereo power. I was enjoying the sounds of Too $hort *"In The Ghetto"* banging in this capsule while keeping my mind on the task I had waiting for me at the house. Everybody is on the edge wondering if I'm going to be back home soon. I was on my own unpredictable schedule and never have been in a rush. The town wasn't dry because too many hustlers was doing their thing and was happy to hear I wasn't in town or my people was not doing anything at the time. There was Duffy and his crew of locals that was putting down and had some pretty decent cocaine coming out of Houston Texas. Duffy considered himself a young Godfather and he could have. He was cool and about his business. I never had any direct dealings with Duffy except a few times when smoking a joint or two of weed with him. I remember him coming by one day to ask where I take my Benz to be serviced. He had taken his Benz to the Mobile, Alabama dealership and was told he would have to bring it in by appointment. I was taking my Benz to Burt Allen Mercedes in Gulfport and my jaguars to the dealership on Pass Road. I called Mr. Pete in the service department and asked him can I send my cousin over there to have his Benz service today and he told me to send him and that he would see that he's taken care of.

BC had went to Texas with Duffy on several occasions while I was on vacation out of the country and had the opportunity to meet who he thought was some good people who had a supply of product. He informed me that they would bring whatever I wanted all the way to my door step for $17,000 a kilo. This did not sound bad when I was paying $14,000 to $15,000 in Miami and had to send my money and pay a driver. This was more for the cocaine but considering I didn't have to pay a driver, expense and the chance that was being taking with the sending of my money on the highway this was much cheaper. I asked about the quality of the dope and BC said what he has been buying from them through Duffy has been very good. I told BC to call them and tell them to bring 10 kilos. I wanted to test the waters with these people BC was talking about. Houston, Texas is five and half hours at the most from the Coast. In seven hours 10 kilos was in

The Enterprise "Testimony"

Jackson County.

The guy that came from Houston with the Columbian connection name was Devo. I had about a total of three or four dealings with him at the most although he would later lie for the Government. I also had a separate connection of my own in Houston which I could and did obtain cocaine. I would send Jenkins to Houston sometimes only to keep the doors open on that end and spread the money around. I didn't believe in changing the channels when it wasn't a problem with the people I'm dealing with. The prices were good and the cocaine was always the best you could find in the United States of America. Again I knew I had what every hustler dream of and that was several solid connections that was loyal and trust worthy. It didn't make sense to trade them in for an unknown commodity that I could probably one day come to regret. The snakes are everywhere.

Antonio Berry

CHAPTER 36

The second day that we was back home from the cruise Jeff and one of our partners from California name Duncan was arrested in Baldwin County Alabama. They were on their way to Pensacola to take some money for repairs Jeff was having done to a couple of properties he owned. Jeff decided for unknown reason to this day to be the one that delivers a small package of cocaine to his brother Dana. Duncan was part of the Cali-Crew who was good people and cool with us. His nick name we gave him was heavy. He was a real dude and they had been coming east to Mississippi for a while when this happened. I gave Duncan and Lucky one of their first major workers in town. His name was Skeeter and he was good and loyal, Skeeter was suppose to be playing football in the NFL and had a promising career but the streets of Carver Village where he was raised would not let go of the grip they had on him. He was exposed at a very young age and exploited with the game.

The Officer that pulled them over on I-10 had noticed Jeff sweated hands. I could have told him Jeff hands stayed sweated but he wouldn't know this because he didn't know Jeff. Then the officer noticed something else that was odd and called for backup. He did not at first let Jeff and Duncan know he had noticed the brown paper bag showing from between the back bumper and the iron plate on the Cadillac. When back up arrived they turn them around on the patrol car and placed them under arrest. Jeff had been careless, in a hurry and it cost him and Duncan dearly. Earlier that day before leaving

Mississippi for Pensacola Jeff had seen his State Probation Officer that morning and was released from probation for the State charge which he served nine months in the R.I.D. program.

There was an incident that caused me to be so angry I could have killed somebody and seriously wanted to. Red and I couldn't put our finger on it but we had our suspicion. We were almost certain Chicken had something to do with it and had formulated a plan to find out. The car was under my garage being packed with money one night for Jenkins to take his usually trip to Miami. Darryl, Nunie and Bryant was there doing the packing. The money was on the floor in the den and they would take one package at a time wrapped to the car and place it in the bumper. As they were accomplishing this task and just placed another package of money in the bumper some would be robbers came from around the corner of the house attempting to rob them. They scattered and it spoiled the robber's plans to have everybody in one room. Janice just so happens to be coming out of the garage door that lead inside the house when she was encountered with one of the robbers who hit her in the head with a pistol.

It was several hundred thousand dollars lying on the floor in the den and they ran away from it. It was a half a million between the house and the car. The question that was never answered was, how did they know the opportune time to make such a dare devil attempt. We had always questioned Chicken because he had insisted that me, him and Red go and get something to eat leaving the others behind to complete the task. The would-be robbers in their escape pursue landed the getaway vehicle in a ditch on a back street close to my house. I recognized the automobile and called Shelia to find out who was in possession of her sister brown ford escort. She said for me to call her back in two minutes. When I called back she said that the Florida Boys had the car. I grabbed my 3 80 and Chicken grabbed the Uzi and we headed for Carver Village. Kilo was in the hide-a-way lounge gambling when we walked upon him. I asked him could we talk for a second. Once I told him what had happened he assured us that he had nothing to do with it and that it had to be the other crew of Florida Boys.

After narrowing it down to the possibilities of who it could be, we set out to find our man/men and straighten this out however it was going to go down. These fools brought the weakest game to the strongest playa on this Coast and it wasn't going to go unanswered. On top of it all they hit my woman in the head with a pistol. All I can see is blood and taste death upon who done this. I have a man insight and it's Florida Boy Tony standing at the back corner of Cat's house on the street over from mines. He's standing there with Cat cousin Bridgett against the wall as if nothing has happened. He didn't see us but I have him in the scope. I reached over from the passenger seat of my truck to fire at Florida Boy Tony and Chicken knocked my hand down and begin to scream take him home. I started to fire off on him but instead called him all kinds of coward punk motherfuckers. I'll deal with him later for sure I thought. He was faking the scene until he seen I was serious about retaliating.

Red and I begin to ride around while I was thinking I should have done Chicken on the spot because something was funny about this scene. Somebody had attempted to rob my house and this is the loyalty he shows? It's coming out now but I'm not paying close attention because of the high grass and blind faith. I went to the avenue and found Buddy Red and sent him to blaze the truck that was parked in the front of Cats house. When the fire truck, Marshall and police arrived, I went to the house and changed vehicle and we was now in Janice Benz. She, Red and I went straight to the fire alarm. Janice continued to say that the guy that hit her with the pistol resembled Duffy. Janice had known Duffy from coming by the store.

When we pulled up on the scene I jumped out the Benz with my pistol in hand telling Janice to point to the one that hit her with the pistol. Florida Tony and the other guys was running around the fire truck asking the officers was they going to stand there and allow me to hold that pistol. I had snapped and lost my mind behind this incident and it's a wonder I didn't get shot by the police. My exact words verbatim was, I'm going to kill one of you niggas for bringing this weak ass game to the strongest MF here. Neither one of you will be able to stay here or make one more dime in this town. I was furious about what had happened and wasn't thinking clearly. Jerome is who Janice thought looked like Duffy and in the dark they did resemble. The police asked me to put away the gun.

Florida Tony called me one day and assured me he had nothing to do with it and didn't appreciate Jerome and the others almost having him killed for something he had no knowledge of. I didn't and never had it twisted because Florida Tony was a cold killer himself and wasn't somebody to be taken lightly and him calling was no way taken as a sign of weakness. I knew he had a trigger finger and would pull it and he didn't have to feel threaten to do it only disrespected and he would kill you. It made sense to me that he didn't have anything to do with it once I calmed down because as he said he wouldn't have done something of that nature and then made himself a target. He also said he knew I had an army and the power to make some dangerous moves and it's no way he would have tried a stunt like that on me. This was another reason we always believed and suspected that Chicken had something to do with the incident but I'm lucky he didn't allow me to shoot the wrong man. Florida Tony I admit I do owe you a truck.

If Florida Tony had wanted revenge the opportunity presented itself in broad day light on a Sunday evening outing. Janice, the children and I had went to church and decided to ride to the Red Lobster in Mobile, Alabama after service. All of a sudden while we're enjoying our dinner and laughing the waiter delivers two margarita's to our table complimentary of the guys sitting over to our left in the corner. I turned and it was Florida Tony, Jerome and another man. The world truly is small and you should always stay ready and alert. I wasn't ready but the look and hand gesture I received from Florida Tony let me know that everything was cool and it wasn't going to be any trouble.

I have slowed my pace down for no other reason except evolving into seriously wanting to stop and exit the street life. Chicken and the others in the Enterprise continue to purchase from Devo not knowing how dangerous he is. I'm deep and falling further in the shadow is why I didn't have any money involved in the $200,000 cake mix scam. Devo came to Mississippi and sold the Enterprise crew cake mix for cocaine. When I awaken the next morning everybody is running around looking crazy and in a daze wondering what to do. Roscoe was the first one I seen that had the long sad angry face. He explained what had happened in the middle of the night while I was in a comatose state of mind. They came to place too much trust and faith in Devo.

I'm now out of the loop as far as the Enterprise day to day activities and I'm assuming they're able to continue it without my guidance and leadership. I discover that everybody has begun to do their own independent dealing and the purchasing of cocaine. Chicken had became involved with this guy from Houston named Neal. Neal was from Houston but had family on his father side that resided in Pascagoula and he was familiar with the area and people. Supposedly Neal had a connection with some Columbians that had good cocaine prices. Everybody was now skeptical after the bad business deal with Devo. Darryl and Roscoe continued to send the car with Jenkins to Florida with the understanding that I-10 was hotter than fish grease. BC for unknown reasons, except out of desperation, has once again begun to associate with Devo. Jeff has been busted and arrested with dope in the bumper of the Cadillac. A Government informant name Troy in Mobile, Alabama has given up the game on the Cadillac and was trying to bring in my friend Steve from Miami. Things were not looking bright as before for the Enterprise but nobody was paying attention to the obvious. Same as I wasn't noticing all the snakes crawling in the grass around my ankles.

When I removed my hands from the day to day running of the Enterprise the glue that bonded the structure unraveled. BC had some problems with one of his female carriers at the Houston bus station. She had been arrested with five kilos of powder cocaine on the greyhound bus heading back to Mississippi. The charges were possession of a control substance with the intent to distribute. BC didn't know if the heat had came from his connection or it was that the bus station was just under surveillance and the DEA got lucky that day. She was given a bond and BC assured her that he was going to make her bond and pay for an Attorney. He wanted to secure a package of cocaine before spending any more money, he talked to her several times and asked her to give him two or three days and she would be free.

BC called and asked me about making a call for him and would I send Jenkins to the connection I had to buy him three or four kilos. I responded that I would make the call but at the same time I hadn't sent Jenkins on a trip in four or five months.

People had begun to seriously believe I was trying to exit the game. The store and rental properties had begin to serve their purpose. I feel great about finally anticipating being able to walk away from the game unscratched is what I'm thinking. BC needed my help and at the time he hadn't done anything wrong or foul for me to refuse his request. I spoke with Darryl and Roscoe to see if they wanted to send for a couple of kilos on this trip.

They too knew the connection was good and trust worthy and could be counted on for good product. I drove BC over to Jenkins house to talk to him. Jenkins agreed to make the trip and understood this trip to be for BC. It was easier to use Jenkins as the driver because he knew the people, route and the do s and don t. Well we thought he did anyway.

Jenkins left for Houston the same night. BC is trying to secure a package of cocaine so he can pursue making bond for his carrier that has been arrested at the Houston bus station. I had no knowledge that Jenkins companion this time was his brother Allen, he would usually take his young girl-friend Felecia for some companionship. They made it to Houston safe and were on their way back with the cocaine at dusk dark. Jenkins and his brother Allen had been speeding and smoking weed when they were stopped in Chamber County Texas. This was something I had always stressed to Jenkins about not doing. I guess he had become to relax. Smoking, drinking and speeding was definitely a no no on the highway while you're riding dirty. The police officer detected the foul odor of the marijuana and called for backup and the drug dog.

The dog alerted and the cocaine was discovered mounted between the gas tank and the body of the vehicle.

Jenkins and Allen panicked and became disruptive with the officers. This caused the officers to become aggressive. The end result was Jenkins and Allen being beat to a pulp and a near death experience. They were placed in isolation until the swelling went down. I was not aware that they had been stopped and arrested. They both begin to cooperate with the authorities immediately after reaching the County Jail. Allen wasn't knowledgeable of the Enterprise detail operation; he knew only what his older brother had told him in a bragging manner. The agents could only use Jenkins because Allen had no direct knowledge of the Enterprise. They wanted Jenkins help in flushing out the owner of the cocaine he had been arrested with. He agreed to help them with this operation snatch and grab. The plan was for Jenkins to make a call saying he has automobile problems and was broke down in Beaumont.

CHAPTER 37

The Agents removed Jenkins from the Chambers County jail to a completely different jurisdiction in Beaumont, Jefferson County. Chambers County is in the Southern District of Texas where the arrest and seizure of the cocaine was made. Beaumont, Jefferson County is in the Eastern District of Texas where no part of the instant crime had been committed. While Allen was in the County jail biting his finger nails scared shitless thinking his life was over, his big brother Jenkins is out playing stool pigeon for the DEA. The agents placed Jenkins in a hotel to begin making his calls. This punk is about to turn a five year sentence at the most and even the possibility of probation into 100 years for the Enterprise. I would have spent whatever it took to keep him out of prison and he knew this from past experience. The thoughts of many hearts will soon be revealed. Luke 2:35

I'm asleep at Angie apartment after we had sexed for most of the night off and on. The phone ring and she sleepily passed it to me saying it was Jenkins. My first thought is, he's about to tell me he made it home safe. At the same time I'm thinking he should be calling BC because that's who has to pay him and that's who the cocaine belongs to. He could have called Darryl or Roscoe because he was very much familiar with them also.

"Hello," I say to Jenkins?

"I'm broke down in Beaumont," said Jenkins.

"Why did you call me?" I asked. "You could have called Bob or even Jr. because you're closer to Houston than me," I emphasized to Jenkins.

"I don't have their numbers," stated Jenkins.

"You have to get a room and call me in the morning," was my only response.

I showed the least concern because it wasn't my trip or my cocaine and I would have to find everybody in the morning. It was almost midnight and I wasn't about to get up and search for them at this time of night. This wasn't an emergency or life or death situation is what I'm thinking not knowing death was knocking at my door. If the cocaine was secured and in a safe spot he would be alright until morning. He should have called one of them first. This was their business not mines and he had agreed with BC to take this trip. I still wasn't about to turn my back and act like this situation didn't warrant attention or show total disregard because he was a good driver for me once. Jenkins called back saying he needed more money. I'm now wondering not about if he has been arrested or if something strange is going on but whether or not BC has given him enough expense money. I always made sure he had more than enough. The next morning he called and I sent him $150.00 through western union for what he said he needed for car repairs. This is what he had me to believe while having the agents believing that it was Todd Caples aka Chicken who was sending him the money. This dude had turned out to be dangerous. Chicken had absolutely nothing to do with this trip nor did he have any idea that it was taking place. Jenkins was trying to hook him with the case.

An hour later he called back saying that when he went to pick up the money from western union there was no money sent from Todd Caples. I said Todd didn't send you any money I did. This is when the agents realized Jenkins had been lying to them and hadn't been calling who he had them to believe he was calling. He had told the agents he was calling Todd aka Chicken. I guess you can assume or think he was trying to save me but if that was the case he shouldn't have made any calls period.

Now, Jenkins is alleging that the car cannot be repaired and that he needed to have it towed back home. I find BC and explained what has been transpiring with Jenkins for the last 12 hours. Angie was scheduled to be in Jackson, Mississippi to take her State Board exam test for her register nursing license. She had to be there and ready in the morning. This was going to be a three day stay for us in Jackson and I needed to make sure help is on the way for Jenkins before I leave town. BC hired old man Dobie to take the trip and tow Jenkins car back to the coast. Nobody was in the dark about anything that was going on. I didn't believe in lying to a person about what I was asking them to do. Mr. Dobie knew he was going to tow a car back that was loaded with cocaine and if there's any doubt ask Joe Watson. Joe was with me the morning when we visited Mr. Dobie at his home where I asked him about taking the trip.

Old man Dobie knew that Jenkins was dirty and had several kilos of cocaine stashed in the car. He actually said that as long as he keeps it in the car he s not responsible for it. All he's doing is what he does for a living and being paid for and that's working on and towing automobiles. This was why he was charging $3,000 to pull him back from four hours away. In his eyes he sees a good pay day and probably

165

a month in his case. After this arrangement was satisfied Angie, Tracy Bingham and myself pull out heading to Jackson. I had no idea or knowledge that Jenkins had been arrested and the entire ordeal with Jenkins is a set up. Trust not in a friend. Micah 7:5.

CHAPTER 38

The entire time we're in Jackson for Angie to take her State exam, I believed that Jenkins was home safe and things had worked out for the best. I hadn't called except to check on Janice and the children and to let her know I was ok. While Angie was in class during the day I would ride around Jackson with Red and Tracy from one location of the City to another, when Angie completed the last day of her exam we had dinner and left for home. Neither BC nor anybody else in the Enterprise had thought to page me for an update on what had happened with Jenkins. I have been away for three days and upon arrival home I'm told that Jenkins had been arrested in Texas. I immediately understood that nothing good could come from this if he hadn't made it home with the cocaine.

Jenkins had called and said that old man Dobie was the cause for the arrest and blamed him for the incident. Jenkins had initially stated that old man Dobie was drunk and acting erratically. I had no reason not to believe him and went to work trying to secure his freedom if possible. At this time I have limited knowledge or understanding of the FEDS as it relates to criminal matters. To give Jenkins some assurance and hope that I had his back, I sent $10,000 to his family to pay some bills and to send money to an attorney in Texas for Jenkins and his brother Allen. It didn't matter which attorney they hired I was going to pay them.

Unbeknown to me at the time, the cowards had begun to cooperate and it was too late to save them this way. Old man Dobie called home saying it was Jenkins fault and that he walked into a set up. I did not have enough understanding of these matters or facts to piece it all together on my own. It wasn't until an attorney was sent to visit Jenkins in jail and reported back that we knew without a doubt it was Jenkins who has turned informant and begin to cooperate with the Government in an effort to set up the head of the Enterprise. This cooperation had begun upon their arrest. In any other organization or enterprise they would have been considered traitors and beheaded. Luke 6:16.

After learning of Jenkins cooperating with the Government, I sent a mutual friend to his family to retrieve the $10,000 I had given as a gesture of sincerity. It didn't make sense to me or good logic to spend the money I was willing to spend, which was any amount, trying to help him if he was cooperating against me. His mother only returned $8,000 of the money and later lied to the Government that I had been harassing her. Now I understand Jenkins better and the analogy saying that a limb doesn't fall far from a tree. The entire family was poison and Jenkins was a limb from that tree. I had no reason to call or harass the Jenkins except for the remainder of the $10,000 they had refused to return. Even with the refusal I would not have allowed $2,000 to cause me a regrettable problem. The raving and wickedness was seeping from their pores. Luke 11:39.

I contacted the Dobie's to determine what assistance I could be in helping their family and try to make amend for a bad situation that I caused them to be in by requesting his assistance. I gave the old man Dobie's wife $3,500 she said she needed for her husband bond. It would later be revealed in court documents that she pocketed the money and did not mention the money to her husband. She used collateral to secure his bond leading him to believe I had not stepped up to help him. Janice and my sister-n-law at the time Irma is GOD witnesses that I gave money each and every time it was needed and on one occasion gave it to Old man's Dobie nephew Lil' Dobie on Landwood Drive. Everybody is money hungry and seeking an opportunity, even the suppose-to-be-Christians which Dobie's wife claimed to be. Dobie had several court appearances where he had to be in Beaumont, Texas. Each trip I provided him with more than $1,500 and as much as $2,000 on some occasion when he stated remaining over night was necessary. Dobie has relatives alone with my sister-n-law that would verify the truthfulness of this statement that I did and tried to do right by him and his family. Did it matter, what do you think? The Dobies were more interested in milking me for as much money as they possible could. The wife was not concerned about her husband welfare. They had missed the mark of the fact that I would have spent whatever was necessary to help him out of this situation in which I felt an obligation and partially to blame. Take heed that no one deceives you. Matthew 24:4

The old man Dobie had a bad heart and was living on a pace maker. His wife was a hag and only seen an opportunity to fatten her pocket at the expense of the possibility of her husband going to prison. The heat was becoming hotter by the day and I could feel it all around me and in the air. It was coming from everybody and ever side imaginable. I'm trying to do the right thing and help as much as I possibly can. Dobie is coming to me once a week trying to get more money and I'm becoming angry at the fact that I'm doing all and willing to do all I can to help this clown and he's not the least concern about what should be important and that's his freedom. I have a strong feeling his wife is behind this behavior.

Dobie had the same knowledge as everyone else that's involved with this. He knows the drugs didn't belong to me and that I was truthful with him up front and did not mislead him into this blindly. With this being known to Dobie I can't understand why he's trying to play me as if I'm live sucker bait on his line. He has caused me now to only want to pacify him.

CHAPTER 39

In the game it was always rumored that one spouse could not be compelled or coerced to testify against the other. After seven and a half years of living together Janice and I decided to marry in hope of eliminating any future problems that could arise from a criminal case. We loved one another and had been living together for years as if we were married. The only thing that changed was it's now official and registered at the court house on file that we're legally bonded. I still haven't purchased any drugs to be distributed on the streets. It has been four months before Jenkins arrest and two months after that I have not been involved. The Jenkins were released based on their cooperation and anticipated cooperation at a later time against the Enterprise. This was the deal they made with the devil. Trust nobody but yourself.

In these days all I'm doing is traveling from State to State and keeping watch of the store and properties. Will Wade and I would sometimes take trips just to get away from around town and out of sight for a moment. Will was maybe six or seven younger than I was but he was cool like Germaine and mature for his age. He was a street gangsta and known in the area for putting in work. His mom used to be very concerned and afraid for him. She was always comfortable with him being with me knowing I wasn't on bull-shit and had, always been considered mature for my age growing up. Xmas has passed and it's January 1992. Will and I decided we're going to take a trip to Norfolk, Virginia and visit with two old friends named Diane and Evette. Evette and I once had a short lived affair until she left to join the military.

On our way to Virginia, Will had been pulled over by a State Trooper in North Carolina and given a citation for speeding. Traffic is slowed down to a snail pace on 1-85 north with motorist stealing glares at the vehicle we're riding in. I know some probably was thinking this was some type of drug intradiction stop. We're in Janice candy blue 190E Benz with the AMG kit and gold package. The only illegal substance we have is a small bag of grade "A" weed that I've hidden well out of sight.

It's somewhere around 7:00pm when we arrived in Norfolk and rent a room at the HoJo on Beach Blvd and Military Circle. There's a mall and my favorite restaurant Bennigan's that sits directly across the highway. I called Evette and Diane and we all meet up and had dinner, it was good seeing some old friends and to be away from the coast for if nothing else a week or two.

They both was taking exceptional care of themselves and looking as beautiful as ever. Evette was originally from D.C and a very energetic woman who loved to travel. Diane was from the Coast of Mississippi and a very warm and humble woman with a heart of gold. Will and I stayed there for four or five more days before heading south again on I-95. Our destination this time is Orland, Florida. I'm going to visit Marka for a couple of days and leave there going back home to Mississippi. This will end our two weeks of get away vacation trip. I doubt if we was gone long enough to be missed.

CHAPTER 40

Will and I arrived home only to see that nothing had changed nor had we missed anything. The flow of traffic and cocaine is still at an all time high in this coast area. The Enterprise is holding it down and keeping a grip on the game. It's a loose net group but it's working for them. Nobody can see the grip coming apart and rather deal with the denial. You have to sometimes be able to see the unseen and accept it for what it is. The obvious will appear to you in many ways, shape and form. Once in the middle of the night while in a deep sleep when living in Orlando I felt a spirit hubbing over me. Our bedroom was upstairs and Janice and I are both lying in the bed sleep. I begin to try and rise up and I'm conscious of my efforts but I couldn't move. When I finally do break loose of whatever it was that had a hold of me I jumped straight up and grab my pistol and begin to check the closet, balcony, under the bed and through the bathroom to the children room. Janice thought I was tripping and had had a bad dream. It wasn't a dream because it was as if I was waked but couldn't move, there was something trying to tell me to stay put.

I didn't understand it at that time. The other voice was Angie wanting to know when I would be coming back to Mississippi. I didn't recognize the signs or warning.

Roscoe and I was riding one day when he revealed to me the new stashed spot they had been using with a different vehicle. The new vehicle was the 80's Jaguar with the two separate tanks.

I'm now curious whether or not this could be a safe enough way for me to try it every once in a while. Roscoe is living in New Orleans. He tells me that BC girl-friend Dwanda has a sister that's gorgeous and that she sells weed. We visit her using the pretext of buying a bag of weed when the truth is I only wanted to see if she was all of what Roscoe had made her out to be. On first sight I cannot close my mouth. This red bone name Angelle with the long jet black hair that's standing before me has to be a goddess. She's 5'6" and thick-to-death and the only thought in my mind is to undress her to see what's on the other side of the garment she has on. I have quickly made a tactical decision to position myself for a door opening opportunity to develop a relationship.

Angie and my intentions were only to visit Roscoe and Tonya for the day and return home that evening. We didn't bring any changing clothes but my mind was made up to spend the night in New Orleans. Angelle had influenced and contributed heavy to that decision. I tell Angie that we're going to spend the night and wake up in the morning and go shopping at the East Mall. She has no idea where this change of mind has come from but she didn't mind spending some more time with her cousin. Tonight all we need to purchase from the store is personal hygiene items. The ulterior motive is for no other reason except to have a second look and another chance to visit Angelle. I couldn't sleep for one hour straight without seeing this goddess face and figure in my mind. You would have never suspected her of doing anything illegal nevertheless selling weed.

I cannot leave New Orleans without establishing future communication with Angelle. The next morning after shopping at the mall and getting fresh, Roscoe and I used the same pretext for a visit to

Angelle as the day before. With Angie and Tonya at the apartment we set out on this mission. Angelle answered the door with a welcoming smile on her face. She must have been thinking the same thing all night as I was – we both wanted to see each other again.

Her glow was as if her last night prayer and dream had just come true. I told her that I wanted to buy another ounce of the weed she had. She knew I was lying for real because her exact words were, "I know you'll didn't smoke all that weed that fast?"

My response was, "No, we didn't. I only wanted to see you again to make sure I wasn't dreaming yesterday."

She recognized the playa and the relationship begin.

Angelle asked me was there any weed over in Mississippi because their area had been dry. If so, could I put my hands on any and would it be good. I assured her that if it's any weed in the area that yes I could put my hands on it and to call me later around 5:00pm and I'll let her know. I asked her how many pounds was she trying to buy and she stated about eight if the price was right. I already knew I could buy them in the range of $750.00. When I quoted this to her she asked was I for real and serious, she had been paying $1,000 and $1,200 a pound in New Orleans and only making a couple of hundred profit off each pound. At 5:00pm sharp she called and I told her to come over and that she didn't need to bring any money with her. At first she didn't understand and was about to question me when I responded for her to trust me. She's about to receive her second taste of the type of playa she has had the opportunity to meet. All I said was I got you just come over and we hung up.

Antonio Berry

It was Angelle and her brother Burt that pulled up in Darryl's driveway two hours later. I dam near had to pinch myself again to make sure what I'm seeing is real and not a dream. I'm forcing myself to contain any signs of excitement at the sight of her. I invited her and Burt into the house where there's cold beer and liquor waiting. Burt had a beer and Angelle refused any alcohol because she was driving. Ok, I'm thinking good decision I say to myself. She's on point because she's the driver and that's a no no in the game. *That* is what got Jenkins arrested and the Enterprise under the microscope of the FEDS—wanting to smoke weed while trafficking cocaine. And, this is what caused a search of his vehicle. I passed her a sack of weed and asked her what she thought and did she like that grade?

She did not smoke but knows the product and after a few seconds of examination said yes. She asked me was this the weed for $750.00 a pound?

I said yes and she wanted to know when she would be able to purchase some of it. I pointed and told her to grab the two bags lying there beside her on the floor between the couch and the wall. "There's ten pounds in the two bags. Give me $750.00 for each when I come over there in a couple of days."

She asked if I was serious.

Baby I don't play games. She smiled and I knew then it was on and we were going places together. She also had cousins across the Mississippi river that she would give weed to sell for her.

It was three days later before I would visit Angelle. The purpose for going to New Orleans wasn't just for the money Angelle had waiting

176

for me. She had already called the next day and said she had the money and I could come pick it up. Angelle and I had talked several times a day since our meeting at Darryl's house. I didn't want to give her the impression that the money was a big deal and that's all I wanted with her and it wasn't because I considered myself a pretty good judge of character and she was good. My intentions were to make her a part of my life. I wanted the money back true because I had made the initial investment for her. We talked as if we had known one another for a life time. She knows I have a wife and children. She also knows a money machine when she encounters one.

Antonio Berry

CHAPTER 41

The real purpose for my being in New Orleans is to purchase this Jaguar I've seen in the Auto-Trader Magazine. Roscoe has given me the game and details on how one of the gas tanks attached to the jaguar is being used to stash and haul the cocaine. The jaguar has two gas tanks, one on each side of the vehicle. These tanks are mounted in between the back fenders/quarter pounds and the frame of the automobile. They sit in a slot specially designed like a glove fitting a hand. I don't know which individual in the Enterprise discovered this idea and never asked. Roscoe said that they had been dropping the tank and cutting a hole at the top side and folding the metal back. This allowed you to place multi-kilos down inside the tank. There has to be a metal strip placed may be about two-or-three inches from the bottom. This metal stripping prevented the cocaine from sitting in the gasoline that remained in the tank. If law snforc6ment was to ever unscrew the plug at the bottom of the tank there would be gasoline dripping from it. The cocaine would always be stashed in the tank on the driver's side which would be directly in the line cf traffic if the vehicle is stopped for any reason.

The jaguar is in the city of Metairie closer to the airport. Metairie is about ten miles north east of New Orleans heading towards Baton Rouge. It's me, Roscoe, Darryl, and Kenny D. that's together on our way to purchase this vehicle. I checked the car out to make sure it's suitable for the purpose I have planned based on what Roscoe has told me. I've owned several jaguars so I'm sure about the tanks but wanted to make certain of its highway condition. There will be too much at stake in this vehicle for it to be broken down on the side of the interstate miles and miles from home. I pay the owner and we're on our way. The title is a savage title because the vehicle had been declared a flood automobile. I would have to obtain a title bond which is simple in the State of Mississippi. My intentions are to have the vehicle registered in the name of the person that will be driving it the most. Angelle is expecting me to stop by on my way heading back home when coming through the east. She and I have been talking on a regularly daily basis. Our relationship is quickly forming and coming into a full circle.

As I'm walking towards her front door I can hear what sounds like a mean killer of a dog barking on the inside. When she opens the door I'm expecting to be rushed by a pit-bull or lion but instead it's a Shar Pei. This was the ugliest, old-looking dog I've ever seen in my life. I asked her, "What the hell is that?? And how old is he?"

She stated he was a puppy and I believe she said he cost somewhere in the range of $2,500. Angelle looked out beyond my shoulders and noticed the blue Benz I was in and called for her brother Burt to come to the door. She wanted Burt to confirm that this was the car they had previous seen a month ago while traveling. Angelle said that she and Burt was on their way to D.C. when we passed them at high speed and then miles later they passed us while we was pulled over by the State Trooper.

It was during the time when Will and I were on our way to Virginia to visit Evette and Diane and was in Janice blue Benz. It's a very small world after all and destiny was in effect.

180

We talked for about another twenty minutes with her handing me the money and I assured her that I would see her in a couple of days. I now need to have the vehicle registered in the name of my going to be driver along with the purchasing of a tag. Due to the vehicle having a savage title and I signed it in the wrong place as the owner I'm now not only required to have a title bond but it has to remain in my name for the time being. I did not want to have this vehicle in my name but, *It Is What It Is*.

Antonio Berry

CHAPTER 42

It's now time to prepare for the new purchased jaguar to make its first trip. Miguel is the driver I recruited and only driver since Jenkins became a Government informant. I have not been involved in the dope game since Jenkins arrest some three or four months prior. The tank has been modified and I think this is a more secure and safer way than the Cadillac. Jenkins and the informant from Mobile have revealed the secret compartment of the Cadillac to all the coastal law enforcement agencies. With Jeff and Duncan's arrest in a Cadillac it didn't help the matter. The bumper of the Cadillac automobiles has probably been the main subject of briefing in law enforcement alone the entire coast. The Cadillac has been laid to pasture.

I didn't waste time dropping the gas tank to place the money to only have to drop it again in Miami to take it out and put the cocaine. Instead I placed the money in the jaguar vents on the hood that's located directly under the front windshield and wipers. Miguel and Bumble Bee will drive the Oldsmobile to Miami while BC and I drive the jaguar. There's only money stashed in the jaguar and I was never uncomfortable riding with any amount of money as long as it was in what I thought to be a secured safe place. The plan is to leave while it's dark and be halfway beyond the turnpike when the sun begins to rise. As we're coming upon the toll plaza booth to enter the turnpike highway in Wildwood, Florida, I noticed a Sumter County patrol car sitting in the median. The occupants of the vehicles also notice us and pull out to follow the Jaguar. Miguel and Bumble Bee are traveling behind me and BC probably about three-or-four car links back. BC and I make it to the toll booth first and were handed a ticket to pay when we exited the toll road. I immediately sped off knowing the patrol car was several vehicles behind. In my review mirror I see the Oldsmobile that's driven by Miguel and it is several cars behind and the patrol car is two or three cars further down the line. I didn't waste any time trying to make it to the next county.

It wasn't until we made it around the Fort Pierce area before Miguel and Bumble Bee finally caught up with me and BC. They said the cops in the patrol car had stopped and questioned them asking were they following that jaguar. At the time I had no reason to wonder why they would automatically assume that the Oldsmobile was following the jaguar when there was other automobiles in between the two cars and the cops wasn't able to see that the jaguar had a Mississippi tag same as the Oldsmobile. In Miami the money is counted and the tank dropped in preparation to load the cocaine. On some occasions I have cooked the cocaine in Miami but this time I'm going to cook some in Orlando before sending it on to Mississippi and the other places it will eventually be distributed. Miguel and Bumble Bee will now be driving the jaguar with their first stop being the City of Orlando. Marka will be waiting to intercept them and park the car somewhere secure until I arrive. BC and I remained in Miami for several hours after Miguel and Bumble Bee leaves.

It's after midnight when BC and I exit on 1-4 into Orlando. Marka has a room at the Days Inn on 33rd waiting for us. I give her a list of items I'm going to need later in the morning for the cooking of the cocaine. Triple beam scales, baking soda, large glass microwavable bowls, plastic sandwich bags, bounce fabric softener, duct tape and brown paper bags. Tomorrow will be a busy day for me in Orlando, the kind I haven't had in long time. This will be the first time I've cooked cocaine in months. There's twelve kilos of cocaine in the gas tank. I'm going to only cook half of it and leave Marka twenty or thirty ounces to distributed to some relatives she has to earn her some pocket change.

I asked Marka to speak with her mother about me using her kitchen to cook. Marka had assured me that she had spoken with her mom and that it was cool. It's me, Marka, BC and Marka's cousin Kim that's sitting in the kitchen with a table full of cocaine when Marka's mom walk through the front door on her lunch break from work. She was so upset until she dam near had a heart attack and said everything under the sun except what the hell is going on. Marka was sitting there looking stupid and crazy like she was a retard and all she could say was, gone mama. My response to this situation because I'm messed up in the head now and told her that Marka said she had spoken with you about this and told me you said it was ok. Marka had lied and here I am sitting here in the wrong and as wrong as a person could be knowing now her mom has no idea what's going on in her house.

She said that Marka did not ask her nothing of the sort and that Marka knew better. She said Tony, Marka know the jump out boys is always across down the street trying to bust them guys hanging around that store and the Melody Bar. I made an attempt to clean and gather everything. She told me that was not necessary but don't ever do this again. Marka's mom, Ms. Henderson, was real sweet, cool and loved me for a. son-n-law. I said thanks and I definitely will not do it again but I'm going to straighten Marka about lying to me. Her mom was crazy about me and said don't worry about it Tony.

185

Here I am with six kilos of cocaine in this woman house cooking and she had no idea when I'm thinking she does. As soon as Marka's mom left back out for work I went into Marka. I wouldn't even allow her to sit in the kitchen with us while I continued cooking the remainder of the dope. I was mad as hell about this stunt and made her stay in the bedroom with the door close. I did not want to see her because this is why and how shit could go all wrong when you're already doing something you have no business doing. This was a dangerous business from every angle. Marka knew she was wrong for this and knew how I felt about this type of BS.

CHAPTER 43

The cocaine is cooked, packaged and placed back inside the gas tank of the jaguar all except the twenty ounces I'm going to let Marka have to give to her people. I have now thought about not doing this because she has really pissed me off with the lie. Miguel will leave at 4:30pm hoping to blend in with the work traffic on the turnpike. Me, BC and bumble Bee will leave an hour behind him. Miguel should be long pass the toll plaza in Wildwood, Sumter County. If not and have any problems he's aware and know that we'll be coming in that same direction shortly.

We say our goodbyes to Marka and the other friend; and begin our trip back to Mississippi.

I reached the toll plaza in Wildwood and pay the exiting fee for traveling this route. I continue my travel in the direction of I-75 north. As soon as I came across the over-pass, the Sumter County Sheriff Department has Miguel and the jaguar pulled over performing what looks like a search of the vehicle. We creped on by unnoticed by either Miguel or the cops. My heart has begun to beat 100 miles per hour. This can't be happening I'm thinking to myself. Bumble Bee is driving when we exit into a rest area a few miles further up the interstate. We waited there for may be ten minutes to determine if this was just a routine stop and if they would eventually allow Miguel to continue on his way. It's doesn't appear that they're going to let him leave.

The only thing I can think of now is to make sure he s alright because if not I also know the next steps that has to be taken. I switch seats with Bumble Bee and become the driver of the Oldsmobile and head back in the direction of the stop but this time we're in the south bound lane on the opposite side of the highway from Miguel. One of the officers happened to look up and notice the Oldsmobile and rush to his cruiser in pursue of us. BC and I jump out the car at a tourist store and tell Bumble Bee to take off and keep going home. We can see from behind the hotel wall we have run to, that they have Bumble Bee stopped. The doors and the trunk of the Oldsmobile are in the open position. They have hauled Miguel off to jail and impounded the jaguar to be thoroughly searched. I called Marka to come and rescue me and BC. She and another friend came and took us to Tallahassee where Darryl will come to take us home to Mississippi. I later learned from Bumble Bee that the cops questioned him about the other passengers. He told them they must have mistaken passengers with the hats that were in the back window.

After making it home I sit and waited for Miguel to call. Three days have passed when I learned that Chicken and a few other associates of his had been busted trying to traffic cocaine from Houston, Texas. It was a deal gone sour from where they had been purchasing cocaine from an undercover agent and the agents allowed the cocaine to travel all the way to Mississippi in an effort to flush out the owners and players in this cocaine deal. Chicken had not volunteered this information to anyone in the Enterprise including me and it would be months later when I find out the reason. It was discovered by a reader of the Sun Herald News Paper. It was not in our local paper the Mississippi Press Register. Miguel said that when the officers called back to Pascagoula to run a back ground check on him and the jaguar, they was told about the gas tank and that they had recently arrested the owner of that jaguar friend in a drug deal using the jaguar model vehicle. This was the concerned problem of mines with the jaguar being listed in my name. My antenna is now in the upright position as high as possible. Why is Chicken keeping it such a secret that he has been busted? Something in the milk isn't clean; the one's you're good to and treat with genuine respect and love will sometimes deliver you to death. Matthew 10:21.

This has caused another setback which time must be taken to re-think. The first time I decided to make another drug deal it ends in trouble. I send word to Miguel that I'm going to do all I can for him. I hired an Attorney in Orlando for a fee of $22,000 to handle the State case. Miguel was able to call collect unlimited to Marka who was only a few miles away in Orlando. Marka also would visit him. He had every number needed to reach me and I made it possible for his wife and children to visit him while he was down there in jail. The State held on to the case and Miguel was eventually sentence to eight months and served somewhere in the range of five months total. More than half of the cocaine was not reported leaves to question the motive for the stop and arrest.

Things are beginning to appear gloomy. I know and can feel that something is very wrong with certain pictures and structure of the Enterprise. A bad spirit has me surrounded and the signs are clear that the snakes are sizzling. For the life of me I cannot place a finger on exactly what and who it is but they're in the mist. In a late night of pillow talk I revealed all the problems I've had lately to Angelle. She's now adamant about assisting me in whatever way possible. She insists that if I needed her to be my driver that she's willing and able to handle it with no problem. We have been spending an enormous amount of time together, when it was Angie who used to travel with me most of the time recently it has been Angelle.

On one of the many occasions when I was preparing for Angelle to take a trip a incident happened that caused me to cancel.

Chicken had given me a bag of money that was supposedly been $80,000 for 5 kilos of cocaine at $16,000 each. When I begin to count the money every $1,000 stack was short. There was $50.00 to $100.00 missing from each stack of money. There s nobody living in the house but him, Sharon and her five year old daughter. He stated to me to return the money and he'll wait until the next time the car would be going to Miami. Chicken had the nerves to insinuate that Will Wade who was riding with me when I picked the money up had somehow gotten inside the bag. Will could have assumed but he had no knowledge that money was in the bag nevertheless the amount. Something did not feel right and my spirit was trying to enlighten me and point me in the right direction. I would never send Angelle or any other driver on a mission with such deep and disturbing feelings.

Angelle has really fallen in love and I'm feeling her but never could I lose touch with reality that I was a married man with a family. I loved my family and family life and why I did what I did in the streets, the only answer I have is, it was easy and simple to do. The women came with the money and life style but not one time did I ever think about leaving Janice and breaking away from my family for the street life. It could have been Halle Berry I wasn't leaving. Truth be told, Angelle was prettier than Halle Berry and all she needed was an opportunity to be placed in a position same as Halle Berry and the world would have had a new black red bone beauty queen. She would visit me in

Mississippi for the entire day sometimes and would even stay for two days depending. Yogi's lounge was the hang out where we would shoot pool for hours. She had a fair stick that was good enough for me to bet with her.

I had to always be mindful because she loved hard. Angelle to, also told me once that the only woman she would accept me having was Janice. She was aware of Angie and believed that Angie should be history. I could sex Angie that morning, clean up and be done bathing twice before going to New Orleans that night. Angelle had the ability to tell each time I had been with Angie. This use to amaze the hell out of me that although I would deny it, the scary part about it is, she would, be correct each time. She professed that her and Angie body chemistry didn't mix and gave off signs. I use to think that she was insane and had someone watching me and reporting back to her.

The pace is slow for me but I'm causing things to happen on the low with distributing cocaine on the streets; none with the purpose or intent of trying to stack more money. There were some people that I felt an obligation to continue to help that needed my involvement for a short period longer. I sought only to supply them with several kilos of cocaine sparingly. Tracy got wind of this and conspired with Jenkins in a jealous rage to begin a conspiracy plot to hand me over to the Federal Government on a silver platter. I made another tactical decision once again to move out of the State of Mississippi. The sporting good and music store the Number One fan Shop is doing great. The apartment units are full. The only major problem now that I can foresee is the hate and enemies are too strong. They hated me without cause. Psalm 69:4 and John 15:25.

The car is prepared for Angelle to travel to Miami. I informed her to page me when she arrived at Darryl house. Two hours later she calls and says she's waiting there for me. I have to give her expense money, reminders and she'll be good to go.

The money for the cocaine has already been stashed in the Lincoln she will be driving. She has no idea where the money is located and stashed. The car- will be turned over to my friends in Miami. They would be responsible for removing the money and replacing it with the cocaine and return the car to her to be brought back to me in Mississippi. Angelle could drive non-stop to Miami and after no more than two hours of rest and maybe sleep while the car is being pack, she could turn around and be on her way back the eleven to twelve hours trip. The understanding we had was that she would always stop and call once she make it to the Marianna, Florida area before continuing on to Mississippi. She would call to make sure it was safe to come on in and not be riding into a trap. I had to answer or she wasn't coming. I always took special effort to keep details of the trips a secret for her safety.

This particular time before she leaves for Miami I pulled up in Darryl's yard to give her the expense money and she wanted to know who it was in the car with me. I'm in Janice's 190E Benz and the windows are tinted. It's dusk-dark and she couldn't clearly make out the occupant in the passenger seat. She was concerned about someone knowing what was going on and stated she wanted to talk to me when she made it back. She had to have kept this thought on her mind the entire trip to and from Miami because it was the first thing out of her mouth upon arrival and seeing me. Before I made it to Darryl house I had already instructed Bumble Bee to take the car to the spot and unload the cocaine from the secret compartment. Angelle begin to quiz me about this and that and who was in the car. I said listen here, Are you stupid? Do you not think I'm going to protect my money and your life any better than that? I screamed on her about the fact that I was doing this shit when I met her and will be doing it when she's gone which seem like it's going to be soon. This was the wrong thing to say to her sensitive ass and it caused her blood to boil. She took off her shoe and threw it past my head barely missing. I picked it up and tossed it towards the woody area of Darryl's yard and jumped in my truck and sped off. She was flipping out for real.

Antonio Berry

CHAPTER 44

I had previous contacted my cousin Jerome about some painting of sport designs I wanted painted on the side and front of the store building; something that will be noticeable and attracts customers when coming towards the building from Highway 63. As soon as I walked in the store Janice say that Jerome called and said for me to come by his mom's house. As I'm pulling out of the store parking lot and begin in the direction to meet Jerome at his mom's house, Angelle is in full throttle speed coming towards the store on Hwy 63. She noticed me and makes a dare devil u-turn in the middle of the highway. I'm like this fool has lost her mind. I mashed the gas and make the turn on the street heading to Jerome and passed him standing in the yard. I called later and explained to him what was happening. He had noticed the Lincoln and the woman driving behind me. We laughed and agreed to meet later.

Angelle made it home and called me with the foolishness and I told her if she had came in my store with that bull-shit in front of Janice that it would not have been a pretty sight for her. I'm really now thinking seriously about letting this broad go because she has attempted to play me too close. I did my thing but I was never going to disrespect Janice and act as if she didn't exist or as if I had carte blanch to do as I pleased. Angelle said she was only going to scare me. It has dawn on me at this moment that she is crazy as a bug and in love.

She and I had traveled to Charlotte, North Carolina together to the factory warehouse of Capitol Graphic. I wanted to get a firsthand look and personally pick some items for the store and to actually see what was available that I didn't have the privilege to see or order in the brochures that was being distributed. We arrived back in Mississippi and I decided late that night to stock the store and have it completed for opening of business in the morning.

Angelle is sitting on a stool behind the store counter. I sensed she was watching me and turned around to be staring her in the eyes. "Why are you looking at me that way?" I asked her.

She stated, "Tony you amaze me. You get in the streets and deal with them dudes like a gangsta, you were in that warehouse of Capitol Graphic with them people like a real business man and now you're in this store like you're serious as hell about this."

I told her, "I am serious because this store is what's going to allow me to come out of the streets."

CHAPTER 45

I traveled to the States of Georgia and Tennessee in search of a home for me, Janice and the children to claim as our new resident. I eventually chose one in Jonesboro, Georgia in Clayton County. This is one of the most racist counties in the United States of America alone with Jefferson County Texas and many more but it was suitable for the time being in comparison to the other locales I had viewed. This move did not set well with Angie or Angelle because both recognized the change in me with trying to distant myself from the streets and street life and that included them. Angie is accepting it more humbly because I have placated her with a down payment of $9,500 on her first home. She still has this home today which I spent more on carpet and has never stepped foot in.

Angelle was beginning to act insane as if she needs to be institutionalized. She would say things like I'd caused her to fall in love with me and now I'm moving away further from her.

I emphasized to her that if she can drive to Miami and sleep/rest for two hours and turn around and drive back to Mississippi then driving to Atlanta from New Orleans is not going to be a problem.

I assured her that we're going to continue to see one another. She doesn't believe this because I've told her I'm retiring from the game completely for good, it's over with. I will not be able or desire to continue with the life style but I will be seeking other means of income that could be just as ludicrous. Janice trained a lady to manage the

Number One Fan Shop and my intentions were to open a You Buy/We Fry seafood market in Georgia. It's over with for me is what I'm think.

Angelle continue to make what was expected to be her last several trips of trafficking cocaine for me. She's very dependable although could sometimes be bugged out. I've placed a nice down payment on the home in Jonesboro with the expectation to pay it off in a matter of months and I know then dam well it will be over for me. Things are coming unhinged in Mississippi and it's hard to tell who's who and their motive. My so called friends and confidants are beginning to appear strange to me and their behavior patterns are of the nature I hadn't seen in all of our years as the Enterprise and hustling. I don't know who to trust so it's best I remove myself from this inner circle. I made another fatal mistake in the game because it's known throughout the underworld that dead men tell no tales. This was a simple task to have done and I failed to do so and if you' re sitting in a jail or prison cell reading this book it means you made the same mistake. Desperate men in the game must take desperate measures to stay alive. Angelle is upset about the move and has begun to act out on her emotions. I tried to convince her that our relationship will remain intact and the only thing that's changing is my location. She wasn't buying it.

It is rumored at the time that Tracy has went before the grand jury in Mississippi and Texas and sold his soul to the devil. I also have a gut feeling that Chicken has done the same. Death is a punishment to some, to some a gift and many a favor.

CHAPTER 46

Janice for the last several weeks has been spending numerous of hours training a person to manage and operate the Fan Shop. I can sense that I've almost burned her out with the continuation of always moving from State to State. I also know and realize that she loves this store and has put her all in it making it a profitable business. She has done great with it because it is making a profit and will support our house hold if all other business ventures fail. This was just another example of a woman willingness to follow her man and allow him to lead. The key is, showing a woman you have the ability and qualification to lead and they'll follow. At the same time I've always believed in a 50/50 relationship with the man having only a small edge with no need to pull some bossy type stunt for his woman to understand and respect that fact. Janice will be alright about the idea of moving once the business I'm going to open in Georgia is up and running.

The day of moving has finally arrived and we have been packing the u-haul all day. Pip-squeak and Lil' Larry are set to drive the u-haul truck. Janice nephew Buck, Kenny D. Bumble Bee and myself will follow and have the u-haul unloaded when Janice and the children arrive in the next couple of days. The six of us will be more than enough hands and backs for this task. Kenny D. and Bumble Bee are driving Kenny's burgundy four-door Cadillac while Buck and I are in the two door white on red Coupe Deville I've purchased for Angelle. The U-Haul is unloaded when Janice and the children pull in the drive-way but Janice is unhappy and it's reflected in her face and spirit.

She's thinking again that I have only moved her and the children away from family and friends to be placed in isolation while I continue the bizarre and promiscuous life style.

Jonesboro police dept had set up a road block in the community entrance in which we had recently moved. The officers stopped Kenny's car that was occupied by him, Pip-Squeak and Lil' Larry. A check was made on everybody in the car and they came back clean and were allowed to proceed on their way. I think it was a racial profiling that prompted a more thorough check. One of the red-neck officers used a pre-empt tech that the ID possessed and used by Lil' Larry R.I.P. had expired and therefore could not be used as a proper valid ID. Although Lil' Larry was only a passenger in the automobile it was illegal for him to use it as identification. I noticed outside in the front of the house seven or eight police cruisers that caused me to almost panic. I'm saying to myself what the hell is happening and could this be it. A lot has been happening lately and the first thing that came to my mind was that my suspicion and all the above was about to be manifested. I was just beginning to think that things had quieted down. What really blew my mind was the helicopter that was hovering over the house. I immediately tell Janice that if they take me to jail she and the children are to pack up as much as they can and leave for Mississippi. She could check on me later from her cell phone while riding the highway.

The encounter with the Jonesboro Police department wasn't a pleasant sight but the end result was I didn't go to Jail.

Lil' Larry was the only one arrested after they discovered the ID didn't belong to hm. The ID belonged to Sipp and he had been using it because they resemble one another. The officers insisted on searching the house after smelling that we had been smoking weed. A warning was giving about us smoking drugs around the children and the police dispense but not without a showing of an attitude and contempt. One of the officers had the audacity on the way out to ask Buck how they could afford the vehicles in the yard. It was Janice Benz, the truck, Kenny's Cadillac and the Cadillac in the back yard. Buck said he had told them that we owned several businesses. To add fuel to Buck response to them I opened the door and said excuse me sir, about the vehicles in the yard, it's one last thing I would like to mention concerning them. They looked like yes. I said they're all paid for and closed the door. I was still a non-believer and figure I had enough money for any bond. I had calm Janice down from almost going to jail. Lil' Larry was hauled off to jail and we would have to prove his true identity.

Janice and the children will be going to Mississippi to bring back the remaining small items that she could place and fit in the trunk of her Benz. She will also have an opportunity to check one last time on the lady that's managing the Fan Shop. We have been gone a couple of days longer than a week and probably want be back after this time for several more weeks. The properties will manage themselves because the only attention they need, unless there are repairs, is the collection of rent each month. Kenny D., Bumble Bee and I will travel I-20 west. We're going to stop in Jackson, Mississippi and speak with Red-Charles before continuing on to Houston, Texas where Angelle will be waiting. I have no intentions or reason to travel I-10, the Coast or visit the City of Moss Point / Pascagoula for many months to come. Janice can visit to check on the business and collect the rent money from the tenants. I'm done with the coast, the snakes and the cut-throats that are there. I still can't shake the feeling that something is not right and the working to bring down the crew of the Enterprise was in the making.

CHAPTER 47

The trip was successful from the stopping to check on Red- Charles to making it back to Jonesboro, Georgia. Angelle had already checked into the Days Inn Hotel on exit I-285 and Jonesboro road. I made a short stop to let her know I'm going home to bath and change and will be back in a couple of hours. The plan was for Pip-Squeak or Bumble Bee to follow her in one of the vehicles. She's taking the Cadillac I purchased for her but she has to also return the rental Lincoln to the place in New Orleans. This eased her mind some because I have provided a means of transportation for her to come back and forth to Atlanta as she pleases. She now has her own very dependable automobile.

As soon as I walked into the house in Jonesboro I picked up the phone to call Janice in Mississippi to inform her that I'm back in Georgia. This was so she and the children could return when she finished with everything she needed to have done or when she's ready. I knew she didn't want to move here in the beginning so I wasn't going to insist that she be here when I wasn't. The phone at the house in Mississippi ranged three times before being answered by a white man's voice. I immediately hung up thinking perhaps I had dialed the wrong number. I looked closely at the phone as I re-dialed the number again to make sure I'm dialing the correct number this time. How could I be dialing the wrong number when it has been the same for years? The phone was answered for the second time and nothing changed, it was the same voice on the other end saying hello. I hung up shaking like a 57

Chevy needing a set of spark plugs.

I called my mom house phone and received the same response and answer. A white voice answered saying hello. The difference was this voice asked if I was Richard, my step-father, and did I want to speak with Shirley, who is my mother. I knew then that the time had arrived for me to make some major decisions. Mama said she was alright and that they were taking her house apart. I hung up and hurriedly fled from the house in Jonesboro. It had been on every news station, broadcasting on the Gulf Coast that the nephew of the State Representative was being sought and wanted by law enforcement in several states. He's the subject of an investigation into one of the largest cocaine distribution network to have ever originated in the Southern District of Mississippi. This investigation includes six to seven States and numerous participants. If anybody has information that would lead to the arrest or conviction of Antonio Berry please contact the numbers at the bottom of your screen or your local law enforcement agency. These red-necks were thirsty and wanted something to quench their thirst and that something was Tony Berry.

Kenny D., Moosie-Cat and the other guys dropped me off at the hotel where Angelle was waiting.

I told Kenny D. that I would call later and that they're to lay low and sit by Howard's house until I call. When I called Kenny informed me that the Jonesboro Police Department had seized everything out of the house including Freeman my talking Amazon parrot. These racist even seized the patio set in the yard, intercoms for room to room, tool sets, soap, towels, hangers and silverware. They wanted it all and to destroy the image of a life style they envy. They seized the money Kenny D and the guys had in their pockets and made them walk. I sent them to Howard's and they called Janice and she sent them a bus ticket to get back to Mississippi. Kenny said the cops was angry and trying to figure out if it was a tunnel in the house because they wanted to know how was I able to come inside the house and make it out and doing this all while they had the house under surveillance. They had to have held their heads down for a sip of coffee and that was the split second window needed to make my escape. Unbeknown to me the window had been left open. I was in and out of the house in five minutes. The thought to call Janice and the response triggered my reaction. If I hadn't decided the first thing to do is call her when coming in the house I would have been trapped like a beast by these hunters. They would have had an orgasm especially after the prior week or so confrontation where I told some on the force to not sit on my couch and do their job and leave. That all the vehicles are paid for and there wasn't one note owed on any of them. This was making not just their day but could better their careers if I'm caught in this house.

The chase had begun with the United States of America being the hunter and Tony Berry being their prey. Everything has been placed under seize: the stores, properties, automobiles and even the children along with Janice and my clothes and shoes. No money or drugs has been found at any location and the walls are being dismantled by the hunters. They're thinking now that I have been tipped off and I was but it was by second nature to survive. The United States Prosecutor arrived on the scene of the house on Charles Street where Janice and the children were and had the nerve to ask her does she think I was with Angie. This was an attempt to cause her to turn on me, but instead, after they seized her Mercedes Benz and $250,000 worth of jewelry, Janice went straight and found Angie. She told Angie to just keep her mouth closed and that we had her if anything happens to her.

Janice had enough sense and knowledge to understand and knew the possibility of Angie knowing a lot of my business. The fact that Angie and I had an affair wasn't important to Janice at this time and I had her game tight. Although I done what I did I was always good to my people. A man's character is the reality of himself. His reputation is the opinion others have formed of him. Character is in him; reputation is from other people that are substance, that is the shadow.

A week passed and I'm still trying to figure out what's going on with the charges. Whenever I would call I was always told that the law enforcement was seizing any of our automobiles they would see Janice driving. The children had begun to complain and have restless nights from the harassment. The truck is in Atlanta parked in Howard's back yard where it's been for weeks prior to me leaving for the trip to Houston, Texas. I tell Janice to only drive one of hers or my Mom's vehicles until we can get a handle on things and find out more. So far it appears to only be the State of Mississippi that has charges and a warrant. Tracy and a few others have gone to the grand-jury and turned informants. I've called Miami and Houston to inform them about what has transpired. I can't reach Rhondetta but I did speak with Tisha. Janice has retained me an Attorney in Gulfport for a fee of $45,000 to find out what's going on and to represent me. A couple of days later he contacted her with the information that it's the State that wants me. It was decided that I would turn myself in Tuesday August 4, 1992 and post bond on said charges. It is the beautiful bird that gets caged.

CHAPTER 48

Angelle and I spent the next week traveling the interstate and the following weekend in New Orleans after traveling from the Carolina's. She did all the driving because it wasn't safe for me to be behind the wheel of any vehicle. The arrangement was for me to meet with the attorney in the parking lot of Singing River Mall in Gautier, Mississippi on August 4, 1992 and he would drive me to the Jackson County Courthouse for surrender. Trials are the true test of mortal men. Everybody was sure and didn't see why I wouldn't be given a bond. A bonding company will be waiting to secure my release. I gave Angelle my watch, ring, link chain and bracelet and told her I'll call later.

The Attorney had notified the local authorities that we were coming in. News Reporters from every local TV Stations and Mobile, Alabama had flooded and saturated the Courthouse. Cameras was flashing and trying to get a good look at this little giant of a man. Some had said they thought I was 6'6" and 300 pounds according to the tales of what this case had been made out to be. It was Election Day because of some re-districting that had been done and Billy was on the ticket to run again after winning the prior year. The story made head line news that the State Representative Billy Broomfield nephew has been arrested as the leader of the largest cocaine enterprise the Gulf Coast has ever seen. This was only an attempt to sabotage his campaign election trying to assure he wasn't re-elected. The tactic failed and he won by a land slide and would remain in office for more than the next

Antonio Berry

20 years.

I'm taken upstairs in the Courthouse by two detectives trying to make small talk in an effort to fill me out. I was finger printed and mug shots were taken. There were never any handcuffs placed on my wrist and why should there be when I voluntarily surrendered myself to the authorities. News reporters is at the ready each time the elevators doors are opened to move me from one section to the other. Cameras are flashing from all direction. I have been advised by my attorney not to utter a word. This was something I've only seen in the movies and now it was like déjà vu with me being the main character in the scene. As I'm being finger printed one of the detectives make a statement as to the allegations for the arrest. I adamantly denied knowledge of any illegal drug dealings and responded with I'm a legitimate tax paying business man in this County. The finger printing and mug shot process is completed. I'm rushed back down stairs to another floor where the courtroom is located and the judge is waiting in his chamber. A crowd of reporters, cops has come off their beats, the bondsman, Janice, Imogene and my attorney are all in the courtroom with the District Attorney waiting to begin with what has turned into a circus.

The District Attorney sought to have bond denied. He argued that I have the financial ability and wealth to flee the Country and has made several trips abroad outside of the United States.

This was a ridiculous argument for him because I had self-surrender when if fleeing is what I had intended or wanted to do I surely would and could have been in another Country instead of standing before a Judge in the Courthouse of Jackson County, Mississippi. He sense he was not going to prevail on the no bond argument and requested that

208

bond be set in the amount of $500,000.00. I'm thinking it didn't matter what it was I wasn't going to jail today. The mentioning of a $250,000.00 bond didn't even cause me to blink and why should it. All I would have to put up is $25,000 cash or property and never see the inside of a jail. My Attorney argued that I should be afforded a reasonable bond in light of the fact that I self-surrendered to the State.

The attorney I retained argued that once I heard that there was a warrant for my arrest I retained counsel and immediately begin negotiating to turn myself in to the proper authorities which bring us to this point. At this very moment one of the detectives hurriedly rushed from the courtroom as if he had just received a 911 call related to the present case or more information for the district attorney's arsenal. The judge hit his grapple and stated bond is set at $100,000.00 and the reporters rush from the courtroom to the printing press. They were the only ones that actually thought I wasn't going to be afforded a bond.

I was then taken down stairs to be processed out and for the bondsman to sign the necessary papers and collect his ten percent. Janice had already spoken to the bonding company and assured them that she had the money no matter what amount the bond was. It could have been a million dollars I say again I wasn't going to jail today. Also the bonding company owner and employees was familiar with me and my family. The formalities are completed with the signing of all the documents of agreement and I'm one door away from freedom. The same detective that abruptly fled the courtroom all of a sudden is back on the scene standing in the doorway. The only thing between me and the sky above is this half-bald headed red-neck racist pig detective. He tells the deputy to place me back in the holding tank because a federal warrant has been issued for my arrest. He had parachuted from the courtroom to notify the FEDS that the State was not going to be able to hold me in custody. I'm screaming and cursing that I've made bond and you have to let me go. I had no knowledge of what was happening or the FEDS and had to be forced into the holding cell.

It was several hours later before I was transported to Biloxi and taken before a Magistrate Judge where a bond hearing was set for within the next ten days. On the way over to Biloxi the two marshals that were transporting me attempted to make small talk same as the two detectives in an effort to extract information while I was being finger printed. They even sought to use the scare tactic. I responded with tell it to your mammy because I'll be out of this shit in a couple of days. I was still fuming from not being released after making bond in the State. The two marshals only smiled and nodded towards one another as if to say I had no idea what was in store for me. To tell you the truth I didn't have a clue. The only thing I knew for sure was, if I was given a bond I was going to be a free man because money wasn't a factor. Other than that I wasn't trying to hear anything else except who do I need to pay. The lawyer seems to be sure I'll be given a bond and this causes me to be more relaxed than I probably would have been otherwise. He has gathered character letters and assurance from several people that they will testify on my behalf at the bond hearing and stand behind me in this ordeal.

The federal hearing took place with the U.S. Attorney arguing for the Government and My Attorney for the Defendant. We have presented family members, teachers, business people and the bonding company all testified that they believed I should be afforded a bond. The Probation Officer alone with several letters stood up in open court and stated before a court room of onlookers that he see no reason I shouldn't be given a bond. The Judge set there for what seemed like an eternity before speaking and stated that bond is denied. He went further and stated that since the charges are stemming from Texas he would let Texas make the bond decision. The fix has to be in because if the people from my community that knows me best will not give me a bond why is it to be believed that Texas where I have no community ties will show any compassion and grant bond. The judge ordered that I be held pending extradition to Beaumont, Texas. I was returned to Harrison County jail.

Antonio Berry

CHAPTER 49

The attorney I've retained for the State charges has limited experience in the Federal Courts. We agree that he would pursue the State matters in the State Criminal and forfeiture proceedings. Angelle has contacted two Attorneys from Louisiana that she thought was some real cowboys and experienced in the Federal Courts. They visited and explained their view on the federal case and what they considered was my best options .Their first concern was to have me extradited to Texas where the battle for my life will ensue. The Louisiana Attorney's had spoken with the Attorney in Mississippi and it was agreed that they would represent me in the Texas federal court and he would remain on the State case while providing any assistance to them that he may be able to render. I signed the retainer agreement to pay them $150,000.00 with half to be paid within the next several days.

The Attorney's was confident based on the lack of evidence so far presented by the Government. The Government description of the case was nothing more than as the Attorney's described it, a bunch of Government stool pigeons and they're going to pick the feathers from this case. There was no hard evidence such as drugs, phone recorded conversations, no sell to an undercover agent, no currency was seized, no photos and not one individual including Jenkins had been arrested with any drugs they alleged belonged to Tony Berry. The Attorney's admitted that they had never seen a federal case this weak and didn't understand why charges was brought without a more thorough investigation. I'm now sleeping better at night believing that it's only a matter of time and this nightmare will be over and behind me forever. If I never knew or was sure before I damn sure know now that if I escape this encounter that the dope game is for real over for me. A close call doesn't get any closer than this if it's only a close call and not a funeral. Angelle is constantly trying to convince me to relax and let the attorney's do their job. They're excellent at what they do and I can trust them. They have been given $90,000.00 which was more than their required retainer as an incentive.

Three weeks later I was extradited to Beaumont, Texas by the U.S. Marshalls. This was the first time I've ever traveled not being on my own free will and it gave me a deep hollow lonely feeling inside. There was something and someone else in control of my life and destiny. The van was loaded for transport with other inmates that were headed for different destinations. Some would be going to other States and Districts to face federal charges, back to prison, transferring and others could be heading to a courtroom to testify against or for another defendant that has decided to load the jury box for a trial. In my case I'm heading to face charges and the devils in Texas. There are times when one would like to hang the whole human race, and finish the farce. This is one of those times for me if there has ever been one.

I was flown from New Orleans airport by the U.S. Marshalls to the federal transit center in El Reno, Oklahoma and processed.

I now have a federal register number of 03256-043 and a federal identification number that will tag me for the remainder of my life. I have begin to realize that the shadow that was hovering over me that night in Orlando while in bed which I didn't understand is, manifesting before my eyes and it's no longer a bad dream it's reality. The

The Enterprise "Testimony"

Government as a scare tactic caused my stay at the Oklahoma transit center to-be no less than three weeks. This was an effort with the hope that I'll be a broken spirit and give in to the Willie Lynch syndrome and sell my soul to the devil and be ready to lie in the bed with them by the time I reach Beaumont, Texas. It's better a thousand times to die with glory than to live without honor. What and who they thought they had arrested I wasn't that man by far.

Once the Government realized I hadn't and wasn't insisting through my Attorney's that a plea negotiation be sought they further implemented tactics in an attempt to break a run-away slave. After several weeks in transit and being incarcerated for almost two months I have yet to arrive in the City of Beaumont, Texas. I could be a bad apple among the stool pigeons that the Government is gradually molding into Government informants. Duffy and I were held miles away from the others in custody at the Beauregard Parish jail in DeRidder, Louisiana. The Federal Government had the game and was running 100 miles per hour with it. Pain makes the man think, thought makes the man wise, wisdom makes life endurable. I was adamant when it came to dying on my feet before begging on my knees.

The Attorney's from Louisiana had visited to discuss the case and thoroughly explained the case and all the options as required an Attorney to discuss with a client. It was understood that I didn't need to retain them for more than $100,000.00 if I had intentions to cooperate with the Government. They visited the U.S. Attorney's Office and requested for the discovery which is the evidence the Government intends to present if the case goes forward to trial. The only evidence known to us at the moment is that the Government has people turning into stool pigeons. Two weeks later my Attorney's

215

visited me again but this time with less confidence than the previous visits.

The antennas in my ears immediately went in the upright position. The Government has mashed the gas and put the fix in once again with my Attorney's at the expense of me paying them. Who's the real gangsta? They to, the Attorney's is, now inquiring and suggesting I plea and cooperate with the Government in exchange for a lesser sentence. They stated that Livingston aka Devo has been arrested down on the border and it's anticipated that he's going to cooperate. The Attorney's tried to sell me on the idea with a story line about the U.S. Attorney being a Christian man and that he can be trusted when mentioning about people are going to throw me in the grease.

I refused any deal and told them that I'll have my family to call because the understanding I had when retaining them was that there would be no negotiations as I said and that you're going to fight these charges for me. The Government hadn't presented anything other than what they had when the Attorney's decided to first represent me in this matter. Weakness of the character is the only defect which cannot be amended. It's time for me to seek other competent representation.

CHAPTER 50

I was placed in contact with another attorney from Knoxville, Tennessee who at the time unbeknown to me was a former attorney teaching at the University of Knoxville. He was retained to fly in to Texas and visit me for a determination of whether or not I wanted to dismiss the two attorneys from Louisiana and proceed with him. I had finally been transferred to Beaumont, Jefferson County Jail. This was an African American attorney from out-of-state requesting to represent an alleged drug dealer from another State in Federal Court. Jefferson County Texas has to be at the top of the list as one of the most racist Counties in America also. Upon seeing this new attorney the first thought that came to mind was Sherman Hemsley of the sitcom "The Jefferson". Everybody including the jailers found the resemblance astounding.

The new attorney had a fighting attitude when it came to this case and I was convinced that he was my best choice with pursuing the federal charges. January 1993 we're continuing to request bond since August 4.1992 the day of my arrest. I was refused bond each request and now wished I had fought extradition based on no part of the alleged crime has taken place in the Eastern District of Texas. A local attorney was retained for another $8,000 with the hope that he may be successful with the securing me a bond on his home playing field with his buddy the good ole Boys. $210,000.00 has now been spent on attorneys and the trial is fast approaching. The only deal that the Government has offered me is a 20 year plea with cooperation and that I assist them in the arrest of several other alleged drug dealers from seven or eight States. I would have to tell them a chronological detail of my first selling of cocaine which would have produced hundred's of indictments. Jenkins, Tracy, Bob, Zeth and even Chicken with the controlled delivery charge from Texas had given statement that consisted of people that I knew. It was going to take me to appear before the grand-jury to produced warrants and arrest. They wanted to use me to capture others whom they assumed through others that I had knowledge of and I wasn't feeling this even if it meant I had to roll the dice. The plea also included seizure/surrender of properties that honestly didn't belong to me nor did the property derive from illegal proceeds. The snitches were lying from both corners of their mouths. An appeaser is one who feeds a crocodile hoping it will eat him last and this is what was going on. The trial date is set for March 22, 1993. On the Government witness list was Jenkins, Tracy, Bob, Zeth. Punkin and other stool pigeons that jumped on the band wagon to lie in order to receive a sentence reduction. Chicken was not on this list because he was a wanted fugitive but he had previously given a statement on me, Kilo, Gold-dog. Pony, Duncan, Lucky and others he had knowledge of in the area. I was sitting here reading this statement that was part of the discovery and couldn't believe it. I took him in when he was a crack head and gave him the opportunity to have more than he would have other-wise ever had in life. He had agreed to help bust me for the DEA, FEDS and local law enforcements. I sent a copy of this discovery home to Irma and his brother Jeff with an inconceivable thought that he could do this to me. These dudes have all turned Government informant for the rest of their lives. Miguel and Bobby were on the list but were not testifying as the Government would have preferred. Miguel and Bobby denied any involvement with Tony Berry concerning the possession and distribution of illegal drugs.

One by one the cowards took the stand to look the most pitiful so called gangstas, playas ever imaginable. These street thugs have been unmasked for the fraud they were. Jenkins and his mother testified. Like mother/like son; ever will a coward show no mercy. Jenkins testified about the trips he had made to Miami and Houston over the years. He re-told the story of his traveling, people he had met as a result of hauling cocaine from State to State all under the instructions and direction of Tony Berry. Jenkins like Tracy was a high school dropout and noticeable illiterate. I know, what does that say about me for having them as a member of the Enterprise? When basing decisions on your emotions these are the results you may obtain. I never had the opportunity prior to learn just how much of a disability or liability they could really be to the Enterprise. Some test are necessary and should always be a requirement that's given serious consideration before going forward with any structure. Jenkins mom testified that she received $10,000 from me saying to pay some of Jenkins bills and send money to an attorney in Texas for representation of him and his brother Allen. Jenkins had been speeding and smoking weed while riding dirty. He knew better and I had assumed he would never do such a thing while trafficking cocaine. Now he wants others to pay for his lack of responsibility. Jenkins and his brother begin to cooperate as soon as the police found the cocaine stashed on top of his gas tank underneath his Grand prix. The stop and arrest was made in Chambers County. Learning of Jenkins cooperation with the Government I realized he needed no retained counsel and asked Tracy to retrieve the $10,000 from Jenkins family. Tracy was a close friend of the Jenkins family and Ms. Jenkins only returned $8,000 of the money. She lied and testified that I made threaten phone calls harassing her about the return of the money. This was a lie because I never talked to this woman and was trying to stay as far away as possible from these people. Tracy did all the communicating and visiting to their home that was necessary. As to this day I cannot honestly say she didn't return all of the money or Tracy is the one that kept the $2,000 because I never asked her about any of it. I had at the time assumed Tracy was telling the truth and he also knew I wasn't going to call her to find out. The use of money is all the advantage there is in having it.

Bob took the stand and was portrayed as a lieutenant in the Enterprise and his testimony carried the most weight than any other witness. Bob gave intricate details of the structure of the Enterprise day to day operation. This included properties, automobiles that was purchased and the names which they were listed. Bob testified concerning an alleged murder plot to kill Tracy. This plot was never substantiated but changed the course of the trial. Bob was trying to send me to death row. He was painting a picture to the jury that was assured to sink the Enterprise and send individuals to their graves with me being the first. He has turned out to be a dangerous enemy. One enemy can do more hurt than ten friends can do good. Bob confirm that metaphor to be accurate. The hit-man was extra Bob gave the Government which I had no knowledge of or any offer made to Tracy in return for him, Tracy not to testify. I was already aware that Jenkins and Tracy had flown to Texas and appeared before the federal grand-jury .The indictment had stemmed from Alex Joe who didn't know me and was not able to point me out to the jury, Old man Dobie, Jenkins, and Tracy appeared before the grand-jury and if any harm to anyone of them would have had to be done it surely was necessary to do it sooner so this was not a thought of mines. A man's action is only a picture book of his creed.

Tracy testified in poor vocabulary a chronologically history of selling his first piece of crack cocaine that him and Zeth had purchased from Tallahassee, Florida. If the indictment had not already been hand down Tracy would have indicted several other individuals in Jackson County as well as other areas with his testimony. You couldn't find courage nowhere in these Government informants Dt. 31:6-7. Tracy was not as deeply involved in the Enterprise as Bob but he was able and not so stupid to not know that the cocaine was coming from Miami, Florida and Houston, Texas. He had an idea that I was giving people in Mobile- Pensacola, New Orleans and Atlanta cocaine. There're many people to this day that do not know that Tracy has been a registered Government informant for more than twenty years. In an attempt to be convincing to the Government that he feared for his life he plotted to burn down the house he had under construction. The plan was foil when the hired amateur arsonist ignited the gas upstairs after they had sprinkled gas downstairs, trapping themselves in the house. They admitted to the authorities that Tracy had hired them to perform this task but he was never charged or indicted for this crime thanks to the long powerful arms of the Federal Government. He had intended to claim and scream retaliation by me as the result of his cooperation with the Government. I admit offers was being made from everywhere for me not to let him live. Some had wanted to snatch him up off the streets to never be seen again but I did not want this on my conscious nor did I want any more problems than what I already had on my hands.

Tracy testified that his reason for becoming a Government witness was because I wouldn't allow him to make any more money. A man always has two reasons for what he does, a good one and the real one. In Tracy's case cowards die many times before their deaths, the valiant never taste death but once. He had only learned of my favor to an individual that really needed my assistance with having funds to complete a project he had begun.

Zeth same as Tracy was one of the biggest liars since the word sin came into existence who took the stand to testify for the Government. Zeth testified for the Government that I had been supplying him with cocaine on consignment for several years. His testimony was, that from 1990-1991, I supplied him with fifty ounces a month at a price of $900.00 an ounce and that Tony Berry was responsible for teaching him how to cook and rock up crack cocaine. This was a total lie and in light of the larger amount of cocaine testified by others who I supplied, the Government allowed this inconsistency and contradictory by Zeth. The Government knows he's lying but it doesn't matter in the pursuit of justifying a means to an end. The only thing that's important to the Government is a conviction and the only thing important to Zeth is a sentence reduction and sending me to my grave alone the way. He would have testified against his own mother if necessary to escape his responsibility as a man for his actions. These were people who called themselves gangstas at one point in their street careers.

It was Chicken who had been supplying Zeth and his crew with cocaine for about a year. Chicken had stopped with Zeth supply because Zeth was always $3,000 to $4,000 short with Chicken's money and Chicken had said on several occasions that if it happened again he was not going to give Zeth anymore cocaine. This is what happened after about the third or fourth time that this occurred. Chicken would be upset and Zeth would not be short for the next two or three times Chicken supplied him with cocaine. As soon as Zeth felt things was ok again for him he would do a repeat and shorten Chicken with his money once again. Zeth had became broke as a result of Chicken not giving r; him anymore cocaine. His lights were out at the house and the water bill was due and would soon be turned off if not paid. Based on Zeth circumstances of living in the dark with the possibility of having no water I supplied him with twenty ounces of cocaine at the price of $700.00 a piece once in my life. He was not one of my workers nor would I have choose him as one based on the way he handled his business. Whatever I had in cocaine I would give it all out to my people because I had a saying that if you're not going to pay me then you want pay regardless of the amount. I had no worker to whom I was only giving fifty ounces.

The Federal Bureau of Prison had accidental sent Zeth to Terre Haute Indiana Penitentiary or it could have been on purpose. At any rate I confronted him about the lie he told about me supplying him with cocaine and his only explanation was he thought I was supplying Chicken so I had to be supplying him. He knew this to be a lie because he was aware that once I placed Chicken on his feet that Chicken was buying his own supply of cocaine. The next morning I was told by other inmates after coming from the kitchen eating breakfast that Zeth had been locked up in protective custody. People who bite the hand that feed them usually lick the booth that kicks them. Zeth same as the others was licking the booths of those that had been kicking them in the ass all of their pathetic lives.

Chicken was indicted but on the lam from prosecution. He was a wanted man by the State of Mississippi as well as the federal authorities. The only reason for Chicken did not testifying for the

Government against the Enterprise was because he was on the run and not in custody. After receiving my discovery I learned that Chicken had been cooperating with the DEA and other law enforcement upon his arrest in Gautier. Several other individuals February 1992 had been tagged as a culprit of an operation sting with cocaine coming from Houston,. Texas. Chicken had given names of major player in the dope game that was distributing in the area who he had decided to throw to the wolves. These names Chicken figure would raise eyebrows and guarantee him a bond on the current charges. The $80,000 that was short changed and the unwelcoming I received from Chicken family I'm now learning neither was coincidental. He had promised the DEA and the Federal Government that he would assist them in building a case on some major drug dealers in Mississippi on the coast and deliver to them Tony Berry on a silver platter. The only way of learning of Chicken arrest in the sting of February 1992 was the article printed in the Sun Herald News Paper.

CHAPTER 51

Miguel and Bobby was the most loyal and courageous witnesses of them all. They refused to admit to the Government that they had been involved in the trafficking of cocaine. The Government had subpoenaed them both as Government witnesses assuming under different circumstances they would to, like the others turn snitch. Miguel and Bobby did not sell their souls to the devils. Jenkins, Bob, Tracy, Zeth, Devo, Chicken, and Joe were all tin men with no hearts who crossed over. Devo had testified against Derrick Brisco and other players from Waco, Texas and was now living in Sanford, Florida. The Government superseded us two times hoping to build a stronger case than the one they had against the Enterprise. Each one of them that took the stand was pitiful cowards and should have been stoned. Exodus 19:13. There was death and life in the power of their tongues. Proverbs 18:21. You couldn't find courage nowhere in them. Deuteronomy 31:6-7.

The jury was up for grabs and it could be any team's ball. The U.S. Attorney's could not be certain that they had secured a conviction with a unanimous verdict even with Bob trying his damnedest to give it to them. The jury took only four hours to return a verdict of guilty after twenty one days of trial. Whom men fear they hate and whom they hate they wish dead. I had been wounced by demon possessed men Act 19:16. A sentencing date was set for June 25, 1993. We had fought a good long fight. Wisdom to often comes, and so one ought not reject it merely because it comes late. I will now wait my faith and the funeral that's being planned with Tony Berry the guest of honor.

June 25, 1993 has finally arrived and I may have had two hours of sleep the entire night prior. After spending over $200,000.00 for what I thought was adequate representation I had also hired NPLA a legal research team from Ohio for another $13,000 to prepare a sentencing memorandum. This was in hope of receiving a lesser sentence than the life sentence recommended by the presentence investigation report prepared by the Probation Officer. I'm a first time non-violent offender but these devils are trying to hide me from society for the remainder of my life with no possibility of parole. My most trusted thought to be friends and confidants had done a casino number job on me and the Enterprise. It had to be an incident in another State and City to bring down the empire I had created. The empire would not have crumble if not for Chicken giving statement after his arrest and Bob turning state. The Government case was weak and we would have all walked out of the courtroom. Jenkins, Tracy, Zeth and Devo did not have enough knowledge of the intricate details to sink the ship of the Enterprise.

Prior to pronouncing sentencing the Judge asked if I had anything to say?

I stated, "Yes, Your Honor. Not really taking nothing from it, Your Honor, not really adding nothing to it, Your Honor, just take a lot of the erroneous information from it."

The Court: All right proceed.

Defendant: And basically the whole PSI report is a bunch of erroneous information and allegations. It's untrue. I dispute the whole PSI report.

The Court: As I am reasonably sure that you dispute the evidence that was admitted during the trial.

Defendant: Well, See, Your Honor. I don't deny that I owned the Number One Fan Shop and I'm Antonio Berry.

The Court: All right.

Defendant: But I deny the allegations about the drugs

The Court: Any drugs

Defendant: Yes, sir.

The Court: At any time?

This went on for several more minutes with my cry falling on deaf ears. The judge proceeded with the objections and stated because of my life style he believed the witnesses quote:

The Court: The evidence has revealed and I'm certain that in the investigation is of sufficient reliability and trustworthiness that I can and do rely on it as to the amounts of money, the number of cars the number of homes, style of life. What he did with the profit, I do not know but it's certainly obviously there were amounts of money in cash in grocery bags that were bandied about, and as the leader, he certainly did profit as to what this court, not what Mr. Berry considers immensely but what the ordinary public would consider immensely.

Antonio Berry

The Court: Pursuant to the Sentencing Reform Act of 1984, it's the judgment of the Court that the Defendant, Antonio Berry, is hereby committed to the custody of the Bureau of Prisons, to be imprisoned for a term of life. The term of life consist of life as to count one and twenty as to count two to run concurrently.

I was sentenced to life in prison based on the testimony of people who I had treated as if they were my blood brothers and family. The one's you're good to and treat with genuine respect and love will sometimes deliver you to death. Matthew 10:21. I was sent to the dungeon of Terre Haute, Indiana Penitentiary as a first time non-violent offender. I'm now lost and hopeless in an unfamiliar world. Always be mindful that one enemy can do more hurt than ten friends can do good. Judge your friends based on character as opposed to personality and you will choose wisely.

Fast forward thirteen years later and Tony has been resurrected from the cross in which he was nailed against by trusted friends and confidants. Tony has crawled from the grave, cleared his sight, removed himself from the cemetery and ascended upon the freeway of life once again.

To many, Tony's resurrection is going to be the second coming. To some it will be the sighting of a GHOST. One thing is for certain and that is, *It Is What It Is*. That's Real!!!!!!!!!!!!

Prior to the Enterprise being edited for publication, Tracy Lee Lett was arrested and charged with the crime of conspiracy to distribute a control substance. The charges/crime carries a maximum sentence of life imprisonment. Will Tracy roll the dice and face the maximum

228

sentence he has delivered upon others? It's very doubtful he will knowing his relation to the parrot family of birds. In life, he who laughs first often times cry later.

APPENDICES

EXHIBIT A	Sun Herald article February 29, 1992
EXHIBIT B	Mississippi Press article August 5, 1992
EXHIBIT C	Beaumont Enterprise Newspaper is this from August 9, 1992
EXHIBIT D	Jenkins' Testimony
EXHIBIT E	Bob's Testimony
EXHIBIT F	Zeth's Testimony
EXHIBIT G	Tracy's Testimony
EXHIBIT H	Privacy Act Statement
EXHIBIT I	Verdict of the Jury, Count 1
EXHIBIT J	Verdict of the Jury, Count 2
EXHIBIT K	Sentencing Transcript
EXHIBIT L	Affidavit to MS Bureau of Narcotics
EXHIBIT M	DOJ Press
EXHIBIT N	Beaumont Enterprise Newspaper article, April 19, 1994
EXHIBIT O	Letter from Supreme Court Regarding Mr. Hubert Johnson, May 21, 1996
EXHIBIT P	Letter from Anthony Lawrence, Asst. DA to Mike Bradford, US Attorney November 14, 1997
EXHIBIT Q	Letter from Kathy Glasgow, NY Times to Antonio Berry, September 1, 2001
EXHIBIT R	Letter from Howell Cobb, US District Court to Antonio Berry, July 8, 2003
EXHIBIT S	Newspaper clipping regarding Roderick Jenkins arrest, December 11, 2003
EXHIBIT T	Letter from Linda Cansler, Attorney to Antonio Berry, April 1, 2005
EXHIBIT U	Letter from John Bales, Asst. US Attorney to Antonio Berry, April 10, 2006
EXHIBIT V	Security Designation, July 2, 2008
EXHIBIT W	Booking document for Tracy Lee Lett, April 5, 2014

SunHerald

Biloxi-Gulf Port and the Mississippi Gulf Coast

SATURDAY   FEBRUARY 29.1992

Traffic Stop Leads To Drug Arrests

More than 13 pounds of cocaine worth $120,000, a 1985 Jaguar, a .25-caliber automatic pistol and $1,656 in cash were seized and four men arrested after a Harrison County sheriff's deputy stopped a traffic violator on Interstate 10, Sheriff Joe Price said Friday.

Booker Tallavaur Carter, 51, of Houston, Texas, was arrested and charged with possession with intent to distribute after a drug dog sniffed out the cocaine, Prince said.

Agents from the Multi-Jurisdictional Narcotics Task Force, the Jackson County Narcotics and Major Crime Unit, and the federal Drug Enforcement Administration were called in, and after a two-day investigation, arrested three other men on charges that they conspired to possess cocaine.

They were identified as Silvio Abello Uribe, 31, also of Houston; Neil Phillip Moore, 23, of 1831 E. Live Oak Ave., Pascagoula; and Michael Todd Ward, 26, of 5406 Gregory St., Moss Point.

Sun Herald February 29, 1992
Exhibit A

232

THE MISSISSIPPI PRESS

AUGUST 5, 1992   WEDNESDAY

Alleged Drug Trafficker Surrenders to Authorities

By ANN PECT
Press Staff

The first person of those whose Moss Point properties were searched and/or seized because of alleged connections with drug trafficking surrendered to authorities in Jackson County Tuesday morning. By Tuesday afternoon, he was in federal custody on related accusations.

Antonio Jerome "Tony" Berry, 27, came to the courthouse in Pascagoula with his attorney, Chet Nicholson of Gulfport. Accompanying them were Moss Point police Sgt. John Gaffney and Mississippi Bureau of Narcotics agents Sgt. Dean Shepard and David Jackson.

The local charge against Berry is conspiracy to distribute more than a kilogram of cocaine. Investigators say Berry's allegedly illegal enterprises were widespread and involved dealing in large quantities of cocaine including major amounts that were brought into Jackson County.

After routine processing, Berry was booked on the sheriff's docket and then taken to his initial appearance before County Court Judge T. Larry Wilson.

Berry is said to have been the owner of No. 1 Fan Shop on Main Street in Moss Point and owner of or connected with owners of several residences in Moss Point. Authorities say the properties searched and seized Friday ware connected to cocaine trafficking.

District Attorney Dale Harkey, at the outset of the brief session in Wilson's court, announced that the U.S. Court for the Eastern District of Texas has two outstanding warrants for Berry's arrest on narcotics-related charges and has placed a hold on him.

US marshals took Berry into custody at the Jackson County Sheriff's Department Tuesday afternoon for appearance before a federal magistrate and possibly for eventual transfer to Beaumont, TX.

Harkey asked Wilson to set Berry's bond at $250,000 to assure the man's appearance for all court procedures.

He said Berry, has resources available on his own and in his family to abscond from the court's jurisdiction.

Harkey said Berry has residences in Georgia, Alabama and Tennessee in addition to an apartment in Gautier and a house on Charles Street in Moss Point.

Nicholson, Berry's counsel, told Wilson his client was not in this area when the warrant for his arrest was issued but he turned himself in and did not wait for law enforcement to find him.

"Besides, he has reason to be here to defend against the forfeitures," Nicholson said.

Wilson said he is aware that Berry turned himself in and that in light of the hold from Eastern Texas, the amount of bond here is not much of a question. He set bond at $100,000.

State and federal investigators allege that Berry has been part of an organization that has been responsible for introducing several hundred pounds of powder cocaine into Jackson County.

Berry told Judge Wilson his home address is 5519 Grierson Street, Moss Point. That, MBN agents say, is the home of his mother and step-father while 4506 Charles Street, Moss Point is Berry's own home in Moss Point.

Harkey alleged that all the furnishings from the Charles Street house had been moved to Berry's house in Jonesboro, GA and the house in Moss Point was bare when it was searched Friday.

According to the MBN, Mississippi authorities also directed the seizure of

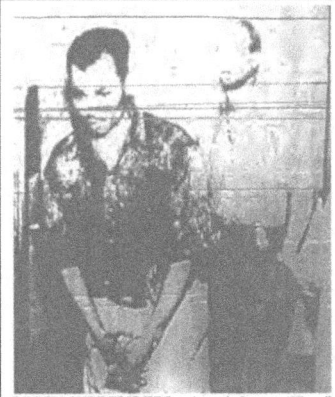

BERRY SURRENDERS – Antonia Jerome "Tony" Berry of Moss Point steps off an elevator at the Jackson County Sheriff's office as state narcotics agent David Jackson provides security. Berry is alleged by authorities to be part of a major drug trafficking operation. He surrendered at the sheriff's office Tuesday and was served with the warrant for conspiracy to distribute more than a kilo of cocaine.

Berry's home in Georgia along with its furnishings and two vehicles.

His house at 4506 Charles Street, Moss Point, and his No. 1 Fan Shop were seized Friday. The Charles Street house is valued at more than $50,000 and the store's inventory was valued at $25,000.

No drugs were seized during the Friday operation in which MBN, the state attorney general's office, Jackson County Narcotics and Major Crime Unit, Moss Point Police, Harkey's office and the Internal Revenue Service took part.

The conspiracy charge, according to MBN, is the out-growth of more than a year's investigation of "a large scale cocaine trafficking organization."

After posting the $100,000 bond on the state charge, Berry was taken into custody on federal warrants. He faces a Friday appearance in federal court on the drug charges brought against him in Texas.

Beaumont ENTERPRISE

SATURDAY   AUGUST 9, 1994

BY SUSAN BORRESON
Staff Writer

Man Will Return, Face Drug Counts

A Mississippi man will return to Beaumont to face cocaine distribution charges after a magistrate in Biloxi, MS ordered him held without bond on similar charges.

US Magistrate-Judge John Roper refused bond Thursday for 27-year-old Antonia Jerome "Tony" Berry. Roper said Berry would be a threat to the community or to flee.

Authorities allege Berry is one of the largest suppliers of cocaine to the Mississippi coast. David Jackson, a Mississippi Bureau of Narcotics agent, said Berry has worked with Texas and Florida contacts, who supplied him with hundreds of pounds of cocaine.

Berry, who faces charges in Mississippi of conspiracy to distribute more than a kilogram of cocaine, surrendered to Jackson County authorities Tuesday morning.

A federal grand jury in Beaumont indicted Berry in June on charges of attempting to distribute cocaine and conspiracy to distribute cocaine, Assistant US Attorney Malcolm Bales said.

Berry posted a $100,000 bond on the Mississippi charges and federal authorities took him into custody on the two Beaumont charges. Bales said authorities will return Berry to Beaumont soon to make court appearances on the charges.

Authorities allege two Texas men, Eddie Garcia dn Devon Livingston, are Berry's main suppliers. Officials allege Michael Todd Ward Caples and Roderick Jenkins, both of Mississippi, have connections with Berry.

Bales said Jenkins is on probation on a state drug conviction stemming from the seizure. Jenkins is cooperating with local law officials in their investigation of the Berry organization, Bales said.

Authorities said Berry dealt cocaine in Mississippi, Texas, Alabama, Florida and Georgia. Berry is the nephew of Mississippi State Representative Billy Broomfield, who defended the suspect.

With reports from the Associated Press.

Beaumont Enterprise August 9, 1992
Exhibit C

Q OKAY. DID YOU ASSEMBLE THE MONEY INTO THE BUMPER LATER ON?

A YES.

Q WHO WOULD GIVE YOU THE MONEY?

A TONY AND THEM, TONY AND TODD.

Q OKAY. YOU MENTIONED TONY AND TODD, AND YOU MENTIONED THIS FELLOW NAMED RED?

A UH-HUH.

Q NOW, ON THAT FIRST OCCASION HOW MUCH COCAINE DID YOU BRING BACK TO MISSISSIPPI?

A FROM EIGHT TO TWELVE KILOS.

Q YOU'RE NOT ABLE TO REMEMBER THE EXACT AMOUNT?

A (NODDING)

Q ON SUBSEQUENT TRIPS, AND YOU'VE MENTIONED THAT THERE WERE MANY, MANY TRIPS, WHAT WAS THE AVERAGE AMOUNT OF COCAINE THAT YOU BROUGHT FROM THE MIAMI, FLORIDA AREA?

A TWELVE KILOS A TRIP.

Q SO, THAT BUMPER WOULD BE FULL OF PACKAGES OF
  COCAINE?

A YES, SIR.

THE COURT: HOW BIG IS A PACKAGE, A KILO OF COCAINE?

THE WITNESS: PROBABLY LIKE THAT, PROBABLY ABOUT
  THAT THICK. (INDICATING)

THE COURT: OKAY.

BOB'S (TESTIMONY) EXHIBIT: E

BY MR. BALES:

Q IS THAT HOW IT LOOKED WHEN TONY SHOWED IT TO YOU?

A WELL, THE LAST TIME I SEEN IT IT HAD BEEN SET
   AFIRE.

Q ALL RIGHT. SO, IT HAD SUFFERED SOME FIRE DAMAGE?

A YES, SIR.

Q THAT IS THE BUILDING THOUGH?

A YES, SIR.

MR. BALES: YOUR HONOR, I WOULD ASK THAT GOVERNMENT
EIGHTY-NINE BE ADMITTED INTO EVIDENCE AT THIS TIME.

THE COURT: IT'S ADMITTED.

BY MR. BALES:

Q DO YOU KNOW WHETHER THE PROPERTY THAT YOU TALKED
ABOUT, THE JACKSON STREET APARTMENTS OR THE DUPLEX
THERE ON PALMETTO, IS THAT IN TONY'S NAME?

A I WOULD SAY IT'S NOT.

Q WHY DO YOU SAY THAT?

A THAT'S SOMETHING DRUG DEALERS DON'T USUALLY DO.

Q WHY IS THAT, MR. CUNNINGHAM?

A TO KEEP FROM CONFISCATING IT.

Q ALL RIGHT. DID YOU EVER YOURSELF ENGAGE IN THAT
  KIND OF ACTIVITY, TRY AND HIDE THINGS THAT YOU
  OWNED?

A YES, SIR.

Q WHAT DID YOU DO ON THAT SITUATION?

A SEVERAL CARS I HAD.

The Enterprise "Testimony"

SKIP AHEAD TO PAGE 766 OF TRANSCRIPT

A SIR?

Q DID YOU TELL TRACY LETT THAT TONY WOULD PAY HIM TWENTY THOUSAND DOLLARS?

A YES, SIR.

Q WHAT WAS TRACY'S RESPONSE?

A HE SAID THAT WASN'T ENOUGH MONEY FOR WHAT TONY HAD DOME TO HIM. HE SAID TONY HAD RUINED HIS LIFE BY TELLING EVERYBODY HE WAS THE POLICE AND NOBODY WOULDN'T TRUST HIM OR NOTHING. AND IT TURNED A LOT OF HIS FRIENDS AGAINST HIM, AND HE SAID THE ONLY WAY HE WOULDN'T TESTIFY IS FOR FORTY THOUSAND DOLLARS.

Q OKAY. AFTER LETT TOLD YOU THAT HE WOULD TAKE FORTY THOUSAND, WHAT DID YOU DO?

A I RESPONDED BACK TO TONY THROUGH ANGELLE.

Q OKAY. EXPLAIN THAT. YOU DIDN'T TALK TO TONY DIRECTLY, YOU TALKED TO ANGELLE?

A WELL, IT WAS LIKE ANGELLE WAS TRANSLATING MESSAGES. AT SOMETIME —

241

MR. JOHNSON: YOUR HONOR, EXCUSE ME. MAY I HAVE THE LAST STATEMENT READ BACK?

THE COURT: WELL, HE SAID TRANSLATING BUT I THINK HE MEANS TRANSMITTING OR TAKING A MESSAGE. YA'LL WEREN'T TALKING IN A FOREIGN LANGUAGE?

THE WITNESS: NO, SIR.

THE COURT: WERE YOU TELLING ONE PERSON TO GO AHEAD AND RELAY A MESSAGE, IS THAT IT?

THE WITNESS: YES, SIR.

THE COURT: ALL RIGHT.

BY MR. BALES:

Q SO, YOU TOLD ANGELLE, WHO TOLD TONY, THAT LETT HAD REJECTED THE OFFER AND SAID HE WANTED FORTY THOUSAND?

A YES, SIR.

Q WHAT RESPONSE DID TONY HAVE?

A WELL, HE SAID, "FORTY THOUSAND DOLLARS, THAT'S TOO MUCH. IT WOULD BE EASIER FOR US TO KILL HIM."

242

Q ALL RIGHT. WHAT HAPPENED AFTER YOU HEARD THAT?

A WELL, ANGELLE BRUNG A GUY FROM NEW ORLEANS OVER
  SO ME AND HIM COULD FIND TRACY, SO THE GUY COULD
  KILL TRACY. Q WHAT RELATIONSHIP ARE YOU TO TRACY
  LETT?

A I HAVE CHILDREN BY HIS SISTER.

Q DO YOU CONSIDER YOURSELF A BROTHER-IN-LAW OR
  SOMETHING?

A SOMEWHAT.

Q WHAT HAPPENED WHEN ANGELLE BROUGHT THIS FELLOW
  OVER FROM NEW ORLEANS?

A AT FIRST I TOOK IT FOR A JOKE, AND THEN, YOU
  KNOW, I SEEN, YOU KNOW, THEY WERE SERIOUS ABOUT
  IT, AND ANTONIA KEPT SENDING ME MESSAGES ABOUT
  "THE MAN IN THE JAILHOUSE, HE DON'T WANT TO BE
  HERE, YOU NEED TO GO AHEAD AND HANDLE YOUR
  BUSINESS," AND SO ME AND THE GUY DROVE AROUND
  LOOKING FOR TRACY FOR SEVERAL HOURS. SO, I
  STARTED THINKING, YOU KNOW, ABOUT DO I WANT TO
  MAKE ONE PROBLEM OUT OF TWO PROBLEMS AND BE
  WORRIED ABOUT THIS AND A MURDER, SO, ME AND THE
  GUY STARTED RIDING IN PLACES THAT I KNEW TRACY
  WOULDN'T EVEN HANG OUT AT. SO, I GOT TIRED OF

HANGING WITH THE GUY, I CARRIED HIM TO A HOTEL AND LEFT.

Q DID YOU HEAR ANYTHING MORE ABOUT TRYING TO DO SOMETHING TO TRACY LETT AFTER THAT INCIDENT?

A ANGELLE CAME BACK OVER AND WOKE ME UP, I WAS STAYING IN A TRAILER, SHE CAME OVER AND WOKE ME UP AND SHE SAID -

MR. JOHNSON: OBJECTION TO WHAT SHE SAID, YOUR HONOR.

THE COURT: I'M GOING TO OVERRULE UNDER BOURJAILY.

BY MR. BALES:

Q YOU MAY ANSWER, MR. CUNNINGHAM.

A SHE SAID, "YA'LL ARE SOME OF THE SORRIEST DOPE

DEALERS I'VE EVER SEEN. YOU KNOW TONY WOULD DO Ii FOR YA'LL." SHE STARTED THREATENING ME, TELLING ME THAT IF SHE HAD TO COME OVER AND HANDLE THE BUSINESS, THAT SHE S GOING TO HANDLE ALL OF US, AND, YOU KNOW, I LIKE THREATENED HER BACK AND TOLD HER, YOU KNOW, THAT HER HEART PUMP BLOOD,

TOO, YOU KNOW.

Q ALL RIGHT.

ZETH'S (TESTIMONY) EXHIBIT: F

APRIL 1, 1993 9:15 A.M.

(DEFENDANTS PRESENT - JURY NOT PRESENT)

THE COURT: WOULD YOU DICTATE YOUR MOTION, MR.
  BALES?

MR. BALES: YES, YOUR HONOR. JOHN M. BALES FOR THE
  UNITED STATES.

THE UNITED STATES MOVES --

THE COURT: NO. NO. HE'S TO STAY ON THE WITNESS
  STAND.

THE MARSHAL: OH, HE'S OKAY THERE?

THE COURT: YEAH.

MR. BALES: YOUR HONOR, WE MAKE A MOTION IN LIMINE
  SPECIFICALLY AS TO THE WITNESS, ZETH RICHARDSON,
  AND WE WOULD LIKE TO LIMINE OUT ANY MENTION OF
  ANY INVOLVEMENT THAT MR. RICHARDSON HAD IN THE
  KIDNAPPING OF SOME PEOPLE OR ASSOCIATION WITH THE
  KIDNAPPING OF SOME PEOPLE IN THE STATE OF
  MISSISSIPPI DURING THE YEAR OF 1992 I BELIEVE.

246

THE UNITED STATES BELIEVES THAT THERE ARE NO
CHARGES PENDING, HE'S NOT BEEN CONVICTED OF
IT,AND THAT IT FALLS OUTSIDE THE RULE OF
IMPEACHMENT, AND THEREFORE, TO PREVENT A SERIES
OF OBJECTIONS IN FRONT OF THE JURY, WE WOULD LIKE
TO LIMINE OUT ANY CROSS-EXAMINATION OF MR.
RICHARDSON CONCERNING THIS MATTER.

THE COURT: IN THAT CONNECTION I'M GOING TO ASK THE
WITNESS A FEW QUESTIONS. THE UNITED STATES
ATTORNEY SAYS THAT YOU WERE ARRESTED OR ACCUSED
OR IN SOME WAY INVOLVED WITH A THWARTED
KIDNAPPING INVOLVING AN ERIC JAMES OR A GOLD BUG,
IS THAT HIS --

WITNESS RICHARDSON: GOLD DOG.

THE COURT: GOLD WHAT?

WITNESS RICHARDSON: DOG.

THE COURT: GOLD DOG? OKAY. ONE OF THE OTHER LAWYERS
HAS TOLD ME THAT SOMEONE IN HATTIESBURG HAS BEEN
INDICTED FOR THAT. ARE YOU AWARE OF THE
TRANSACTION OR THE EVENTS I'M TALKING ABOUT?

WITNESS RICHARDSON: I'M AWARE OF WHAT YOU'RE

SPEAKING OF BUT I'M NOT AWARE OF ANYBODY THAT'S
BEEN INDICTED ON THAT CHARGE.

THE COURT: ALL RIGHT. BRIEFLY TELL ME WHAT IS
   SUPPOSED TO HAVE OCCURRED.

WITNESS RICHARDSON: SOME GIRLS, WELL, SOME PEOPLE
   OWED GOLD DOG SOME MONEY AND HE HAD HIRED ME TO
   TRY AND GO COLLECT THIS MONEY FOR HIM, AND IN THE
   PROCESS, WE ABDUCTED SOME GIRLS TO TRY TO OBTAIN
   INFORMATION TO LEAD US TO PEOPLE THAT OWED MR.
   JAMES THE MONEY.

THE COURT: DID YOU DO THAT?

WITNESS RICHARDSON: YES, SIR.

The Enterprise "Testimony"

TRACY'S (TESTIMONY) EXHIBIT: G

BY MR. BALES:

Q GOOD MORNING, MR. LETT. PLEASE INTRODUCE TO THE JURY BY TELLING THEM YOUR FULL NAME AND YOU'RE FROM.

A MY FULL NAME IS TRACY L. LETT, I'M FROM MOSS POINT, MISSISSIPPI.

Q HOW OLD ARE YOU, TRACY?

A THIRTY.

Q HAVE YOU BEEN RAISED YOUR WHOLE LIFE IN MOSS POINT?

A YES.

Q DID YOU LIVE ANYPLACE ELSE BESIDES MOSS POINT?

A YES.

Q WHERE ELSE HAVE YOU LIVED?

A NEW YORK CITY.

Q HOW LONG DID YOU LIVE IN NEW YORK CITY?

A ABOUT FOUR YEARS.

Q WERE YOU A CHILD THEN OR WHAT?

A I WAS A CHILD THEN, YOUNG.

Q DID YOU GO TO SCHOOL IN MOSS POINT?

A YES, SIR.

Q DID YOU GRADUATE?

A NO, SIR.

Q HOW FAR DID YOU GET?

A ABOUT THE NINTH GRADE.

Q WHY DID YOU LEAVE SCHOOL IN THE NINTH GRADE, MR.

The Enterprise "Testimony"

SKIP AHEAD TO 1380 of transcript

DRUGS?

A NO, SIR.

Q DO YOU HAVE SOME SORT OF AGREEMENT WITH THE
  UNITED STATES OF AMERICA CONCERNING YOUR
  TESTIMONY HERE?

A YES, SIR.

Q I WANT YOU TO TELL THE JURY WHAT YOUR
  UNDERSTANDING OF THAT AGREEMENT IS.

A MY UNDERSTANDING IS THAT IF I GET INTO THE
  COURTROOM TODAY AND TESTIFY TRUTHFULLY, THAT NO
  CHARGES WILL BE BROUGHT UPON ME.

Q AND NO CRIMINAL CHARGES HAVE BEEN BROUGHT AGAINST
  YOU?

A NO, SIR.

Q MR. LETT, THIS CASE IS ABOUT SOME PEOPLE NAMED
  TONY BERRY, GERALD DUFFY AND EDWARD KING. DO YOU
  KNOW TONY BERRY?

A YES, SIR.

Q DO YOU SEE HIM HERE IN THE COURTROOM?

251

A YES, SIR.

Q WOULD YOU PLEASE DESCRIBE SOMETHING THAT HE'S
  WEARING FOR THE RECORD?

A HE'S WEARING A LIGHT BLUE SHIRT AND A BLUISH TIE.

Q ALL RIGHT.

MR. BALES: YOUR HONOR, I WOULD ASK THAT THE RECORD
  REFLECT THAT HE HAS CORRECTLY IDENTIFIED ANTONIA

SKIP AHEAD TO PAGE 1382 OF TRANSCRIPT

YOU KNOW, HE TOLD ME I COULD MAKE MONEY, AND I HAD
  A LITTLE MONEY AND WAS GOING AND BUYING DRUGS,
  YOU KNOW.

Q ALL RIGHT. WERE YOU WORKING BACK IN 1986?

A THE EARLY PART I WAS, THE LATTER PART I WASN'T.

Q THAT WAS FOR THE CITY OF MOSS POINT?

A YES, SIR.

Q DIB YOU GET LAID OFF OR WERE YOU FIRED OR WHAT?

A GOT LAID OFF.

The Enterprise "Testimony"

Q SO, DWIGHT ASKED YOU IF YOU WANTED TO SELL DRUGS
   AND YOU AGREED?

A YES, SIR.

Q HOW DID YOU AND DWIGHT DO THAT?

A WE WAS GOING TO A GUY BY THE NAME OF BIG DADDY
   WITH A HUNDRED, TWO OR THREE HUNDRED DOLLARS,
   JUST KNICKKNACK AND DIMING, YOU KNOW.

Q KNICKKNACK AND DIMING MEANS SMALL AMOUNTS OF
   DRUGS?

A YES.

Q WHERE IS BIG DADDY FROM?

A HE'S FROM FLORIDA.

Q WHAT PART OF FLORIDA?

A TAMPA.

Q TAMPA? WHO KNEW BIG DADDY?

A DWIGHT JACKSON DID.

Q DO YOU KNOW BIG DADDY'S REAL NAME?

A I JUST KNOW HIS NAME IS RICHARD.

253

Antonio Berry

SKIP AHEAD TO PAGE 1445 OF TESTIMONY

A YES.

Q NOW, YOU'VE TESTIFIED HERE TODAY. DID YOU EVER COME OUT HERE ON OTHER OCCASIONS IN COOPERATING WITH THE GOVERNMENT?

A YES, SIR.

Q AND WHAT DID YOU DO ON THAT OCCASION?

A EXCUSE ME, I DON'T UNDERSTAND THE QUESTION.

Q WHEN YOU CAME TO TEXAS, DID YOU MEET WITH ME?

A YES .

Q DID YOU DO ANYTHING ELSE BESIDES MEET WITH ME?

A NO, SIR.

Q DID YOU TESTIFY BEFORE A GRAND JURY?

A YES, SIR.

Q NOW, EVENTUALLY BERRY WAS ARRESTED ON THE CHARGES THAT HE'S HERE FOR TODAY, IS THAT CORRECT?

A YES, SIR.

The Enterprise "Testimony"

Q DID YOU KNOW ABOUT THAT?

A YES, SIR.

Q AND HOW DID YOU KNOW ABOUT IT?

A DID I KNOW HE WAS ARRESTED?

Q YES, SIR.

A THROUGH YA'LL.

Q ALL RIGHT. DID YOU HEAR ABCUT IT THERE IN YOUR
   TOWN?

A NO, SIR.

Exhibit H

8. Pursuant to a written plea agreement, Bob Cunningham appeared before U.S. District Judge Howell Cobb on November 5, 1992, and entered a plea of guilty to a single count Information charging him with conspiracy to possess with intent to distribute cocaine, in violation of 21 U.S.C. § 846. As a part of the plea agreement Cunningham agrees to provide substantial assistance to the Government in he investigation and prosecution of others involved in the trafficking of controlled substances. Should Cunningham provide substantial assistance, the Government agrees to file a U.S.S.G. § 5K1.1 motion for downward departure at the time of sentencing. Also, the Government agrees to dismiss the Indict 1-92-CR-93 against Cunningham at the time of his sentencing. The Court accepted Cunningham's plea and adjudged him guilty. At the time of this report, Cunningham is awaiting sentencing.

9. Pursuant to a written plea agreement, Delvin Livingston appeared before U.S. District Judge Howell Cobb on March 1, 1993, and entered a plea of guilty to a one-count Information charging him with conspiracy to possess with intent to distribute cocaine in violation of 21 U.S.C. § 846. As a part of the plea agreement, Livingston agrees to provide substantial assistance to the Government in the investigation a, prosecution of others involved in the trafficking of controlled substances Should Livingston provide substantial assistance, the Government agrees to file a U.S.S.G. § 5K1.1 motion for downward departure at the time of sentencing. The Govern, in also agrees to dismiss the Indictment, cause number 1:92-CR-

93, against Livingston at the time of sentencing. The Court accepted Livingston's plea and adjudged him guilty. At the time of this report, Livingston is awaiting sentencing.

10. Michael Todd Ward remains a fugitive in this case.

The Offense Conduct

11. Investigation of this case was initiated by James Kuykendall and Rick Humphreys, Special Agents of the U.S. Drug Enforcement Administration. The DBA initially obtained information from the Chamber's County, Texas, Task Force on November 5 1991 that two individuals, Roderick Jenkins and Allen Jenkins, had been arrested and were in possession of cocaine. At that time, Roderick Jenkins was willing to cooperate with the Chamber's County Drug Task Force and the Drug Enforcement Administration. As a result of his cooperation, a large scale investigation was conducted concerning the illegal drug trafficking activities of several individuals in the Miami, Florida; Pascagoula, Mississippi; Mobile, Alabama; and Houston, TX areas The investigation revealed that Antonia Berry, Edward King and Gerald Duffy were involved in a large scale cocaine trafficking operation between Miami Florida, and Pascagoula, Mississippi, as well as between Pascagoula, Mississippi, and Houston, Texas. The activities of Berry, King and Duffy are as follows.

12. Roderick Jenkins and Antonia Berry grew up together in Moss Point, Mississippi, a small town located near Pascagoula. During the summer of 1988, Berry propositioned Jenkins about earning some "fast money." Berry advised Jenkins that he needed him to drive from Mississippi to Miami, Florida, for the purpose of obtaining cocaine. Jenkins was to transport large sums of cash to Miami in exchange for cocaine and transport the cocaine back to Mississippi. Jenkins accepted Berry's proposition.

13. Shortly thereafter Jenkins prepared to make his first trip to Miami. Berry provided Jenkins with $150,000 which was placed in the bumper of a Cadillac, a vehicle Jenkins used to transport the drugs and money. This was the standard procedure for all of the trips Jenkins made. Jenkins left Mississippi and proceeded to Miami. Berry and an individual known as Bobby Tate followed Jenkins in a different vehicle.

14. Upon arriving in Miami, Jenkins went to a specific location, as directed by Berry. Jenkins was instructed to take the $150,000 out of the car and wait for an individual known as Corey Johnson, who was Berry's main source of supply for cocaine in Miami. Johnson arrived a short time later and provided Jenkins with eight kilograms of cocaine in exchange for the $150,000. Jenkins placed the eight kilos in the bumper of the Cadillac and proceeded back to Mississippi. Jenkins transported the drugs back to a house located in Gautier, Mississippi, where it was given to Berry.

15. After the first trip, Jenkins made at least 50 additional trips to Miami for the purpose of obtaining cocaine powder for Berry. Jenkins made approximately two trips per month and would receive eight to twelve kilos of cocaine powder from Corey Johnson, which was ultimately delivered to Berry. Jenkins would transport cocaine powder from Miami to Gautier, Mississippi, where Berry would pick it up. All totaled, Jenkins transported at least 400 to 600 kilos of cocaine powder from Miami Florida, to Gautier, Mississippi, for Berry. The majority of the 400 to 600 kilos was converted into crack cocaine. On one occasion in Orlando, Florida, Jenkins witnessed Berry "rock up," a term used to describe the conversion of cocaine powder into cocaine base, eight kilos of cocaine powder. Jenkins transported the eight kilos of crack back to Mississippi.

16   During the early part of 1990, Jenkins began making trips to Houston, Texas, to pick up large amounts of cocaine for Berry. The source of the cocaine in Houston was Edward King, aka Junior. Jenkins also continued to make his trips to Miami to purchase cocaine for Berry. Berry accompanied Jenkins during his initial trips to Houston to show Jenkins the proper procedures on how to obtain the cocaine.

17   After learning the procedures, Jenkins began making trips to Houston on his own Berry instructed Jenkins to take someone with him, as to not raise the suspicions of law enforcement officials. Jenkins was often accompanied by his girlfriend, or his brother Allen Jenkins. Upon arriving in Houston, Jenkins would secure a room at the Days Inn, located off the 610 Loop. Jenkins would call King to notify him that he was in town. King would go to the Days Inn, where Jenkins would follow him back to a ranch where the cocaine was located. King rented horse stables at the ranch, which were often used to store the cocaine. This procedure was done until Jenkins learned how to get to the ranch on his own.

18   From the beginning of 1990, until November 5, 1991, Jenkins made at least 35 trips to Houston, where he purchased at least eight kilos of cocaine powder per trip from King. Jenkins was given $150,000 by Berry on each occasion, which was given to King in exchange for the cocaine. All totaled, Jenkins received at least 280 kilos of cocaine powder from King.

19   On November 5, 1991, Jenkins was stopped by the Chamber's County, Texas, Sheriff's Office for speeding, while traveling eastbound on Interstate 10. Upon approaching the vehicle, officers detected the odor of burnt marijuana in the vehicle. Jenkins consented to the officer's request to search the vehicle. A subsequent search of the vehicle, recovered three kilos of cocaine powder located near the gas tank, underneath the vehicle. Jenkins usually transported the cocaine in the bumper of a Cadillac because it was capable of storing large amounts of cocaine. However, due to the arrest of Corey Johnson and Jeffrey James, both of whom

utilized Cadillacs to transport cocaine, Jenkins decided to use his own vehicle, a 1981 Pontiac Grand Prix. Jenkins felt that because of the arrest of Johnson and James, utilizing a Cadillac was too risky, as he felt law enforcement officials had targeted Cadillacs Jenkins was arrested on this date, and this was the last time he transported cocaine for Berry.

20   Berry initially paid Jenkins $300 for his trips to Miami. However, as time went on. Berry began to increase the payments to Jenkins. Before his arrest, Berry was paying Jenkins $3,000 for every trip he made to Houston.

21   Prior to his arrest on November 5, 1991, Jenkins also transported drugs for Berry from Moss Point, Mississippi, to an individual known as "Punkin," aka Earl Shinn, who lived in Prichard, Alabama. Berry instructed Jenkins on how to contact "Punkin" once he arrived in Prichard. Jenkins made 10 to 20 trips to Prichard, in which he transported 40 to 80 ounces of crack cocaine per trip. The crack was fronted by Berry to "Punkin." Berry paid Jenkins $100 per trip. All totaled, Jenkins transported at least 400 to 800 ounces of crack cocaine for Berry to "Punkin."

22   After Jenkins was arrested on November 5, 1991, he was questioned by law enforcement officers as to the ownership of the cocaine. Jenkins first stated that the cocaine belonged to Michael Todd Ward, because at that time, he did not want to implicate Berry. Jenkins thought Berry would get him out of jail. Jenkins later told - the officers and DEA agents the truth, which was that Tony Berry was the organizer of a large cocaine network in Moss Point, Mississippi.

23   Through instructions from the DEA, Jenkins phoned Berry and explained to him that his car had broken down, and he would need help getting back to Mississippi. Berry told Jenkins that he (Berry) would not come to Beaumont because it was a "hot spot," meaning a place where a lot of people get stopped on Interstate 10 hauling cocaine. Berry sent Charlie Doby to assist Jenkins in getting him

back to Mississippi. Doby arrived at the motel where Jenkins was placed by the DEA on November 6, 1991. Doby was accompanied by Gerald Causey.

24   After entering Jenkins' motel room, Doby and Causey were shown a duffle bag, which supposedly contained cocaine, when in fact it was counterfeit cocaine placed in the bag by DEA agents. Jenkins kept trying to show the bag of cocaine to Doby and Causey. However, Doby did not seem to be interested in looking at the cocaine and told Jenkins not to worry about it, they needed to get going. As Doby and Causey left the motel room to go to their tow truck, DEA agents and officers moved in and secured their arrest.

25   After Jenkins was arrested, his mother, Janie Mae Jenkins, received a call from Berry who advised her that Jenkins has been arrested in Texas and was in jail. Berry sent $10,000 to Ms. Jenkins and advised her to pay some of his bills and send money to an attorney in Texas to get Jenkins released from jail.

26   After learning that Jenkins was cooperating with law enforcement officials, Berry called Ms. Jenkins and demanded that she return the $10,000. He told her to have her husband deliver the money to him. For fear of his safety, Mr. Jenkins refused. Berry sent an individual known as "Biglet" to Ms. Jenkins' house to get the money. After returning the money, Berry kept calling Ms. Jenkins and harassing her. This lasted for approximately two weeks before Ms. Jenkins was forced to change her phone number.

27   Sometime in 1988, Bob Cunningham began distributing drugs while "hanging out" in the Carver Village Housing Projects in Pascagoula, Mississippi. He began by selling small quantities, specifically $100 quantities of crack cocaine. His principle source of cocaine was Earnest Tell, who supplied. Cunningham and other gang member in Carver Village. Cunningham worked for Tell for approximately one year, at which time Tell moved back to Los Angeles, California.

28   Cunningham began associating with Michael Todd Ward, aka Todd Capels. Ward was supplying Cunningham with several ounces of crack cocaine at a time. Cunningham was not a courier of drugs for Ward. Cunningham dealt with Ward for approximately one year, at which time Cunningham met Antonia Berry through Ward. This meeting occurred when Ward took Cunningham to Berry's house in Orlando, Florida.

29   A few days later, Berry, Ward, Cunningham and Roderick Jenkins drove from _ Mississippi to Miami, Florida. Upon arriving in Miami, Jenkins met with Corey Johnson in Miami to complete a drug transaction. Jenkins received eight kilos of cocaine powder from Johnson in exchange for $150,000. Jenkins transported the cocaine powder back to Mississippi, where Cunningham, Ward and Berry converted it into crack cocaine.

30. Cunningham accompanied Berry and Ward to Miami on at least ten other occasions. Jenkins would again pick up the cocaine powder from Johnson in Miami. Jenkins...

Antonio Berry

SKIP TO PAGE 9

37.   Berry was subsequently arrested on August 4, 1992. After his arrest, Berry, through Cunningham, offered Tracy Lett $20,000 not to testify against him. Lett refused and wanted $40,000. Berry thought $40,000 was too much money and advised Cunningham that it would be easier to kill Lett. Subsequently, Angelle introduced an unknown male to Cunningham, who was from New Orleans, Louisiana, and had come to Mississippi to kill Lett at Berry's request. Cunningham drove the "hit man" to places in the Mississippi area that he knew Lett would not be. Cunningham did this because he did not want to be involved in a murder. Because of this, Cunningham was threatened by Angelle because he did not assist in the murder of Lett and allowed Berry to remain in jail.

38.   Through his dealings with Gerald Duffy, Cunningham had an occasion to meet Delvin Livingston in Houston, Texas. After working with Duffy, Cunningham maintained contact with Livingston, and in June, 1991, Cunningham, convinced Livingston, Eddie Garcia and Andrew Routt to come to Mississippi. Cunningham stated that Berry and Ward were capable of purchasing large quantities of cocaine.

39.   Approximately two weeks later, Livingston, Garcia and Routt flew from Houston to Mississippi. Once in Mississippi, they went to Cunningham's house in Gautier, Mississippi. Joe Nelson, a driver for Livingston, ' subsequently arrived at Cunningham's house with ten kilos of cocaine powder. Cunningham, Berry and Ware- purchased the ten kilos from Livingston for $19,000 a kilo. Nelson transported the $190,000 back to Houston for Livingston. After this transaction, Berry told Livingston that they could do business in the future.

40.   A few weeks later, Livingston, Garcia and Routt made another trip to Mississippi. Upon arrival, they went to Ward's house

264

and negotiated a ten kilo deal with Ward, Berry and Cunningham. During this transaction, Livingston counted the money and found it to be short. Berry provided an additional $8,000 to help purchase the cocaine. During the transaction, Berry agreed to trade Livingston a green Mercedes Benz in exchange for a kilo of cocaine. Livingston subsequently sold this Mercedes to a drug dealer in Waco, Texas.

41. Livingston, Garcia and Routt continue to make trips, approximately two times per month to Mississippi for the purpose of supplying Berry, Cunningham, Ward and other Mississippi drug dealers with large amounts of cocaine. Livingston made at least one trip to a house owned by an individual named "Red," who lived in Jackson, Mississippi. During this transaction, Livingston, Garcia and Routt supplied Berry, Ward, Cunningham, "Red," and others with ten kilograms of cocaine powder per trip.

42. All totaled, Livingston, Garcia and Routt made at least ten trips to Mississippi in which they supplied Berry, Ward, Cunningham and others with at least ten kilos of cocaine powder per trip. Berry advised Livingston that he converted all of his cocaine powder into crack cocaine. Ward and Cunningham also "rocked up" the cocaine they received from Livingston.

43. On two occasions while dealing with Berry, Livingston had large amounts of cash seized. On August 5, 1991, the U.S. Customs Service engaged in a surveillance after receiving information from a confidential informant that money laundering was occurring at 10044 Coral Ridge in Houston, Texas. This was the residence of Eddie Garcia. Surveillance led customs agents to 1001 Kempwood, Apartment 119, in Houston, the residence of Maria Lopez, aka Carmen. A search of the apartment was conducted and officers recovered $354,247, along with a money counter.

Antonio Berry

44.   On October 1, 1991, Joe Nelson, a courier for Livingston, was
       stopped for a traffic violation in Gulf Port, Mississippi. A
       subsequent search of Nelson's vehicle determined that he was
       in possession of $145,000 in cash. The money was the result of
       a drug transaction between Livingston and Berry, Ward and
       Cunningham.

45.   In October, 1990, Berry began supplying crack cocaine to Zeth
       Richardson. Richardson and Berry had grown up in the same
       town of Moss Point, Mississippi. Richardson became
       associated with Berry in the drug business through Michael
       Todd Ward, who had previously been supplying Richardson
       with large amounts of crack cocaine. From October, 1990, until
       June, 1991, Berry supplied Richardson with at least 50 ounces
       of crack cocaine per month, totaling 450 ounces. Richardson,
       who at that time was residing in Mobile, Alabama, was a
       source of supply to several street level dealers in the Mobile
       area. Richardson received crack from Berry on a front. After
       receiving income from the redistribution, Richardson paid
       Berry $900 an ounce for the crack.

46.   In July, 1991, Richardson moved back to Moss Point,
       Mississippi. Because of the amount of crack he was
       distributing in Mobile, Richardson felt he needed to leave that
       area. Richardson began receiving ¼ of a kilo of cocaine
       powder from Berry. This eventually increased to kilo
       quantities. This lasted until Miguel McNair's arrest in Florida
       on February 26, 1992. During this period of time, Richardson
       received a large, but undetermined amount of cocaine powder
       from Berry. Berry did not front the cocaine powder to
       Richardson, but rather charged him $20,000 a kilo at the time
       of the transaction.

47.   Berry was responsible for teaching Richardson how to rock up
       cocaine. Initially, Berry charged Richardson $1,000 to rock up
       a kilo of cocaine powder.

266

48. Richardson employed Victor Oliver as a courier of crack cocaine. Oliver would pick up the crack from Berry in Mississippi and transport it back to his (Oliver's) apartment in Mobile, where it was eventually picked up by Richardson. Also, Berry employed Bobby Tate and Irma Jean Watson to travel to Mobile, Alabama, to deliver large amounts of crack cocaine to Richardson.

49. During 1990, Delvin Livingston met Gerald Duffy at the Yale Village Apartments in Houston, Texas. Duffy was dealing with Overton Randall, who was working with Livingston. Livingston was trying to cut Randall out of the business. Livingston got Duffy's business by offering him a better price. During this meeting, Livingston sold...

SKIPS TO PAGE 16

87.   During the course of his drug trafficking activities, Berry was responsible for providing large sums of money to purchase cocaine, as well as receiving a large amount of money for the distribution of crack cocaine. Jenkins made at least 85 trips in which Berry provided him with at least 150,000 per trip to purchase drugs. Zeth Richardson received at least 450 ounces of crack cocaine from Berry at the rate of $900 an ounce, which totals $405,000. This is not including the undetermined amount of cocaine powder received by Richardson, for which Berry charged him $20,000 a kilo. Berry also pooled his money with Michael Todd Ward, Bob Cunningham and others to purchase the 120 kilos from Delvin Livingston, who charged them $19,000 a kilo.

88.   During his involvement in the trafficking of controlled substances, Gerald Duffy was responsible for the purchase and/or distribution of at least 10 kilograms of cocaine powder and 5½ kilos of crack cocaine. Duffy employed Alex Joe and Lonnie Perryman as couriers, who were responsible for transporting the cocaine from Houston, Texas, back to Mississippi. Duffy provided at least $186,000, which was used to purchase cocaine.

89.   From the beginning of 1990 until November 5, 1991, Roderick Jenkins made at least 35 trips to Houston, Texas, and purchased cocaine from Edward King for Berry. During this period of time, King provided Jenkins with at least 280 kilos of cocaine Jenkins provided King with $150,000 on each transaction. King also supplied Angel with at least 25 kilos of cocaine powder, which were delivered to Berry. All total, King is responsible for the distribution of at least 305 kilos of cocaine powder.

Victim Impact

90.   There are no identifiable victims of the offense.

268

Adjustment for Obstruction of Justice

91.   After Berry's arrest on August 4, 1992, he offered Tracy Lett $20,000 not to testify against him. Lett refused and wanted $40,000. The defendant thought $40,000 was too much money and advised Bob Cunningham that it would be easier to kill Lett. Subsequently, Angelle LNU introduced an unknown male to Cunningham, who was from New Orleans, Louisiana, and had come to Mississippi to kill Lett, at the defendant's request. Cunningham drove the "hit man" to places in the Mississippi area that he knew Lett would not be. Cunningham did this because he did not want to be involved in a murder. As a result, Cunningham was threatened by Angelle because he did not assist in the murder of Lett and allowed Berry to remain in jail.

Adjustment for Acceptance of Responsibility

92.   During the interview with the probation officer, the defendant denied any involvement in drug trafficking. He stated that the people that testified against him were coerced to do so by the Government. He states that people picked him at random because of a dispute he was having with Tracy Lett. The defendant maintains his innocence and challenges what he terms the circumstantial evidence against him.

Offense Level Computations

Count One—Conspiracy to Possess with Intent to Distribute Cocaine

Count Two—Possession with Intent to Distribute Cocaine

93.   Pursuant to U.S.S.G. § 3D1.2(b), counts are grouped together when the counts involve a conspiracy and a substantive act which is part of the conspiracy. Therefore, Counts 1 and 2 are grouped together for the purpose of guideline calculations.

94.   Base Offense Level: The United States Sentencing Commission Guideline for violation of 21 U.S.C. § 846 is found in U.S.S.G § 2D1.1(a)(3) and calls for a base offense level of 42. Investigation of this case revealed that the

defendant was responsible for the purchase and/or distribution of at least 833 kilograms of cocaine powder and 82 kilograms of crack cocaine. Eighty-two kilograms of crack cocaine is equivalent to 8,200 kilograms of cocaine powder. This amount, added to the 833 kilograms, produces a total of 9,033 kilograms of cocaine powder that is attributed to the defendant. According to the Drug Quantity Table, located in U.S.S.G. § 2D1.1(a)(3), 1,500 kilograms or more of cocaine results in a base offense level of 42.

42

95.   Specific Offense Characteristics: None.

96.   Victim-Related Adjustments: None.

97.   Adjustments for Role in the Offense: The defendant was the organizer and leader of a large scale cocaine distribution operation, which involved at least four states and numerous codefendants and co-conspirators. The defendant employed Roderick Jenkins, Miguel McNair. Angelle LNU, Bobby Tate and Irma Jean Watson as couriers to transport money and cocaine. The defendant also utilized Charlie Doby, Matthew Jones and Kenny Davis to further his drug distribution activities. The defendant was the ultimate decision making authority and claimed a larger share of the proceeds from the distribution of cocaine. Pursuant to U.S.S.G. § 3B1.l(a), the offense is increased four levels.

+4

98.   Adjustment for Obstruction of Justice: After his arrest on August 4, 1992 the defendant offered Tracy Lett $20,000 not to testify. When Lett refused his offer and demanded $40,000, the defendant indicated that it would be easier to kill Lett. At the defendant's request, an unknown male from New Orleans, Louisiana, came to Mississippi with the intent to kill Lett.

270

However, Cunningham took the hit man to places where he knew Lett would not be. Because of this, Cunningham was also threatened. Pursuant to U.S.S.G. §3C1.1, two levels are added.

$+2$

IN THE UNITED STATES DISTRICT COURT

FOR THE EASTERN DISTRICT OF TEXAS

BEAUMONT DIVISION

UNITED STATES OF AMERICA	*
	*
VS.	* CRIMINAL NO. 1:92-CR-93-1,6
	*
ANTONIA BERRY	*
EDWARD KING, JR.	*

VERDICT OF THE JURY

We, the Jury, find as to Count One of the indictment:

ANTONIA BERRY _____guilty_____ GUILTY _____ NOT GUILTY

EDWARD KING, JR. _____guilty ✓_____ GUILTY _____ NOT GUILTY

_____
Presiding Juror

_4-8-93_____2:50 pm
DATE

Verdict of the Jury Count One
Exhibit I

Antonio Berry

UNITED STATES OF AMERICA   *

VS.   * CRIMINAL NO. 1:92-CR-93-1,6

ANTONIA BERRY   *
EDWARD KING, JR.   *

<u>VERDICT OF THE JURY</u>

We, the Jury, find as to Count Two of the indictment:

ANTONIA BERRY   _guilty_ GUILTY   _____ NOT GUILTY

Rhodda Frazier
Presiding Juror

4-8-93
DATE   2:00 pm

Verdict of the Jury Count Two
Exhibit J

274

SENTENCING TRANSCRIPT beginning on page 3
Exhibit K

WITH HIM EITHER IN PERSON OR BY PHONE SINCE
THE TIME THAT YOU RECEIVED IT?

THE DEFENDANT: ONCE OR TWICE WHEN I WAS READING
IT THROUGH AND JUST RAN ACROSS SOME THINGS
AND I CALLED HIM AND ASKED HIM SOME
CONCERNS ABOUT IT.

THE COURT: ALL RIGHT. HAVE YOU REVIEWED THE
PRESENTENCE INVESTIGATION REPORT, MR.
JOHNSON?

MR. JOHNSON: YES, SIR, YOUR HONOR, I HAVE.

THE COURT: BEFORE I MAKE MY FINDINGS AND RULE
ON THE OBJECTIONS, FIRST, MR. BERRY, IS
THERE ANY ADDITION, CORRECTION, ANYTHING
THAT YOU WISH TO ADD TO THE PRESENTENCE
INVESTIGATION REPORT?

THE DEFENDANT: YES, SIR.

THE COURT: ALL RIGHT. PLEASE PROCEED.

MR. JOHNSON: YOUR HONOR, ON BEHALF OF --

THE COURT: I WANT TO FIRST HEAR FROM THE

DEFENDANT, THEN I'LL HEAR FROM YOU, MR.
    JOHNSON.

MR. JOHNSON: VERY WELL.

THE COURT: IT IS THE DEFENDANT WHO IS IN
    JEOPARDY, AND I WISH TO GIVE HIM SUCH
    LATITUDE THAT HE WISHES TO BRING UP, THEN
    I WILL, OF COURSE, HEAR FROM YOU.

THE DEFENDANT: NOT REALLY TAKING NOTHING FROM
    IT, YOUR HONOR, NOT REALLY ADDING NOTHING
    TO IT, YOUR HONOR, JUST TAKE A LOT OF THE
    ERRONEOUS INFORMATION FROM IT.

THE COURT: ALL RIGHT. PROCEED.

THE DEFENDANT: AND BASICALLY THE WHOLE PSI
    REPORT IS A BUNCH OF ERRONEOUS INFORMATION
    AND ALLEGATIONS. IT'S UNTRUE. I DISPUTE
    THE WHOLE PSI REPORT.

THE COURT: AS I AM REASONABLY SURE THAT YOU
    DISPUTE THE EVIDENCE THAT WAS ADMITTED

DURING THE TRIAL.

THE DEFENDANT: WELL, SEE, YOUR HONOR, I DON'T
    DENY THAT I OWNED THE NUMBER ONE FAN SHOP
    AND I'M ANTONIA BERRY.

THE COURT: ALL RIGHT.

THE DEFENDANT: BUT I DENY THE ALLEGATIONS ABOUT
    THE DRUGS.

THE COURT: ANY DRUGS?

THE DEFENDANT: YES, SIR.

THE COURT: AT ANY TIME?

THE DEFENDANT: YES, SIR.

THE COURT: OR WHAT THE WITNESSES WHO TESTIFIED,
    WHO WERE CO-DEFENDANTS CUNNINGHAM AND
    LIVINGSTON, AND OTHERS, TESTIFIED TO?

THE DEFENDANT: YES, SIR.

THE COURT: AND JOE AND JENKINS?

THE DEFENDANT: YES, SIR. I EVEN, YOUR HONOR, I
    EVEN ASKED THE PROSECUTOR DURING THE

COURSE OF THE TRIAL DID HE BELIEVE THE
TESTIMONY, ALL THE TESTIMONY THAT THE
WITNESSES WERE GIVING, AND HE TOLD ME, HE
STATED NO HIMSELF, BUT HE STILL ALLOWED
THEM TO CONTINUE ON WITH THE LIES JUST TO
OBTAIN A CONVICTION. I ASKED HIM THAT
DURING THE TRIAL PERSONALLY MYSELF, I
SAID, "MR. BALES,

DO YOU BELIEVE ALL THE TESTIMONY" AND HE SAID,
"NO."

THE COURT: MR. BALES, DO YOU WISH TO RESPOND TO
THAT?

MR. BALES: YES, I DO, YOUR HONOR.

THE COURT: THEN PLEASE DO.

MR. BALES: TONY BERRY IS A SELF-DECEIVED
PERSON. I FEEL SORRY FOR HIM. HE'S NOTHING
BUT A GANGSTER, HE'S STILL ACTING LIKE A
GANGSTER, AND IF HE CAN'T ACCEPT THE
TRUTH, I'M SORRY FOR HIM, BUT I NEVER SAID
THAT. I WOULD NEVER PUT ON TESTIMONY THAT
I THOUGHT WAS A LIE, AND I KNOW IN MY
HEART OF HEARTS THAT HE IS GUILTY AS THE

JURY DECIDED.

THE COURT: MR. JOHNSON, WHAT ADDITIONS OR
   EXCEPTIONS OR CORRECTIONS DO YOU WISH TO
   MAKE?

MR. JOHNSON: YOUR HONOR, FIRST OF ALL, LET ME
   APOLOGIZE TO THE COURT AND COUNSEL, MR.
   BALES, THE PROBATION OFFICE DID TRY TO
   REACH ME AND WAS UNABLE TO REACH ME. AS A
   RESULT OF THAT, I DIDN'T RECEIVE A COPY OF
   IT UNTIL EARLY THIS MORNING, BUT I'VE HAD
   OCCASIONS TO GO OVER THE PRESENTENCE
   REPORT THIS MORNING WITH MY
   TRUSTWORTHINESS THAT I CAN AND DO RELY ON
   IT AS TO THE AMOUNTS OF MONEY, THE NUMBER
   OF CARS, THE NUMBER OF HOMES, STYLE OF
   LIFE. WHAT HE DID WITH THE PROFITS I DO
   NOT KNOW, BUT IT'S CERTAINLY OBVIOUS THERE
   WERE AMOUNTS OF MONEY IN CASH IN GROCERY
   BAGS THAT WERE BANDIED ABOUT, AND AS THE
   LEADER, HE CERTAINLY DID PROFIT AS TO WHAT
   THIS COURT, NOT WHAT MR. BERRY CONSIDERS
   IMMENSELY BUT WHAT THE ORDINARY PUBLIC
   WOULD CONSIDER IMMENSELY. I FIND IT'S
   CORRECT AND BASED UPON INFORMATION OF

SUFFICIENT TRUSTWORTHINESS AND
RELIABILITY, AND I DO LELY ON IT, I FIND
IT BY A PREPONDERANCE OF THE EVIDENCE, AND
IT IS — THE OBJECTION IS OVERRULED.

I ASSUME THAT THE OBJECTION NUMBER "X" ON PAGE
8 THAT REFERS TO PARAGRAPH FORTY-THREE, I
ASSUME THAT IT IS ONE FORTY-THREE, AND THE
OBJECTION IS DENIED AND OVERRULED AS TO
THE LEGAL CONCLUSION.

THE OBJECTIONS, THOUGH FILED LATE,
NEVERTHELESS HAVE BEEN RULED UPON. PLEASE
PLACE THEM IN THE FILE, MA'AM.

The Court: ARE THERE ANY OTHER CORRECTIONS OR
ADDITIONS THAT YOU WISH TO BRING TO THE
COURT'S ATTENTION, MR. BERRY OR MR.
JOHNSON, BEFORE I MAKE MY FINDINGS?

MR. JOHNSON: YOUR HONOR, THE ASSAULT CHARGES --
YOU'RE NOW ADDRESSING YOURSELF TO MR.
BERRY, YOUR HONOR?

THE COURT: SIR?

SKIPS A PAGE HERE (21 MISSING)

ONE, THE OFFENSE AND THE OFFENSE CONDUCT ARE
    CORRECT,

THAT IS, PARAGRAPHS ONE THROUGH EIGHTY-NINE
    ARE CORRECT, AND I ADOPT THEM AND SO FIND
    BY A PREPONDERANCE OF THE EVIDENCE.

I DISAGREE IN PRINCIPLE THAT THERE ARE NO
    IDENTIFIABLE VICTIMS OF THIS OFFENSE.
    HOWEVER, I ACCEPT THAT AND I SO FIND.

AS FOR THE ADJUSTMENT OF THE OBSTRUCTION OF
    JUSTICE IN PARAGRAPH NINETY-ONE, I FIND
    THAT THAT IS BASED UPON INFORMATION OF
    SUFFICIENT RELIABILITY AND TRUSTWORTHINESS
    THAT I CAN AND DO ACCEPT IT, AND SO FIND.

I FIND THE SAME AS TO PARAGRAPH NINETY-TWO,

FROM WHAT THE DEFENDANT HAS STATED BEFORE ME
    TODAY.

I FIND THAT, ALTHOUGH MR. BERRY WAS CONVICTED
    ON TWO COUNTS, THAT THEY SHOULD BE GROUPED
    AND THEY ARE GROUPED, AND THAT THE BASE

OFFENSE LEVEL IN THIS CASE, BASED UPON THE
PURCHASE OR DISTRIBUTION OF EIGHT HUNDRED
AND THIRTY-THREE KILOGRAMS OF COCAINE
POWDER AND EIGHTY-TWO KILOGRAMS OF CRACK
COCAINE, WHICH IS THE EQUIVALENT OF
EIGHTY-TWO HUNDRED KILOGRAMS OF COCAINE
POWDER, PRODUCE NINE THOUSAND AND THIRTY-
THREE KILOGRAMS OF COCAINE POWDER
ACCORDING TO THE DRUG QUANTITY TABLE, AND
THAT THAT PRODUCES A LEVEL OF FORTY-TWO.

I FIND THAT THERE ARE NO SPECIAL OFFENSE
CHARACTERISTICS.

The Enterprise "Testimony"

SKIP AHEAD TO PAGE 23 OF TRANSCRIPT

AND ACCORDING TO THE PRESENTENCE REPORT, THOSE
    TWENTY-FIVE KILOS IS AN AMOUNT THAT WAS
    MENTIONED BY SOMEONE NAMED ANGELLE TO
    EITHER MR. CUNNINGHAM OR TO SOMEONE ELSE,
    AND THERE IS NO INDICATION, BECAUSE THIS
    PERSON, ANGELLE, WAS NOT A WITNESS DURING
    THE COURSE OF THE TRIAL, WHERE HER
    RELIABILITY SHOULD BE ACCEPTED, SHE'S NOT A
    CO-CONSPIRATOR, SHE WAS NOT NAMED IN ANY
    WAY OR DIRECTED IN ANY WAY AS BEING PART
    OF THE CONSPIRACY, AND --

THE COURT: I'M NOT SO SURE THAT SHE WASN'T A
    CO-CONSPIRATOR THROUGHOUT THE ENTIRE
    COURSE. YOU'RE TALKING ABOUT ANGELA
    VIVARETTE?

MR. ANDERSON: NO. THIS IS SOMEONE ELSE,
    ANGELLE.

THE COURT: OH, ANGELLE, THE ONE FROM NEW
    ORLEANS?

MR. ANDERSON: RIGHT.

THE COURT: ALL RIGHT.

MR. ANDERSON: BUT THERE HAD BEEN NO TESTING OF
    THIS WITNESS' CREDIBILITY NOR AN
    OPPORTUNITY, UNLIKE BEING ABLE TO CROSS-
    EXAMINE MR. JENKINS, UNLIKE BEING ABLE TO
    CROSS-EXAMINE MR. CUNNINGHAM, TO CROSS-
    EXAMINE THIS PERSON.

THE COURT: WELL, DISREGARDING THAT TWENTY-FIVE
    KILOS, IT WOULD STILL BE - IN EXCESS OF A
    HUNDRED AND …

The Enterprise "Testimony"

SKIP AHEAD TO PAGE 27 OF TRANSCRIPT

TIME.

BASED UPON THAT, AND BASED UPON THERE ARE NO
FURTHER ADDITIONS, NO FURTHER CORRECTIONS,
AND YOUR HONOR WAS CORRECT THIS MORNING
WHEN YOU RECITED THE RECORD, THE RECEIPT
OF REPORTS, THE REPORTS HAVE BEEN READ IN
TOTO TO COUNSEL ON THE PHONE, ALL OF THAT
RECITATION BY THE COURT WAS ENTIRELY ONE
HUNDRED PERCENT CORRECT.

WITH REFERENCE TO MR. BERRY'S BACKGROUND AS
SET FORTH IN THE PRESENTENCE REPORT, YOUR
HONOR HAS GOME OVER, YOUR HONOR HAS READ
THAT, AND BASED UPON EVERYTHING THAT IS
BEFORE THE COURT THIS MORNING, BASED UPON
EVERYTHING THAT IS KNOWN TO COUNSEL, WE
WILL SUBMIT.

THE COURT: WHAT IS YOUR AGE, MR. BERRY?

THE DEFENDANT: TWENTY-EIGHT AND A HALF.

THE COURT: PURSUANT TO THE SENTENCING REFORM
ACT OF 1984, IT'S THE JUDGMENT OF THE

285

COURT THAT THE DEFENDANT, ANTONIA BERRY,
IS HEREBY COMMITTED TO THE CUSTODY OF THE
BUREAU OF PRISONS, TO BE IMPRISONED FOR A
TERM OF LIFE. THE TERM OF LIFE CONSISTS OF
LIFE AS TO COUNT ONE AND TWENTY YEARS AS
TO COUNT TWO, TO RUN CONCURRENTLY.

IT IS FURTHER ORDERED THAT THE DEFENDANT PAY A
FINE IN THE AMOUNT OF SEVENTY-FIVE
THOUSAND DOLLARS,WHICH IS TO BE PAID
IMMEDIATELY.

SHOULD THE DEFENDANT EVER BE RELEASED FROM …

SKIP AHEAD TO PAGE 29 OF TRANSCRIPT

FROM THIS DATE.

IT IS FURTHER ORDERED THAT THE DEFENDANT SHALL
    PAY TO THE UNITED STATES A SPECIAL
    ASSESSMENT IN THE AMOUNT OF A HUNDRED
    DOLLARS, WHICH SHALL BE DUE IMMEDIATELY.

AS JUSTIFICATION, I FIND THAT THE DEFENDANT
    WAS AN ORGANIZER AND LEADER OF A LARGE-
    SCALE COCAINE DISTRIBUTION NETWORK THAT
    INVOLVED AT LEAST FIVE STATES AND NUMEROUS
    CO-DEFENDANTS AND CO-CONSPIRATORS.

THE DEFENDANT WAS RESPONSIBLE FOR THE PURCHASE
    AND DISTRIBUTION OF AT LEAST EIGHT HUNDRED
    AND - THIRTY-THREE KILOS OF COCAINE
    POWDER, AS WELL AS AT LEAST EIGHTY-TWO
    KILOS OF CRACK COCAINE. THESE FIGURES ARE-
    VERY CONSERVATIVE IN RELATION TO THE
    TESTIMONY PRESENTED AT TRIAL.

IN HIS ROLE AS AN ORGANIZER AND LEADER, THE
    DEFENDANT EMPLOYED SEVERAL PEOPLE AS
    COURIERS TO RECEIVE AND DISTRIBUTE
    COCAINE.

287

THE MONEY PROVIDED BY THE DEFENDANT TO
PURCHASE COCAINE IS WELL INTO THE
MILLIONS.

INVESTIGATION OF THIS CASE REVEALED THAT THE
DEFENDANT WAS A MAJOR SOURCE OF SUPPLY OF
COCAINE IN THE STATE OF MISSISSIPPI .AND
IN THE MOBILE, ALABAMA, AREA.

AFTER HIS ARREST, THE DEFENDANT OFFERED A CO-
DEFENDANT A SUBSTANTIAL AMOUNT OF MONEY
NOT TO TESTIFY AGAINST HIM. WHEN THIS CO-
DEFENDANT REFUSED THE OFFER, THE DEFENDANT
TOOK AFFIRMATIVE STEPS TO ATTEMPT TO KILL
THE CO-DEFENDANT. HIS BEHAVIOR IS
INDICATIVE OF THE EXTENSIVENESS OF THIS
CONSPIRACY.

IT IS APPARENT, IN REVIEWING THE TRIAL
TESTIMONY AND THE DEFENDANT'S PRIOR
EMPLOYMENT, HE ELECTED TO ENGAGE IN THE
DISTRIBUTION OF COCAINE AS A MEANS OF
FINANCIAL LIVELIHOOD.

CONSIDERING ALL OF THESE FACTORS, A SENTENCE
OF LIFE IMPRISONMENT IS JUSTIFIED, AS WELL
AS REQUIRED BY THE SENTENCING GUIDELINES.

The Enterprise "Testimony"

BECAUSE THE TESTIMONY PRESENTED IN THIS CASE
REVEALED THAT THE DEFENDANT HAS NUMEROUS
ASSETS WHICH WERE OBTAINED FROM THE
PROCEEDS OF DRUG DISTRIBUTION, ORDERING
THE DEFENDANT TO PAY A FINE IS JUSTIFIED.

THIS SENTENCE WILL PROVIDE JUST PUNISHMENT,
ADEQUATELY SANCTION THE DEFENDANT'S
CONDUCT AND PROVIDE PROTECTION TO THE
COMMUNITY.

HIS ACTIVITIES ARE SUCH THAT WITHIN THE
COUNT'S DISCRETION I CAN REFUSE AND I DO
REFUSE TO ALLOW HIM TO OBTAIN ANY FEDERAL
BENEFITS FOR A PERIOD OF FIVE YEARS.

SHOULD THE DEFENDANT EVER BE RELEASED FROM
PRISON, A FIVE YEAR TERM OF SUPERVISED
RELEASE IS REQUIRED BY STATUTE. THIS WILL
ALLOW THE PROBATION OFFICER AN OPPORTUNITY
TO MONITOR THE DEFENDANT'S...

Antonio Berry

TO THE MISSISSIPPI BUREAU OF NARCOTICS

I, Rhondetta T. Nelson, duly Designated Representative for Antonio Berry, hereby acknowledge receipt and take possession of goods seized by the Mississippi Bureau of Narcotics from Antonio Berry and his business known as The Fan Shop, a listing of these items known as Exhibits "A" and "B" in Cause No. 92-5343(2) in the Circuit Court of Jackson County, Mississippi.

Furthermore, I agree to take these items without new inventory and as is, holding the State of Mississippi and Mississippi Bureau of Narcotics harmless, and indemnifying the State of Mississippi and Mississippi Bureau of Narcotics against any and all future actions with reference to said items.

_____   5/17/00
RHONDETTA T. NELSON   (date)

Witnessed:

_____ 0845 hrs   5-17-00
CAPT. DAVID JACKSON   (date)
Mississippi Bureau of Narcotics

NOTARY:

_____
S. Yvonne Young McGrath
My Commission Expires: December 22, 2003
Bonded Thru Dixie Notary Service   (seal)

FL &ll N425-738-66-553-1
14047 NE 2 Ave.
N. Miami, FL 33161-0000
exp. 2/15/01   DOB
                 2-13-66

Exhibit L
Affidavit to MS Bureau of Narcotics

➡epartment of Justice

FOR IMMEDIATE RELEASE
June 28, 1993

Contact: Daryl Fields
(409) 839-2538

FEDERAL PRISON IS PERMANENT HOME
FOR MISSISSIPPI DRUG LORD

(BEAUMONT, TX) A Pascagoula, Mississippi man, who authorities believe is the most significant crack cocaine dealer on the Mississippi Gulf Coast, will spend the rest of his life in federal prison.

This afternoon, United States District Judge Howell Cobb, also ordered 28-year-old ANTONIA "TONY" BERRY to pay a $75,000.00 fine.

On April 7, 1993, a federal jury in the Eastern District of Texas convicted Berry on one count of conspiracy to distribute five or more kilograms of cocaine and one count of possession with the intent to distribute cocaine. From mid 1987 to mid 1992, authorities believe Berry was responsible for the distribution of some 800 to 900 Kilograms of cocaine to areas all along the Gulf Coast.

Today, Judge Cobb also sentenced two of Berry's co-defendants in this case. Berry's former brother-in-law, 36-year-old EDWARD KING, JR., of Houston, TX, received a 324-month sentence in federal prison and was ordered to-pay a $50,000 fine. GERALD DUFFY, 24, of Pascagoula, was sentenced to 30 years in federal prison. While King was convicted by a federal jury .of conspiracy to distribute five or more-kilograms of cocaine, Duffy-pleaded guilty to the charge.

This case resulted from information obtained during several drug interdiction stops along Interstate 10, the first of which was made in Beaumont back in September of 1991. This case was investigated by the Mississippi Bureau of Narcotics, agents with the Federal Bureau of Investigation, Drug Enforcement Administration and officers from the Jefferson County Narcotics Task Force and Department of Public Safety Narcotics Unit. Assistant United States Attorneys Malcolm Bales and Melissa Baldo prosecuted this case.

Beaumont
ENTERPRISE

TUESDAY | APRIL 19, 1994

Man appeals conviction after attorney gets in trouble

BY SUSAN BORRESON
Staff Writer

A Mississippi man whose attorney faces a murder charge in Tennessee contends two drug convictions should be reversed because his attorney was not properly licensed.

Antonia Barry contends in an appeal that lawyer Hubert Johnson, 50, fraudulently obtained a certificate from federal court officials in Beaumont to represent Barry at trial.

Barry went to trial this past spring in Beaumont on charges of conspiracy to distribute cocaine and possession with intent to distribute cocaine.

U.S. District Judge Howell Cobb in June sentenced Barry to life in prison plus 20 years after jurors convicted Barry on both counts.

Beaumont lawyer Doug Barlow, who now represents Barry, contended on appeal that Johnson was not a lawyer in good standing when he represented Barry at trial.

Cobb on April 15 presided at a hearing on Barlow's contentions and will issue an opinion to the 5th US Circuit Court of Appeals in New Orleans. The appeals court then will issue a ruling, Barlow said.

A Knox County grand jury in Knoxville, TN indicted Johnson in January on charges of first degree murder and attempted murder, a criminal court clerk in Knoxville said Monday. Johnson remains in the Knox County jail, a jail spokeswoman said.

Documents introduced into evidence show Johnson was licensed to practice in New Jersey until December 1982, when the New Jersey Supreme Court suspended him from practice for miss-appropriating $20,000.

A Knox County grand jury in Knoxville, TN indicted Johnson in January on charges of first-degree murder and attempted murder, a criminal court clerk in Knoxville said Monday. Johnson remains in the Knox County jail, a jail spokeswoman said.

The court in April 1991 reinstated Johnson to practice under the guardianship of another lawyer and ordered him to complete law courses within two years.

Barlow said Johnson never completed the courses and began practicing law in Knoxville, TN. Records from the State Bar in TN show Johnson never obtained a license to practice in that state.

"He perpetrated a fraud on the court here when he represented himself as an attorney licensed in good standing in New Jersey, when in fact he hadn't practiced in New Jersey since that reinstatement," Barlow said.

Assistant US Attorney Malcolm Bales introduced into evidence a letter from a New Jersey Supreme Court clerk stating that Johnson was eligible to receive a certificate of good standing.

The clerk wrote that the requirements of the New Jersey court's order did not apply to Johnson while he practiced law in Tennessee.

Barlow said Barry testified at the hearing that another lawyer referred him to Johnson. Barry testified he paid Johnson $60,000 to represent him.

The Enterprise "Testimony"

EXHIBIT C

May 21, 1996

Mr. Antonio Berry
03256-043
Box PMB
Atlanta, GA 30315

Re: In the Matter of Hubert Johnson

Dear Mr. Berry:

I am writing in response to your letter dated May 6, 1996 which was received in this office on May 15, 1996. I really have nothing to add to what I told you in my letter dated April 16, 1996. Neither would I change anything I said in that letter.

As you have been told before, and as I explained in the certification I provided for the United States District Court, the ability to obtain a Certificate of Good Standing means that the attorney is licensed to practice in New Jersey, is not currently suspended or disbarred and is current in payments to the New Jersey Lawyers' Fund for Client Protection. There may be reasons why an attorney who has satisfied all those requirements still would not be eligible to practice law in New Jersey, such as by not having the required bona fide office for the practice of law within this state. Such an attorney still could obtain a Certificate of Good Standing.

Similarly, at the time in question Mr. Johnson would not have been eligible to practice law in New Jersey because he did not maintain a bona fide office here and because he had not provided proof of his satisfactory completion of the Skills and Methods Course within two years of his reinstatement as directed the Supreme Court.

Very truly yours,

Gail G Haney

Letter from Supreme Court
Regarding Mr. Hubert Johnson
May 21, 1996
Exhibit O

293

OFFICE OF THE DISTRICT ATTORNEY
Nineteenth Circuit Court District
Jackson, George, Greene Counties

JACKSON COUNTY COURTHOUSE
PASCAGOULA, MISSISSIPPI 39567
601-769-3045 -- FAX 601-769-3545

MAILING ADDRESS:
POST OFFICE BOX 173
PASCAGOULA, MS 3956

DALE HARKEY
DISTRICT ATTORNEY

November 14, 1997

Mike Bradford
United States Attorney
350 Magnolia Ave., Suite 150
Beaumont, Tx 77701-2237

SAMPLE

RE: State of MS EX REL, MBN
vs
Two Parcels of Real Property Located
in Jackson County; The Contents of A Business
Known as the Fan Shop, Owned and Operated
By Antonio Berry, See Exhibit "A"; and various
items of Personal Property Seized From The
Residence of Antonio Berry and Wife, Janice Watson Berry,
See Exhibit "B"

Dear Gentlemen:

I am writing this letter to you to advise that Antonio Berry has cooperated with this office in resolving the forfeiture action which has been pending for some time now. Mr. Berry contacted this office, by letter, advising that he would... I prepared the necessary paper work and advised Mr. Berry that I would write this letter. I further advised that I would do no more than write this letter and more importantly, that I had no control over his sentence nor could I guarantee to him any reduction. I simply ask that you take whatever action you deem necessary, as a result of Mr. Berry's cooperation in resolving this matter. If you have any questions or if I can be of any further assistance, please contact me at your convience.

Thanking you in advance for your assistance, I am,

Sincerely,

ANTHONY N. LAWRENCE, III
Assistant District Attorney

ANL/ac

November 14, 1997 Letter from
Assisant DA to Mike Bradford, US Attorney
Exhibit P

LETTER FROM MEDIA

NewTimes

EDITORIAL
P.O. Box 01SH
Miami, Florida 33101-1561
303 970 8000
fax 305 371 7576

September 1, 2001

Mr. Antonio Berry 03256-043
Federal Correctional Institution
P.O. Box 779800 Unit C
Miami FL 33177

Dear Mr. Berry,

My boss gave me your recent letter, and I read it with great interest. This past Thursday I called your uncle and spoke briefly to him, and he said he would convey to you our interest in your case the next time he was in contact with you.

I would like to be able to speak with you in person. Could you call me collect and let me know if I can visit you at the prison? My direct line is 305-571-7570. I can't tell you for sure when I'll be at this number, but it would probably be better to call between noon and 7:00 p.m. Tuesdays through Fridays. If you don't call I will be requesting an interview through the federal authorities anyway. I do hope soon we can discuss your story and the possibility of my writing an article about you.

Sincerely,

Kathy Glasgow
Staff Writer

September 1, 2001 Letter from
Kathy Glasgow, Staff Writer for NY Times
Exhibit Q

Antonio Berry

Exhibit_____

United States District Court
Eastern District of Texas
H.O. Box 037
Beaumont, Texas 77701

Howell Cobb
U.S. District Judge

July 8, 2003

Telephone
(409) 65-1-2810

Mr. Antonio Berry
No. 03256-043
Federal Correctional Institution
P. O. Box 779800 Unit/A
Miami, Fl, 33177

Dear Mr. Berry:

Thank you for your letter dated June 21, 2003, and for a copy of Judge Cahill's opinion. However, on appeal by the Government, the Eighth Circuit Court of Appeals reversed, remanded, and the mandatory minimums were upheld. The United States Supreme Court has denied certiorari.

You are wrong in your assumption that I must hate you. I disapprove what you did, and the manner in which you did it. I disapprove what you must have done to uncounted young people for the sake of big money fast.

If the Sentencing Guidelines had not permitted or required a life sentence, I would not have imposed it in your case. Any relief must come from Congress, not district judges. The 100 to one ratio of crack cocaine to powder cocaine was not addressed by Attorney General Reno, or any other Attorney General, or Congress; and I am not sure it ever will be. But until it is, harsh mandatory sentences must be imposed by federal trial judges.

Yours truly,

Howell Cobb

July 8, 2003 Letter from Howell Cobb, Sentencing Judge
Exhibit R

Moss Point man arrested on Texas warrant

MOSS POINT — Police here arrested Roderick Jenkins, 41, of 4513 Jackson Ave., Moss Point at his residence without incident on Tuesday. Jenkins was wanted by the Chambers County Sheriff's Office in Texas on a probation violation. Jenkins is being held at the Moss Point city jail pending extradition.

Anyone with information regarding this incident or other incidents is asked to call Moss Point Police Department at 475-1711 or the Moss Point TIPS line at 474-8477.

12-11-03 — From Staff, Wire Reports

Newspaper clipping, December 11, 2003
Regarding Roderick Jenkins arrest
Exhibit S

LINDA C. CANSLER
ATTORNEY AT LAW
P.O. BOX 693
BEAUMONT, TEXAS 77704-0693

(409) 835-5920   FAX (409) 835-4105

April 1, 2005

Antonio Berry 03256-043
Federal Correctional Institution
P.O. Box 779800 Unit/A
Miami, Florida 33177

Dear Antonio,

I'm very pleased to forward to you a copy of the Order entered by Judge Cobb. He signed the ordered on March 29, 2005. I had a little bit of trouble getting a complete copy of it until today so that's why there is a couple of days of delay in sending it on to you.

I know that you would be happier if it were less time then 360 months, but I am happy for you that you have hope of a life, that you would not be in the Federal Prison System for the rest of your life .

I wish you the very best in the future. I know that you became depressed and impatient when such a long period of time went by without hearing anything. That is unfortunaly what has to happen before a decision many times.

Sincerely yours,

Linda C. Cansler

April 1, 2005 Letter from
Linda Cansler, Attorney to Antonio Berry
Exhibit T

298

The Enterprise "Testimony"

415 S. First Street, Suite 201
Lufkin, Texas 75901

Commercial/FTS
(936) 639-4003
Fax (936)639-4033

April 10, 2006

Antonio Berry
Register Number: 03256-043
Federal Correctional Institution
P.O. Box 779800 Unit 1A
Miami, Florida 33177

Dear Tony:

It has come to my attention that you are still hopeful that I might make additional filings which would result in your receiving further reductions in your sentence. I have given thoughtful consideration to this matter, and unfortunately, not only can I find no legal justification for this type of filing, I also do not feel it is appropriate in light of the facts surrounding your conviction.

I know my decision may seem harsh, but your current sentence is appropriate for the crimes you committed. I still recall that your PSR offense level score was the highest that I have ever encountered in one of my prosecutions. I also remember, as I know you do, how many opportunities I gave you to reclaim your life before the trial.

I applaud the changes you have made in your personal life, and do not want you to allow this news to cause setbacks in the strides you have made since your incarceration. But the fact remains that you committed the offenses, you were justly convicted for these crimes, and your punishment is warranted.

Sincerely,

Matthew D. Orwig
United States Attorney

April 10, 2006 Letter from
John Bales, Assistant US Attorney to Antonio Berry
Exhibit U

Antonio Berry

```
  YAZ88  600.00 *                SECURITY/DESIGNATION          *        07-02-2008
PAGE 001 OF 001 *                        DATA                  *        10:43:16
    REGNO: 03256-043   NAME: BERRY, ANTONIA                                 ORG: CHN
RC/SEX/AGE: B/M/43  FORM D/T: 07-06-1993/0834   RES: MOSS POINT, MS 39563
OFFN/CHG..: CONSPIRACY TO POSS. COCAINE & ATTEMPT TO POSS. COCAINE
            LIFE CCCA
CUSTODY...: IN          BIL:              SEN LIMT: NONE
CITIZENSHP: UNITED STATES OF AMERICA  PUB SAFETY: GRT SVRTY,SENT LGTH
CIM CONSID: SEPARATION                                      USM: E/TX BEAU
JUDGE.....: COBB          REC FACL: 0                REC PROG: 0
DETAINER..: MODERATE      SEVERITY: GREATEST         LENGTH..: 84 PLUS MOS (540)
PRIOR.....: MINOR         ESCAPES.: NONE             VIOLENCE: 5-10 YRS MINOR
PRECOMMT..: N/A           V/S DATE:                  V/S LOC.:
                          SEC TOTL: 18              SCORED LEV: HIGH
CCM RMKS..: US CITZ-LEADER/ORGANIZER OF GROUP RESPONSIBLE FOR 833 K COCAIN
            E POWDER (CRACK) OVER SEVERAL YR PERIOD.THREATENED TO KILL WIT
            NESS.PEND POSS 1 K COCAINE MISSSISSIPPI.PRIOR ASSAULT,DISTURBI
            NG PEACE-FINES.RECKLESS DRIVING-5 DYS JAIL.CIM SEP,SCA DRUG
FACL DESIG: TERRE HAUTE FCI        DESIG: SCR KMR 07-06-1993 DESIG REAS: LEVEL
MGMT: N/A                    MV EXP: N/A          SEN: N/A
DESIG RMKS: NO JUDICIAL RECOMMENDATION NOTED.  NO MED PROBLEMS NOTED.

G0005       TRANSACTION SUCCESSFULLY COMPLETED - CONTINUE PROCESSING IF DESIRED
```

Security Designation, July 2, 2008
Exhibit V

The Enterprise "Testimony"

Booking document for Tracy Lee Lett
April 5, 2014
Exhibit W

ABOUT THE AUTHOR

The Author, from 1992-2006, served 14 years of the life sentence in the Penitentiaries of USP Terre Haute, USP Atlanta, USP Edgefield and Medium High FCI Miami. This was during a time when officers, same as inmates, were being butchered like wild animals for what most in society would find unbelievable and label as petty, but very serious senseless, crimes. Respect was the key to survival in these dungeons.

It was rumored by credible official sources that the author's sentencing judge stated that he had always been troubled by the case and the sentence that the author received. March, 2005, the same judge reduced the author's sentence to 360 months/30 years. Six months later the judge passed.

If not for this intervention of mercy the author would still remain to serve what's considered a death sentence in the federal system. A year later in 2006 the author was transferred to Yazoo City (low) in the State of Mississippi where he remained for more than seven years before being transferred to Yazoo City (Camp) where he is now.

At the time of the publishing of "The Enterprise" The author is in custody at Yazoo City Camp waiting months before entering the Residential Drug Program to complete a 9 months process that will restore the author's long awaited freedom after serving 22 years. Don't do the crime if you can't or don't want to do the time. I'm a living testimony that it's definitely not worth the penalty you could have to pay.

Antonio Berry

www.ingramcontent.com/pod-product-compliance
Lightning Source LLC
Chambersburg PA
CBHW070223260626
47160CB00002B/660